For All It's Wo

Second Chances Series #2

Jax Stuart

Edited by Kristen

Cover Art by Covers By Jo https://www.facebook.com/groups/coversbyjo/

Title Credit - Busy-Bee on Discord

https://jaxstuartauthor.wixsite.com/website

jaxstuartauthor@gmail.com

This is for Stacey who spent countless hours with me in the library as we wrote what were probably truly horrific romance books in our teens. I still have flashbacks of my attempts at poetry. Her poems though should have been put out there somewhere.

About This Book

Charlie needs a second chance at life
Mugged, beaten, and left for dead. Charlie gets the wake-up call that he so desperately needed.
Rehab, a new path, and second chances. As Charlie works to reset his life.
Max has missed Charlie like a piece of himself was lost but hated the destructive path Charlie was on. He cut his best friend out of his life until Charlie changed his ways.
This new Charlie? This one, he wants to take a second chance on. To finally confess what's in his heart.

Friends to lovers, second chances, and family healing. For All It's Worth is the second book in the Second Chances series and features Will's brother Charlie and his best friend Max whom you met in So Worth More. This book can be read as a standalone but may be best enjoyed as part of the series and is told in dual pov.

Content warning for discussions about alcohol dependency and a brief violent scene. The couple also kiss someone outside of their relationship while the other partner is present.

Prologue

One Week Earlier - Charlie

After hours of sitting in this club, the heavy bass had waned to background noise, the feeling still reverberating in my bones the only indicator that it still thudded its repetitive beat. The meeting with the owner was a distant memory, drowned in champagne and shots as I reclined back on the comfortable sofa with a sigh. This whole day had been a waste of time, but at least the drinks were decent. Nothing but top-shelf liquor.

I flagged down the hot waiter, giving him a suggestive look as he took my order. "Another round for the table."

The "friends" I'd accumulated cheered, and the little twink that had been up in my space leaned closer to press his lips to my cheek. He fake stumbled, his hand landing on my groin, and caught the edge of my mouth. My lips quirked at how hard he was trying. He was cute, he didn't have to work that much.

My best friend Max, rolling his eyes, caught my attention and I grinned at him as I wrapped an arm around my new friend, pulling him almost into my lap.

"Shots!" I called out as the waiter returned with a full tray and a pout at the guy trying to grind his ass on my leg. Cute as the twink was, the waiter was more my speed and I winked at him as he passed me a shot with a napkin and his number.

I tried handing a shot to Max but he indicated the bottle of hard cider he was nursing. "I'm good."

"Oh come on! Just one," I cajoled.

"You said that two shots ago. I have work tomorrow," he reminded me, his tone even though there was some stress in the way he held himself. He tried to get the waiter's attention but was ignored as the guy went to take another order. With that kind of attitude, he was risking his tip. I balled up the napkin with his number and tossed it onto the low table between me and Max.

Noticing the gesture, Max graced me with a real smile and I relaxed and downed my shot. The alcohol burned as it went down, warmth seeping into my perpetually cold body. I reached for another and caught Max frowning, but ignored it.

My buzz was building into something mellow. The edges of my vision were blurring and everything was slowing, becoming less frantic. Within minutes, my guests and I had finished the tray and I was on my way to being wasted.

The waiter returned with a pitcher of some cocktail that I couldn't remember ordering and sneered at the guy nearly in my lap, which made me glad I'd ditched his number. "Here you go, courtesy of management." His customer service skills needed brushing up on. I wouldn't have had that shit in my clubs.

Being reminded of my clubs was a pang to the heart, but I pushed it aside and poured some of the unnamed drink. Hopefully, the alcohol would continue to do its job and make everything soft and warm.

The pounding music faded the more that I drank and the twink moved off with someone else when I wouldn't dance with him. I shrugged, he didn't matter.

I checked on Max, who was still sitting with the same bottle - it was the same bottle, right? - and looking off into space. I'd made myself a promise to take better care of him after leaving him in a bar a few weeks ago. I still felt panicked when I thought about what could have happened. I'd left him vulnerable. As the alcohol hit, I felt that promise fading as I justified my actions. Max was old enough to look after himself. He was being more careful with his drinks. It would be fine.

"More shots!" I shouted when I noticed my glass and the pitcher were empty.

"No!" Max said fiercely, his words not meeting the waiter in the din of the club.

"I want more." My words didn't quite come out right; I was pretty sure that I slurred them in his direction.

Max got up and grabbed at my arm. "Come here," he demanded, leading me towards the bathrooms.

"Max, come on, let's just go get some more then we can head out, maybe get some food," I suggested, leaning against the cool wall of the corridor. The music was quieter here, the lighting brighter, and I could see the frustration in his face. The world started to feel very far away like I was watching from the outside and it was on TV.

"No, Charlie. You have any more and you'll be too wasted for anything else and I'll have to get your ass home."

I shifted suddenly, losing my balance and grip on reality, and missed the way that Max flinched as I moved into his space. I missed the brief flash of fear before he wiped it away.

"Just one more," I pleaded.

"It's always just one more, Charlie. You're drinking too much."

My head began to pound, the light too bright and a buzzing noise in the background too loud. "I'll be fine," I promised.

Max wiped his hand over his face. "I can't do this anymore, Charlie."

"What?"

"Be around you while you drink like this. It's too much, you're drinking too much. You're not yourself anymore and I hate it."

The vehemence in his voice shocked me.

"I'm fine. I don't drink too much." I heard the defensiveness in my tone. Anger rose at him and his judgment. Who was he to decide how much I had to drink? "Stop being a dick, Max, come on, let's go back to our friends."

"Do you know any of their names?" I saw the fire in his eyes, Max didn't argue often but he was mad, and at me. My stomach fell, the contents curdling until I worried about getting sick.

"I, uh...it doesn't matter. Look, we were having a good time." I couldn't grasp thoughts properly, they ran like water through my fingers.

Max was speaking but I couldn't understand.

"What?" I asked.

"You're starting to remind me of her. In the end, you'll be the same as her. Bitter, lonely, and drunk," Max spat at me.

A distant part of me thought that he looked like an angry cat. Feeling that little bit soberer, I didn't let those words escape. Self-preservation had won out, but I didn't know what to do.

I stood staring at him for an unknown amount of time.

"Don't you have anything to say?" His anger took me aback.

He made a noise of frustration and grabbed my hand. Taking me back through the club, he made me settle the tab with a hefty tip as I tried to find the words. Something was very wrong.

Outside, Max took a long breath and tapped on his phone.

"I've called you a ride," he told me plainly.

"Where are we going? Another club?"

He let out a garbled scream. "No! Fuck!" He paced back and forth, people moving out of his way in a hurry.

"Max?"

My words had him pausing in front of me. "I'm done, Charlie. Just done."

"What?"

"I need a break from you. Give me some space. Don't call. Don't come to my place or my business." He wouldn't meet my eyes

"What's happening?" Tears threatened as a car pulled up.

"Ride for Charlie?" The driver called out of the open window.

"Until you get yourself sorted, we can't be friends anymore." Max looked at me with eyes filled with tears and I watched one slip free.

"We can't?"

"No. Get help, Charlie. Then we can talk. Until then, leave me alone."

With that, he turned and walked away.

Chapter One

Charlie

Stumbling free of the beefy security guy's hold, I offered a slurred, "Fuck you!" as he kicked me out of the club.

Time passed as I tried to decide if I wanted another drink or to take some company home. The thought of dealing with more people had me curling my lip into a snarl and I decided I wanted another drink.

Traipsing the city streets with no real direction in mind, I caught sight of a group who looked like they were party-goers and attempted to follow them. There was one guy in their party that looked familiar and I was reminded of the hookup from the other day.

My phone buzzed in my hand. Another text from Max with a not-so-gentle reminder to, "Leave me the hell alone," after I'd sent him a plea for company when I'd gotten into it with that guy's boyfriend at the last club. There was a blank in my memory there for a bit, as the next thing I knew I was being shown the door.

My foot hit something and I staggered. Getting my bearings, I noticed that I'd lost sight of the group I was following and I crashed into a group of guys that had been trying to walk around me. Vaguely, I heard insults and taunts thrown but they rolled off me, unable to penetrate the fog of confusion clouding me.

I found myself down a side street that I hadn't intended to go down and there was another gap in my memory before I found myself pushed face-first into a wall, the cold, damp brick abrading my face.

At six feet, I wasn't a small guy. I was lean though, and the taller man pushing at me had about thirty pounds of muscle on me by the feel of him.

He held me still and I didn't fight him while he took my phone and emptied out my pockets of all the cash I had on me, jamming my wallet into his dark jeans. I'd stopped taking a credit card with me after the last time I'd lost it so I wasn't worried. A rideshare I could usually pay for with my phone. Not this time though. Getting home was going to suck.

There was no fight in me, I was utterly resigned to being mugged until he took the watch I was wearing, one of the last things I had from my father.

He unleashed something dark and frightening in me and I swung my fists and kicked out at him, fury at the audacity of my attacker fuelling my punches until his lookout stepped in.

Hits rained down on me, sending me to my knees. They turned to leave, taking my watch with them and I got back up to try and chase them. I grabbed one in a firm grip and he shouted at the other for help.

I saw the flash of silver and felt the burning pain in my abdomen. Blacking out for a second, I wobbled on my feet. I still held onto one of the men, until he spun, lobbing a fist at my head. I yelled out as I hit the pavement and it all went black.

The sounds of the street faded in and out with my consciousness. I couldn't feel my fingers and toes and the parts of my body that I could feel made me wish that they were numb, too. Agony shot through me as I tried to move.

"Holy shit! There's someone here. Dude? Are you okay?" I heard someone ask distantly.

"Is he alive?" A different voice queried, tinged with anxiety.

Pain exploded as someone nudged at my shoulder, trying to see my face. I couldn't hold back my groan at the way everything hurt from that small touch. The light from their phone had me squeezing my eyes shut tight.

"Careful," came the second voice, possibly female. "You could be hurting him. I see blood. We should call an ambulance."

Other voices mingled with the ones next to my prone body. I could feel the freezing damp street through my clothes but was too tired to move, talk or even shiver. I was utterly done.

I passed out again for a while and was roused once more when I was already on a stretcher being loaded into the ambulance. Unable to answer any of their questions, I let myself slip away again.

Coming to briefly in the hospital, I had vague memories of the nurses and doctors trying to treat me, asking me questions I didn't answer. I was pretty sure that I tried to leave, not getting far before I was crumpling to the floor and being helped back onto the bed again. I was sure I told them that I just wanted to go home, and demanded that they get Max.

The next time I slipped into consciousness, aware but unable to open my eyes, I heard the nurses say that they'd finally identified me. My I.D and discarded wallet had been found a few streets away from where I'd lain in the street half-frozen and losing blood.

I was aware enough to pick up a thread of disdain in the tone of their voices as they discussed me. Clearly being mugged and left to die wasn't enough to endear me to them. I'd obviously pissed them off with my escape attempt.

There weren't enough fucks left in me to give a shit. It'd been a long time since I'd had any left to care what people thought of me.

I gave myself over to sleep again.

Everything hurt as I opened my eyes to a bright and private hospital room. I felt someone holding my hand, carefully avoiding the scrapes and cuts there.

Gingerly turning my head, I glimpsed my oldest brother, Alex, against the far wall looking somber, before my eyes landed on Mom, her gently-lined face so worried, blue eyes filling with fresh tears.

"Oh darling, you're finally awake! We were so worried!" Mom's voice trembled with the effort it took to push back her sobs.

I tried to speak but my dry throat closed around the words and I choked on them. Then I was startled as a hand pressed a cup with a straw to my parched lips. My brain couldn't truly comprehend who I was seeing.

Taking a few sips, I managed to get out, "Will?" He was absolutely the last person that I thought would be here. My brother's expression was conflicted and I half expected him to leave the room now that I was awake. I wouldn't blame him if he did.

This was the first time that I'd been in the same room as either of my brothers since after the Ethan incident and the tension was thick between us.

My throat constricted as I thought of all the things that I'd wanted to say to them, Will in particular, over the last few years, but the only thing that mattered was the word I choked out, "Sorry."

I watched the word land and Will weighed it, judging the authenticity and in my haste to apologize again, my throat spasmed around his name and had me coughing.

He reached over with the cup again, allowing me to take a few sips before withdrawing.

"I really am sorry, Will." I managed.

Will visibly flinched before restraining his reaction and I wanted to try and apologize yet again but all the energy had fled from me and darkness rushed back in.

When I woke again, only Mom and my sister Matilda were with me.

"Where?"

"Sorry darling, but your brothers had to go home. Alex has Joe, and Andy was looking after him so that he and Will could be here. They'll come back in the morning," Mom told me unconvincingly. I doubted that they'd come back now that they knew I was going to be fine. I shared a look with Matty that suggested we both knew that it was wishful thinking.

It was then that I noticed it was dark outside. The blinds were open, showing the city beyond under the glow of street lights.

Trying to move into a sitting position, I winced as pain flared along my ribs and I was stopped by both my mom and sister pushing me back into the plush pillows.

"Stop, Charlie!" Mom scolded, "You'll pull your stitches!" Seeing my confusion, she continued. "You were stabbed! Luckily it wasn't deep and didn't hit anything. You've also got some nasty bruises and cracked ribs." She paused, looking at me with a worried expression. "Do you remember what happened?"

I wished that I didn't but I did. I'd been drunk pretty much solidly since the weekend before, when Max, my best friend of ten years, cut all ties with me until I got myself figured out. Demonstrating some tough love, as he called it. He'd never pulled anything like that before so I knew he was deadly serious about it. That didn't stop me from calling him or texting when I was drunk and lonely, as I'd been before I was mugged.

Unfortunately, I didn't lose my memory when I was drunk, so I remembered with too much clarity all the shitty things that'd happened or that I'd done...

Max pressing pause on our friendship until I sorted myself out.

The manager of one of my clubs quit because I drunkenly served some new friends some top-shelf liquor, not charging anyone for it.

My housekeeper also quit after finding a used condom on the floor. Again. I admit I felt bad about that. Jessie had always been sweet to me every time she came to clean when I was hungover and I knew that I had to get her back with a massive raise.

A brief flash of memory flickered in my mind of being punched by a jealous boyfriend before I was kicked out of a club, not one of mine since I was persona non grata in my establishments for multiple reasons, and then mugged and left for dead on the street.

"I was mugged." I finally said my tone flat.

"You nearly died!" Mom's tone was scandalized. "And you don't seem to care, Charlie! I couldn't bear to lose you," she cried as fresh tears flowed down her face.

"I'm sorry, Mom." My voice lacked any emotion. I was too tired at this point to care. Everywhere on my body ached and burned.

I wasn't sure that I really was sorry. My life of late was empty and lonely and it was all my own doing. I wasn't sure that if I had died anyone would miss me. Mom would for a while but she had two other boys and her baby girl, even if Matty was almost an adult herself.

Would Max miss me? Had he spent this last week feeling like he had lost a limb as I had? Missing Max was like having a gaping wound in my chest and trying to take a full breath. How hadn't I realized how much I needed him?

"Charlie?" Mom touched my shoulder gently as if it wasn't the first time that she had tried to get my attention.

"Yeah?"

"I think you should come stay with me for a bit until you heal up."

"Mom, no. I'll be fine at my apartment. I have work."

"No, Charlie. You need proper care and you're only going to get that at home with your sister and me."

Dread at the thought of having to live in that house again filled me. "I'm not staying with you."

"Listen to me!" Mom snapped. The rare show of anger cut off my words and doused the spark of panic. "You nearly died from the blood loss and hypothermia. You've been drinking so much lately that I'm not sure you know what day it is."

"I'm not an alcoholic Mom, I can go without a drink."

"I find that unlikely since you've had to be treated for alcohol withdrawal since you were brought in. The amount of alcohol in your system worsened the hypothermia and the bleeding from your wounds. Right now you're lucky to be alive."

I resisted the urge to make a caustic remark or roll my eyes. Being alive seemed to be a punishment for a long list of crimes.

Sensing I wasn't going to win this one, I gave in. "Fine, I'll come stay with you." I heard the petulance in my voice and Matty winced in the corner of my eye. Sensing my mom gearing up to berate me, I changed the subject. "When can I leave here?" My tone was resigned.

She sighed and looked hesitant to share something. "A couple of days still." There was a pause and a glance at Matty, who shrugged. "We only found out about it this morning." Her expression was sad but turned reproving. "You've been here three days but weren't able to answer any questions when they tried. Your blood alcohol level was dangerously high, which made treating you so much harder."

My breath hitched at the realization that they hadn't known I'd been here for so long. Had anyone noticed?

"Max?" I managed to squeeze out.

"Will is going to bring him tomorrow, sweetheart. You were asking for him earlier but only family are allowed to visit now."

"Max is my family," I stated firmly.

Out of the corner of my eye, I saw Matty smile. She loved Max almost as much as I did. Though she was closest to Will out of all of us, she had tried not to take sides when it had all gone down with Ethan. I did get a lecture from her, and Max too, for sleeping with my brother's boyfriend.

Truth be told, Ethan had been a dick and I hadn't been the only other person he'd been sleeping with, but I'd let Will blame me for it all. To him, I'd stolen Ethan. Not what actually happened but there'd been no point in saying anything different.

Chapter Two

Max

It was early Sunday morning when I was woken by someone ringing the bell of the apartment that I shared. I was tempted to leave it for my roommate to answer before I remembered that he'd stayed with his girlfriend the night before, having gotten sick of my whining.

I wasn't whining, or pining, or moping, or anything of the sort. Taking a break from Charlie was necessary, though it tore my heart out.

Pulling myself from the nest of blankets I'd made on my bed, I went to get the door.

"Just a minute," I called to the person on the other side of the door as I began unlatching and unlocking. It wasn't the best area of the city to be living in and we'd been burglarized before. Charlie had tried to get me to move into his apartment and I'd considered it before his dad died and he started to spiral.

Opening the door to a tense-looking Will, my heart dropped. If Will was here, then something had to be wrong with Charlie. Guilt ate at me for all the missed calls this last week, all the ignored texts. It hurt me to push him away, but I couldn't help him. More importantly, he didn't want my help.

"Charlie! Is he okay?"

"He's in the hospital, but he'll be fine. I'm heading there now. Do you want to come with me?"

"What happened?" I asked, motioning for Will to come inside the apartment.

Will looked uncomfortable but whatever it was, it must have been serious to get him to go to the hospital.

"There's no easy way to say this, but Charlie was mugged and stabbed. He nearly died from blood loss and hypothermia." We stood inside the tiny living room for a moment while I processed that information. My legs felt like they didn't want to hold me up and it took all of my effort just to stay standing. Will shifted guiltily on his feet. "I'm sorry Max, I did tell my family what you said the last time I saw you."

I flushed and lowered my head, embarrassed at the reminder of the last time I'd seen Will when I'd gotten sick in the gutter after Charlie had ditched me. The night that I'd probably been spiked. There was no other explanation for what had happened.

"It's fine, I think you know Charlie well enough to know that he'd have ignored any sort of intervention over his drinking."

"Well, we've been talking about it and we think rehab is the only choice now. He hasn't been told but he's going to rehab after Christmas, so if you want to see him, it might be best to go now. He'll be staying with our mom while he heals. He could go right away, but mom needs him home for a bit. It really shook her, y'know?"

Dumbly, I nodded. I could only imagine what it had been like for his mom. I'd been half-expecting something like this to happen, but I was still terrified for my best friend. I'd nearly lost him and the last time that we talked, we fought and I'd asked him for space. For ten years we hadn't gone a day without talking. Even at his very worst, I'd had his back and then it had just gotten to be too much. Watching the man that I loved lash out at everyone in his life had been heartbreaking, but I'd stayed until he'd started to turn on me. I just couldn't let him hurt me because he was broken inside.

I didn't know what he was going to make of the rehab conversation and was glad I wouldn't have to be there for it.

A pit of dread formed in my stomach. I hadn't spoken to Charlie in just over a week. There was a chance that he wouldn't want me there. "D'you think that he'll want to see me? We fought last week and haven't been speaking."

"Pretty sure that he asked Mom about you, but I can check. Mom had to go home for a bit, but Alex is there now. I'll give him a call while you go and get dressed."

I wondered how I'd cope if Charlie said that he didn't want to see me. Knowing that he could have died had grief over my mistakes welling up inside me. I wanted to see him with my own eyes, have proof that he was going to be okay. If he didn't want me there, I wasn't sure what I'd do. I felt like I could sob at the thought of it.

In the safety of my room, I allowed a few tears to flow before I pushed them back. I grabbed at the closest pile of clothes and started to put them on until I realized I had two t-shirts and no pants.

Will knocked on the door. "Max? Charlie wants to see you. Are you nearly ready to go?"

Relief hit me hard and I couldn't stop myself from sagging onto the bed. The tears that I'd managed to push away were back and I sobbed into my hands, huge heaving sobs that must have been loud enough for Will to hear through the closed door.

"Max, can I come in?"

Will didn't wait for an answer, which just as well since I couldn't speak. He carefully pushed the door open and crossed the uncharacteristically untidy room. I should've felt embarrassed at the state of it. I'd let everything slide this week, unable to focus on anything. He gingerly sat next to me and awkwardly put his arm around my shoulders, pulling me in for a hug.

"He's okay, I promise." His voice cracked and I looked at him questioningly. "We only found out about it yesterday.

He's been there a couple of days."

My heart stuttered and threatened to stop at the idea that this had happened days before and no one had known. Charlie had been alone in the hospital for days and no one had questioned where he'd gone. I'd thought that he was finally giving me the space that I'd asked for, not that he'd been lying in some hospital bed after being stabbed.

My stomach contents rose and I struggled to keep the bile down.

"Wh...When...When did it happen?"

"Wednesday into Thursday." Will looked shame-faced.

"What!" Oh my god! Three days alone!

"We only found out yesterday morning. Charlie had lost his I.D. and someone handed it in and then we were contacted. I would have come to get you yesterday, but we had Joe and only family were allowed to visit."

"I get that, but Jesus. No one knew anything about it for days! That's insane."

Will shuddered as some unknown emotion crossed him. His face filled with guilt. I couldn't even put myself in his place. He and Charlie had such a tense relationship. What would he have done if Charlie had died and things hadn't been resolved between them?

"Come on, we better get going. I heard him in the background asking for you."

A sob threatened to break loose again. Even after everything, he still thought of me. Though probably not in the way I wanted him to.

I felt like the worst friend in the history of friendship. I'd known he was struggling but hadn't had anyone to help me deal with it. Not to mention I'd been putting things off at work to deal with him and my business had suffered for it. I'd chosen my stuff over him and then he'd gone and gotten hurt. If he'd died...I couldn't go down that road. Just couldn't think about what would have happened. The guilt alone would have buried me.

After I'd calmed down and dressed, Will drove us to the hospital. Nerves flooded me at the thought of seeing Charlie. At the same time, I felt like I would come out of my skin with my need to see he was okay with my own eyes.

The door to the private room was open, and I could see Alex looking out at the city from where he stood at the window.

As we rounded the corner, the bed came into view. Charlie was propped sitting up with a mound of pillows, a meal on a tray over his lap.

His eyes lit up when they landed on me and all the breath in my body whooshed out with sheer relief at the hopeful gleam in those navy depths.

I studied him, taking in his pallor, all the more stark when I considered his half-Greek heritage from his father's side of the family. Usually, his olive-toned skin glowed, but now it was dull and pale. His beautiful eyes were sunken and shadowed. Cuts and bruises littered his face; his lip was split. He was shirtless, pebbled with goosebumps in the over-warm room. How had I not noticed how much weight he'd lost? Charlie was lean, but now he was bordering on emaciated. I took in the bandages that covered him and thanked whatever deities there might be for Charlie's continued existence.

I wanted to make some sort of witty remark to try and lighten the tension in the room. More than that, I wanted Alex and Will to leave us alone because Charlie was always defensive when they were around.

The words died on my lips and I rushed to his side, grabbing his hand and just holding it gently, like spun glass that might shatter at the slightest bump.

Sniffing to hold back yet more tears, I tried to think of something to say when Charlie broke the silence.

"I'm glad you're here. I was worried that you might not want to come."

Throwing a glance at Will and Alex, Charlie seemed to read my thoughts and his tiny smile showed that he too wished that they weren't here to witness this uncomfortable conversation.

Will must have picked up on our brief, silent conversation, "Alex, you want to come to get something to eat? Maybe some better coffee than that vending machine swill?" He gave me a sympathetic smile.

Alex grunted in acknowledgment, and the pair left the room. Will briefly returned to ask if we wanted anything, glancing at us in turn. My stomach was too tied in knots for eating so I shook my head. Charlie gestured to the tray at the bottom of the bed. Will left again with assurances that they'd be gone a little while so we could talk.

I let go of Charlie's hand briefly, my knees no longer willing to keep me standing. I went over and pulled the closest chair up to the bed, sinking into it carefully, my muscles tight with tension. We just stared at each other for a minute.

It was soothing to settle into the regular pattern of us. We've always been like this, never needing words to understand what was going on with each other. Even our argument couldn't stop that.

There was warmth in his expression, the easy affection that we always shared but he never gave to anyone else, and not a single trace of anger. That lack of anger had me relaxing, letting out a sigh, and gaining me a smile from Charlie. I reached over the bed and squeezed his hand gently and he grasped at my fingers before I could pull my hand away and twined them together.

While Alex and Will were away, instead of talking about all the issues that we really should be talking about, we sat in silence.

I was overjoyed to be able to have this. Just to be able to soak in his presence and feeling so glad he was okay and happy to see me. Talking about heavy stuff would have to wait, he wasn't up to it, and I felt too fragile to discuss how much he hurt me.

"You look good," I teased.

Charlie groaned. "I feel amazing, too. Nothing like roadkill." He rolled those gorgeous eyes, but there was a twinkle within them.

Chuckling, I looked over the contents of the tray to avoid looking into his eyes. "Anything good?"

"You know what they say about hospital food..." he trailed off.

"And what do they say? You've got a private room, this is a great hospital, surely the food is decent?"

"I miss your cooking," he muttered under his breath, but I caught the words.

Giving him a soft smile, I steered us into other, safer, topics.

When it came time to leave I didn't want to go, knowing that I would have to stay firm and tell him to give me space. Now that I knew that he would be fine, he had a lot of things to do before we could try to be friends again.

I think he saw that all in my face as he said, "It's cool, Max. I know we aren't there yet, but I want to work at it. Is that okay?" When I nodded he asked hesitantly, "Can I call you now and then, Christmas and stuff?"

I was hesitant to allow that, but the hopeful look he sent my way had me relenting slightly. "Once a week on a Sunday night, but Christmas and New Year don't count. You get those free and you better call me to wish me Happy New Year, or there'll be trouble!"

"I promise."

Chapter Three

Charlie

After a week in the hospital, I returned to my family's house, a place I hadn't lived in since just after college some seven, eight years ago. Staying in my old room did nothing for my mood. The reminder of who I'd been before I royally fucked up my life was sobering, pun intended.

Mom fussed over me after settling me into my bed, fresh sheets carefully folded back. She'd hired a nurse even after I'd reminded her I wasn't an invalid. I could go to the bathroom with no help and wasn't going to keel over at a moment's notice, no matter what she thought.

I'd lain there in that space, with memories of life before it started to go wrong haunting me.

This wasn't home to me. It was a gilded prison. The place where I was meant to conform to what my family wanted me to be. Home had been college with Max. The dorm, and then the apartment while we took classes. It was the tiny run-down house we'd shared with two other guys until Father insisted I at least lease something in line with my job.

In the back of my mind, there had always been a hope for some sort of job that wasn't as soul-sucking as finance, so I'd been trying to save every penny so I could go out on my own. I'd thought I was finally onto something good with the clubs, but even that was being taken from me.

As I lay in bed, I reflected over the uncomfortable meeting that I'd had with Alex the day before. He had confirmed with my doctors that I was getting out of the hospital and into my family's care, before going over what was going to happen to me after I'd healed more. He and Mom had a conversation in the corner before Mom came to break the news.

Rehab.

No questions. No option of saying no. My mom was utterly firm in her decision.

"You need to learn how to express how you feel without using alcohol and anything else to numb your pain." Her voice was soft, the words sad.

The comment struck me hard and I stopped to consider her words. Is that what I'd been doing? Using endless nights of partying and sex to push away what I was feeling?

After Father had died, my anger at him, at Alex and Will, had exploded. I don't think that I was sober for weeks. It was during that time that I'd met Will's boyfriend, Ethan. It had been ridiculously easy to get him into bed the first time; Ethan was desperate for attention and Will was distracted. By the time I figured out that he wasn't just getting it from me, he'd gotten what he'd wanted. Stupidly, it didn't stop me from making a repeat of it, though. Ethan had been more than willing to hold my mistakes over my head when I tried to break it off. Ethan had been an addiction; knowing that I had the power to hurt Will with what we had been doing. There was a time that I used to get a sick sense of satisfaction when I remembered the look of horror on Will's face when he caught us. I'd enjoyed hurting him, making him feel just a fraction of the pain I'd felt. Usually, it was then followed by a feeling of shame that I drowned with vodka. Now I just felt empty. It had been a hollow victory and made things so much worse.

As the third son, I'd always been overlooked and ignored. Alex and Will never really had any time for me, so when Alex took Will's fiancee, Helena, from him, I thought I could fill those shoes, but Will ignored me. I tried time and time again to step up and be the friend that he needed, but he didn't want anything to do with me.

When Father died, Alex rose into his role in the company. The man had it all - the wife, the son, the job. I was pushed aside. It was made clear to me that I had to be like Will and forge my own path.

Except I wasn't as talented or smart as Will. He was Mom's favorite. The one that was a gifted artist, too.

"Darling." Her voice interrupted my thoughts. "I think that you need this. You've been lost for so long and I've never known how to help you."

I wanted to rage at her. Shout about feeling unimportant enough to her to do anything to help me. Rant about how I'd gone about destroying the life I'd managed to build for myself because no one seemed to care, aside from Max. He was my only constant. I cut those words off though because there was no point in causing more pain.

"I don't want to go to rehab, Mom."

"Charlie, my love, you're not getting a choice in this. I won't lose you to your demons."

Then she made her excuses to leave to sort out her house for my return, leaving me alone with my oldest brother.

I was pretty sure that no one in my family knew that Alex and I hadn't been alone like this for years.

Ever since my brief fling with Ethan, Alex hadn't spoken to me any more than was necessary if we happened to be in the same room.

It was why I'd given up going to family events. Will got out of them because of Alex and Helena, and then me, but Alex had made it clear that I wasn't welcome in any place that he was.

I didn't understand him. What he had done was so much worse. He'd married his own brother's fiancee after getting her pregnant. My thing with Ethan was nothing in comparison.

Alex had glared down at me until his anger burst out of him. His tirade about how irresponsible I was, how lucky I was to be alive, yadda yadda, went on and on until he had to sit down and take a breather.

Once he had calmed down, he outlined the steps he'd taken to look after my clubs while I would be in rehab. No choices were given to me; I was just to accept it and move on.

Guilt filled me when I thought of Alex's prematurely lined face and the flecks of gray in his dark hair. Stress had worn at him and while I knew that a lot of his problems were of his own making, I couldn't help but take on some guilt at the burden I was placing on him with the clubs.

I hadn't given the clubs more than a passing thought since I'd been hurt. How they had managed until Alex stepped in and sorted everything out, I had no idea. There was a small burning flame of anger aimed at Alex. He hadn't come back to the hospital after Max had visited. Not until he had a solid reason to. Alex still seemed to feel like it was his place to interfere in my life.

After spending the entire day in bed, when I woke the next morning I was bored and frustrated at looking at the same four walls.

If Mom thought all my time here would be spent with me in bed and getting served food on trays, she had another thing coming. I'd go out of my mind and end up hunting down some booze if I had to stay here much longer.

I'd had an all too short talk with a doctor who was pleased with the rehab plan, but less amused at how much Mom was coddling me.

Slipping downstairs, I joined Matty at the breakfast table. Out of all my siblings, she was most likely the least messed up of all of us. Father had spent less time with her and had died just after she started high school. His lack of influence at such an important time in her life had left her less damaged, I guess.

"Hey, Tilly."

She let out a growl. Her name was all too easy to poke at since we all knew Matilda hated it but couldn't decide if she wanted to change it. With Father gone, she could use her middle name, Eleni, if she wanted, but I think she loved the nickname that Will had given her. Truth be told, Matty suited her.

Mom was at the stove making dinner and I got the impression that she had something to say. Matty gave me a look before making an excuse to leave the kitchen.

"Charlie, darling..."

Well, here we go.

"It won't solve everything, but perhaps three clubs is too many for you." She paused, assessing before she spoke her next words carefully. "Have you considered the offer?"

I wanted to snap at her that thinking about it was all I'd done recently, but I didn't want to give up on the clubs or let my staff down. She must have seen something in my expression because she let it go.

I wanted to dig my heels in and tell her I was fine, that I could keep the clubs and didn't need to go to rehab, but she clearly knew where my thoughts were headed and cut me off before I could open my mouth.

"Darling, I think rehab is what you need to get well. All the drinking is just making it worse."

Pondering her words, I had to admit that maybe I could learn something by going to rehab. Drinking wasn't doing anything to get me out of my head. At least it would get me away from the city and my problems for a while.

Chapter Four

Charlie

While I didn't think I really needed rehab, since I wasn't dependent on alcohol to get through the day, I had to admit that often there was a niggle of need when I got stressed out and pissed off. I'd taken to avoiding Mom because conversations with her were only tolerable with vodka. I guess she had a point. I point blank refused AA, though. I'd do rehab and regular therapy, but not in a group setting. People were part of the reason I'd used alcohol in the first place, so sitting me in a room with a ton of people who all liked a drink was a disaster in the making.

Alex closed on a house for himself and his son, Joe, in the week before Christmas, and since I was at loose ends, I helped him pick out furniture and set the place up.

Conversations with Alex were stilted and stiff, even more so than with Will, which was frustrating. He accepted my help, but it was grudging, our interactions tinged with frustration that I couldn't understand. I spent most of the days helping with Joe since I couldn't really lift anything and got tired easily. Alex had no reason to hate me, but he'd cut me off after Ethan like he wasn't a giant hypocrite.

Part of me understood it; he was protective over Will in a way that he'd never been over me or even our sister.

It burned at me, though. Shame and anger tested my resolve to put the past behind us all. If Will could forgive

Alex, then he could forgive me. If Will did forgive me, then Alex had no reason to hate me, right?

Maybe there would be a time soon where we could all get along and maybe act like the close brothers we were before our father made it a point to pit us against each other. It was going to be a long time coming if nothing changed.

The move went smoothly. Money certainly made shit like moving go much easier, that was for sure. Alex had wanted to move in before Christmas if it was at all possible so that he could give the kid the best day possible considering the circumstances.

"Grandma! Auntie Matty!" Joe yelled as Alex opened their door late Christmas morning. "Santa came! He knew where our new house was!" He looked up at his father with a look of adoration that even affected the usually stoic Alex. "Daddy says it's 'cause Santa is magic!" Joe was practically bouncing on the spot and I wondered if Alex had fed him pure sugar for breakfast or if Christmas just had that effect on kids.

Mom laughed and picked the squirming kid up so she could kiss his cheek before handing him over to his father and kissing Alex, too.

"Merry Christmas, my darlings. Joe, come show Grandma what you got for presents. Auntie Matty has gifts from us."

I stood in the vestibule, unsure what to do. No one had noticed I was even there until Alex put down Joe and I caught the little boy's attention. "Hiya Uncle Charlie," Joe's voice was timid. I hadn't spent nearly enough time with him and I felt bad about that. It wasn't his fault that his family was so messed up. There was always something more important, with running the clubs and general life crap when Mom had him and Helena worked or did whatever.

"Hey there, little man. Happy Christmas. How'd you like your new house? Did you get the bed we picked out?"

Joe's face lit up. "Daddy, can I show Uncle Charlie my room?"

"Presents first with Grandma and then you can take Uncle Charlie upstairs, okay?" It was like seeing a whole new Alex, watching him playing the doting dad. He'd made time for Joe in the past, but with a sabbatical at work, he had much more quality time with him. He was going for full custody with Helena being less than interested in the poor kid, what with her new boyfriend's kids and a new baby on the way.

"Okay, Daddy!" Joe hollered as he rushed off with Alex following behind him, leaving me to wander inside and close the door. I rolled my eyes. It seemed our shopping trip and Joe's acceptance of me wasn't working any magic on Alex.

Mom sat in a chair by the tree with Joe on her lap. She had a new energy about her, like she was finally coming out of the grief that had dimmed her shine since losing Father. She'd known what a difficult man he was and tempered him as best she could. I think that's the only way that we got through our childhoods as well as we did. Sure, we had rough edges, but just the fact that Alex and Will had been able to have relationships, even if they were with flawed people, meant that it hadn't all been bad. There were happy times. I had some good memories of my father, at least.

With us all together, Mom was in her element. Cooking for so many people and spending time with us all was the highlight of her year, as she kept reminding us whenever Matty or I grumbled.

Honestly, we just did it to make Mom laugh; I'd almost forgotten the sound of it. It rang clear, unrestrained, and free all day as Joe tugged on her hand to get her to play with him, and it made being uncomfortable around my brothers so much easier.

Spending Christmas day as a family meant that I got to meet Will's new guy. The one that Mom and Matty had been raving about.

From the moment I met Andy, I got it. He and Will just fit and I'd never seen Will so at peace.

They hadn't been together long, just getting together the week before my mugging. Andy meeting the family and them all spending the day together may have been the catalyst for the binge I went on that weekend. The seething jealousy at them all playing happy families coursing through me led to my argument with Max. Not that the rest of the family knew that, though. They thought I was just a stumbling drunk and that was how I spent all my time.

They didn't see me as the successful businessman that I was. I'd worked hard to make something of myself, but they didn't see that side of me.

It hurt that Andy seemed to have been accepted into the family already, almost like he was taking the spot meant for me. The way that he fit twisted my insides with envy as I remained an outsider. With Alex, Andy was quiet and reserved, but he clearly adored Joe, so that meant Alex would be cool with him. Since they'd been introduced, Mom had spent some time with Andy and Will to get to know Andy better with him being so important to my brother. Mom and Andy had a sweet bond and jealousy burned as I watched them bustling around the kitchen together.

"Oh, they are adorable!" Mom said, cooing over cookies Andy had made.

"Would you believe me if I told you that Will helped make them?" Andy joked, tossing a wink in Will's direction. My brother stood in the doorway watching them with a fond smile on his face.

"Not a chance!" Mom joked. "Will is a kitchen disaster waiting to happen. There's no way he helped with these. He can burn water!" Her laughter filled the room and Will smiled rather than getting upset.

"He's a work in progress," Andy teased and tiptoed over to Will, kissing him on the cheek before returning to Mom's side. Mom put her arm around Andy's waist and squeezed him to her, showing a lightness that I hadn't seen in years. It burned that he was the cause of it.

In the afternoon, in the plushly appointed living room, Matty and Andy chatted about shows they'd watched like old friends. Andy had brought his twin and her partner to the holiday meal, since they usually spent it together. Matty had an instant friendship with his sister, Abby. They just clicked. They gossiped about the theater and the shows that Abby had worked as a costume designer on. Abby shared the technical aspects of some of the elaborate costumes she'd made as Matty looked up photos on her phone. I'd forgotten that Matty loved musicals. I used to take her or get tickets for her often, another thing that had stopped in all this family mess. It made me feel more and more like I didn't belong than ever before and I desperately wished that I hadn't fucked things with Max so badly, or he'd be with me now. He'd know exactly the right things to do and to say to make everything easy for me. Max was my wingman, my best friend, and my social buffer. Tears stung my eyes just thinking about him being alone today. He couldn't bullshit me, I knew that he had no other plans. I'd done that to him and how would I ever be able to make up for that?

Andy was a breath of fresh air, breathing life back into our damaged family. Helena and Ethan had never been like this, which is how I knew this was the real deal for Will.

Over the day I made an effort to get to know Andy instead of being an asshole like usual. It was difficult to get a chance to speak to him; Andy drew people to him, but when we got a quiet moment I made a point to draw him into conversation. I listened to stories of him growing up, and I envied his close bond with his twin. Andy had me laughing at things he told me about when he'd met Will and I could picture them easily. Eventually, his mood shifted and he withdrew into himself. He admitted that the loss of their mom made Christmas hard for him and Abby.

My petty jealousy vanished immediately when Andy quietly asked, "Could we light a candle for my mom? We do that every year." He glanced at his sister, who gave him a little nod.

"You do it this year," she said, equally quiet, as if not wanting to intrude on the moment.

Mom's eyes sparkled with unshed tears. "Of course, sweetheart. I think I have just the one here." We waited a moment as she looked through the present bags she'd tucked in a corner of the room, far from the chaos of all the gifts that Joe had received. Returning with a beautiful multi-colored jar candle and a soft smile on her lips, she handed it to Andy. "Is this okay?"

"It's perfect, thank you. Are you sure it's okay?"

Will appeared at his elbow with matches and he shared a look with Mom. "It is. Here, love."

Andy lit the candle with a soft, "Thinking of you. Mom." It occurred to me that his whole family was in the room with us, even though that was just Abby and Josh. I could stand to be less selfish and share mine with him. I had a feeling he'd be joining my family officially at some point in the near future.

In my room, I'd found my digital SLR camera discarded on a shelf at the start of my forced stay at home, and had started playing around with it again for something to pass the hours. I'd taken a photography course in college and it all came flooding back, so I had taken it with me to Alex's and offered to capture the day for everyone, much to Mom's appreciation. Her eyes had filled with tears at my quiet offering. I needed to make the effort to do better, to be better for her if something so small could make her so happy.

Preferring the honesty of candid shots, I lurked and watched everyone celebrate while getting some great pictures of them. It felt good to be useful for a change, and it kept me out of conversations.

Hiding out in the kitchen after dinner, I made myself useful by cleaning up the detritus of the massive meal we'd consumed while the others chatted in the large living room. Needing something to do and feeling restless, the usual feeling of wanting to escape came over me. When Will came in, an intent look on his face, I knew there was no skipping out on this conversation. Though I didn't want to, it was past time that he and I cleared the air.

"Look," he said firmly, resting against the kitchen counter with his arms folded across his chest. "I don't want to talk about everything that happened. There's no changing the past and you've said that you're sorry, so it's done."

"Still though, I am sorry." I put the last plate in the dishwasher and set about switching the appliance on. Shame over my past behavior made me avoid Will's eyes. "Ethan was a dick and you deserved better. It wasn't just me he was with, there were at least two other guys. Did you know that?"

As the words registered, I realized that he hadn't known.

"Seriously?" Will's face said that he didn't believe me.

"I'm not just saying that to make it sound like I didn't do anything wrong. I should have told you when I found out he was seeing other people. Instead, well, you know what happened."

Will looked green and I rushed to get him a glass of water and stood to the side while he drank it and processed what I'd told him.

"I'm so sorry, Will. It's inexcusable, what I did, especially after Helena."

He flinched at the reminder, but I noticed that he wasn't reacting as strongly as I'd expected to. The emotions were hollow. He was shocked but not devastated over what I'd told him.

After finishing the glass, he handed it to me to set by the sink for the next dishwasher load.

"I'm sorry, too. I let you down, not seeing that maybe you needed someone. Then after it all happened.." His color was returning, anger causing heat to rise on his cheeks. "Not letting you explain even when you tried. I pushed you away instead of seeing that. Punished you, since I couldn't do anything about Alex and Helena." He paused and flushed further, this time with embarrassment. Rubbing the back of his neck nervously, he continued, "Sorry, since you ended up in the hospital I've been talking to my therapist about everything. There was a lot to process."

I wanted to make some sarcastic comment about therapy, but Will was the happiest that I'd ever seen him, so who was I to mock him? He had his shit together and I was being packed off to rehab to save my clubs, my relationships, and likely my life. Plus, I had my own therapist now, so I had no room to talk shit.

Thinking about my businesses soured my mood. Although I'd been cut off from the world, somehow the developer that'd been hounding me managed to call me after I'd ignored his emails.

I pushed that aside to concentrate on what Will was saying and cut in, "Still though, it doesn't excuse what happened. But if you're willing to draw a line under it, then we could just not talk about it anymore."

"I can do that," he said with a contented smile on his face. "It's not like I have any feelings for Ethan now."

Giving a significant glance in the direction of Andy, who was sitting next to Matty with Joe on his knee, I said, "Nope, you've got someone so much better."

"You like him?" Will didn't seem concerned about my opinion, but unthreatened, like he was completely sure of how Andy felt about him.

"For you, yeah. He just seems to fit." I shrugged. I could see the appeal of Andy but he wasn't quite my type.

I didn't have a type per se, and the one person that I could stand to be around for any length of time wasn't talking to me. We'd had the most awkward of conversations at the hospital at the end of his visit and a couple of short calls since then, but Max wanted to leave trying to be friends again until after I'd sorted myself out a bit. Telling him about rehab had been hard. His voice was quiet and firm as he talked me into believing that it was a good idea.

The best part of my week was the call each Sunday. I was saving my Christmas call until a little later so I could tell him all about the meal with Alex and Will. He'd be over the moon that I'd managed a whole day with my family without a drop of alcohol. Not that there was any in the house for me to drink. I wished again that Max could have been here with us and that I hadn't messed up so badly.

Will let the conversation go, talking about other things for a minute before he rejoined his boyfriend. Mom had served all non-alcoholic drinks at the meal and I felt ashamed at the relief of not being tempted. While I'd been resistant to rehab to begin with, the longer I went without a drink, the more it burned and itched at me.

Lurking in the kitchen away from the others and the pressure of socializing, I could admit that I turned to alcohol a lot after a stressful day. I ran three clubs, so there were always drinks at meetings with suppliers or on training days. With everything as it stood, I didn't know how I could go back to being hands-on with the clubs. How could an alcoholic in recovery be a good fit to run nightclubs or bars?

My staff didn't know what happened to me to the best of my knowledge, though I'm sure there were rumors about it. Part of the reason I'd been drinking more was the stress of the clubs. I'd been keeping it from them, but one club wasn't in the best shape. Financially, it was doing okay, but there was a ton of work that was needed to get the building up to the new codes that were coming in. They were going to be costly and difficult to implement, possibly causing us to close briefly to get the work done. A developer had been on my case about buying the building and one of my other clubs. He was unwilling to take just the one and I was torn over it.

If I gave in and sold them, it would still leave me with my best performing club. It was the one where the manager had quit but had come back after Alex had bargained with him. It was also the one that didn't need me there. What would I do with my days if I didn't have them to oversee? What would happen to my staff if I agreed to the sale?

I'd been holding out, partly because the stubborn part of me wanted to keep them even if they were going to cost me a fortune to renovate. The real reason though was the people that I'd hired. Most, if not all, of the staff were handpicked for my clubs. While I wasn't the best at dealing with the general public, years of sitting back and observing had taught me a lot about what made people tick. Human behavior was easy to predict. After working for me a while, I knew these people well and didn't want them to lose their jobs just after Christmas. I could be a dick, but I wasn't a bastard.

Aside from that one manager who I'd made the mistake of sleeping with, all of my employees seemed to enjoy working for me. We didn't hire often, so I must have been doing something right.

As the party started to wind down, with Alex putting Joe to bed and Abby and Josh taking their leave, Mom noticed that I was flagging and said her goodbyes, pushing me and Matty out of the door.

I hurt all over, my body still healing from the beating it'd received. While I'd put on weight, I was still far too skinny.

For so long I'd been caught up in running away from my problems, and I'd neglected to look after myself. Eating and sleeping were regularly forgotten. Passing out drunk and having a liquid dinner didn't count for much, it seemed.

The house was warm and scented with vanilla when we returned, Matty having driven us in her new car. Next Christmas she would be in college, so Mom justified spoiling her with something practical but safe, not that any of us minded.

"I'm just going to call Max and then probably go to sleep," I told Mom, giving her a brief hug and saying goodnight. I still felt sleepy and full from the feast we'd eaten.

"Okay honey, wish him a Merry Christmas from me and a thank you for the gift. It was beautiful."

"Sure thing."

Upstairs, in the safety of my room, I took a breath, toed off my shoes, and sat at my desk, pulling my phone out of my pocket.

I was grateful that I had always automatically backed everything on my phone up to the cloud because I had a ton of pictures of me and Max just hanging out that I would have been gutted to lose. I could deal with losing numbers and random things, but I wanted those photos.

Putting off the call a little longer, feeling guilty at how I knew Max had spent his day, I scrolled through the recovered photos, smiling at happier times and wondering where it had all gone wrong for us.

On my desk, there was a framed photo of the two of us from college. We were both smiling up at the camera with my arm around his shoulders. It'd been a gift from Max early on in our friendship when we still didn't quite know each other's likes and dislikes as well as we did now. Or at least, as well as I thought we did.

Unpacking my camera bag carefully, I got the memory card out, ready to back up the pictures and pick the best ones out for a photo book for Mom. It would be a great gift for her. I'd bought her a spa experience, which was a cop-out gift if I was honest. I'd lost touch with stuff that my family liked and saw the brief flicker of disappointment in her eyes when she'd opened it. After so many Christmases apart, I really should have done better.

My laptop fired up quickly. Clicking on the memory card, I waited as the contents loaded. After a minute, I was stunned at discovering photos from my university days with Max. I couldn't believe that I'd set these aside and forgotten them. There were maybe hundreds of Max. Him sitting in fall leaves, laughing up at me without a care in the world. Max cooking, on one of the many vacations we took, or just hanging out.

If I did my rehab and we figured things out, would Max let me take photos of him again? He used to love posing for me. Often it was just silly poses, but I'd get him to pretend he was a proper model. He was pretty enough for it, and he'd strut around while I took tons of shots. He'd stare into the lens moodily and then we'd crack up with laughter. We would wander the city looking for great backgrounds for him, the park, museums, old buildings, anywhere that caught my eye. He was crazy photogenic, the light always hitting him just right, turning his white-blond hair silver so he looked otherworldly. He hadn't lost any of that now we were older, if anything he was more beautiful.

I was aware I was running out of excuses to put the call off, but I couldn't help feeling nostalgic and guilty. The argument with Max was my fault. I'd messed up with him royally and it'd taken days for me to figure out where I'd gone wrong. I'd gotten careless with him. It niggled at me that it might be something more than that. It wasn't like Max to react so strongly, so maybe it was something else? I scoured my memories of the last few weeks and couldn't come up with anything, leaving me frustrated.

When we were out partying, I always had to keep half an eye on him. He was like catnip to a lot of creeps. They mistook his smaller stature for weakness. They saw him as vulnerable because he looked so angelic and though he could hold his own, it never hurt to have back up.

A few months ago we'd been out and I'd lost track of him. I'd left him alone in a club and went to a new bar looking for a hookup. Stress had been piling on and I was drinking more and more to take the edge off and I'd just... left him. I was lucky that Will had found him and made sure he'd gotten home safely. My brother was a far better man than I'd given him credit for.

Max was the best friend that I could hope for. While he hadn't condoned my actions with Ethan, I'd suffered many of his lectures, he stood by me when others hadn't. I think that he'd been relieved when Ethan and I fell apart quickly after it all came out. There had been no chance that we would stay together since Ethan and Max didn't get along.

Pulling up the contact for Max, I hesitated before pressing the call symbol. It rang a couple of times before he picked up.

"Merry Christmas, Charlie."

"Merry Christmas, Max."

Chapter Five

Max

I'd visited with Charlie's mom before he got out of the hospital and gave her the small gift that I'd gotten her, as well as the gifts for Matty and Charlie.

She looked at me with concern when I'd let her know that I wouldn't be spending Christmas with them, but thanked her for the invitation. Usually, Charlie and I would spend Christmas together. While he didn't open for customers on Christmas Day, he still opened the doors to staff. They had always held a potluck for those without families to celebrate the holiday together.

When she asked me about my plans, I'd been vague, unwilling to make her feel bad. If Charlie and I had been in a better place then I'd have loved nothing more than to spend it with his family again. I knew it'd never be like it was before Alex and Helena got married and the fall out of that, but I could see them getting past it all eventually. They may have had difficult times, but there was a lot of love between them.

Nerves filled me as I waited for our Christmas call. I both did and didn't want to speak to Charlie, to hear his familiar voice. I wanted to believe that he was missing me as much as I missed him, but the anxious part of me worried that I'd be forgotten in the healing he was doing with his family.

Charlie called in the evening on Christmas, making sure that he'd have plenty to say.

"I met Andy today," he said.

"Andy?" I squashed the bitterness at feeling left out, trying not to let it show in my tone.

"Will's new boyfriend."

I sucked in a breath as I had a brief flashback of the time I think I was spiked. I had to have been, I hadn't had much to drink. Certainly not enough to make me vomit in the street like I did. I vaguely recalled Will telling me something about Andy as he took me home, though I hadn't been in any state to talk to him much. "What's he like?"

"He's cool." I could almost hear Charlie's shrug. "Fits in great with everyone." It gave payment to my fears until Charlie said. "I wish you'd been there though, it wasn't the same without you. I get why you weren't, but Max, it sucked until I could get over myself. I did a lot of the damage here. I know it's my fault that things are rough and that's why you didn't come, but I just wanted you with me."

My heart swooped and soared. I hated hurting Charlie, but this would be good for him long-term. It was enough that he'd wished for me, it had to be. It soothed my worries.

I evaded questions about what I'd done all day, turning them back on him. He knew as well as I did that I had no family and I'm pretty sure that he could guess how my day had been, he just didn't call me out on it and for that I was glad. My mom had been young when she'd had me and I'd grown up with the knowledge that as soon as I was eighteen, I was on my own.

Charlie and I had been roommates in our second year of college. I was a poor scholarship student and he was the popular rich boy.

Charlie should have had that rich boy charm, being graced with smiles everywhere he went, especially with how he looked. His Greek heritage combined with those stunning dark blue eyes should have had people agreeing to anything. He'd been given the best of everything since birth, including a private school education, but he failed miserably when dealing with people he didn't need to. The man was a leader and hated to conform.

We were an odd match. He had zero people skills and the talent of pissing people off, whereas I was voted "Actual Ray of Sunshine" in high school. My high school was weird and I think the guidance counselors were in some sort of hippie cult or something because we weren't allowed to have negative categories. In short, I made friends easily and went around after Charlie smoothing ruffled feathers so he'd keep me around. In return, he looked after me like an overbearing bodyguard when we were out getting drunk and trying to get laid.

While it wasn't the best Christmas ever, it wasn't the worst either. Deciding not to throw myself a pity party and maybe gain a little perspective, I volunteered at a homeless shelter serving meals for those less fortunate than myself. I'd been invited elsewhere but didn't want my low mood to bring anyone else down. So, okay, maybe I didn't have any family, but I had some great friends, my own business, and a home. Which was more than most of these people had, so I should be grateful right?

I didn't have a lot of close friends. Great ones, but not friends as close to me as Charlie, anyway. Recently I'd become close to my assistant manager at my café-bookshop, Books & Biscuits. Acting as my sounding board, she listened to me talk about Charlie a lot over the last couple of weeks. Kristen has had to pick up the pieces after the fights that we had, which couldn't help but make us closer. Kristen had been a godsend in the couple of years since I'd taken her on. I was lucky that I could afford to hire an assistant manager and take some time off not too long after opening. It was hit and miss with cafés like mine, but I'd been fortunate. Maybe I'd relied on Kristen a little too much during all this crap with Charlie, but knowing her as I did now, she'd tell me if I was getting on her last nerve. She was forthright to a fault. I kinda loved that about her.

She was quick enough to say that she didn't understand why I wasn't spending all my time at the hospital with Charlie, but it was difficult to explain my feelings and how we had left things, or why tough love was needed.

I didn't think that she understood addict behavior until I explained it. Addicts will always be full of promises, assuring you that they'll change, that it won't happen again, that the addiction isn't in control of them. I'd been down this path with my mother, her medicating with alcohol to make up for her frustrating life, being saddled with a child at such a young age, and having no support.

Charlie could promise to me all that he liked but in the end, until he worked on himself, his addiction would win out. Our friendship was the only bargaining chip that I had. It's not like I enjoyed being separated from him. It hurt. A lot. So had being dumped in a club for the flavor of the week or being ignored because he'd gotten caught up arguing with some random person.

There were other red flags but I didn't have the mental energy to dwell on them. I wanted Charlie to figure it out.

Will rescuing me from a handsy creep had been a bit of a wake-up call for me. I'd been far too drunk, and not entirely sure I hadn't been slipped something, so I'd started only drinking from bottles I'd seen opened or having soft drinks. It had been all too easy to be swept up with Charlie and it was affecting the rest of my life. Unfortunately, being sober highlighted how much Charlie was drinking and how little he was listening to me.

Rehab would be the thing that would make or break our friendship. If he ducked out of going, then that would be it for us. If he went, but started drinking again, then I didn't know what I'd do.

I wanted the sweet Charlie from the start of our friendship back, but I often wondered if I was wishing for the impossible.

Chapter Six

Charlie

By the time the first week of January came around, I was more than happy to go to rehab just so that I could get away from my family. I felt smothered by their well-meaning attention.

I'd been "encouraged" to let my apartment go. Giving Jessie, my housekeeper, a huge severance and an apology, I'd packed up my belongings and donated my furniture, hoping that some good karma was on its way.

My therapist had agreed that a fresh start once I came out of rehab was a good idea since I was in the position to do that.

"I know you don't see it this way, but where possible, I encourage all my clients to do this. Severing ties to your past that you don't want to bring into your sober future will help long term." Evan must have seen my snort rising. "Yeah, I know it sounds like bullshit." For all his alternative vibe, he didn't curse often and that was what stopped me from interrupting. "I'd look at getting a job that wasn't in a nightclub if I were you, and find somewhere new to live once you're home. Try it. A clean sweep will help your recovery." I still must have looked doubtful, but he didn't push it further.

Being realistic, I'd always known that I would end up selling two of the clubs but had managed to come to an agreement with the developer and he was looking at finding similar jobs within his portfolio for my employees. Word of what had gone on with the clubs had gotten to him and he played hardball over the negotiations, but I could more than afford to hold out. I'd hire other managers if I couldn't handle being in them, but I'd protect my staff either way. In the end, it was decided that some could stay with me and work my remaining club, but that was all down to the manager who had returned with a hefty raise. Honestly, it was lucky I wasn't being sued, since I'd been his boss and had taken advantage of that.

Alex had grudgingly taken me to a few appointments with my lawyer to sign over the clubs and sort out the mess with the manager so he couldn't come back and sue me later. I'd endured more than one lecture from my eldest brother over the whole mess, then spent a full hour of my twice-weekly therapist visits ranting and raving over what a dick Alex was.

It was glaringly obvious there were more than a few issues between Alex and me since he didn't have Will to use as an excuse.

Selling had hurt, and just because I'd saved jobs, it didn't mean that I was happy with all of this. It went against the grain to have to ask for help, to grovel to get people to do their jobs and look after their own interests as well as mine.

"How did you come by the clubs in the first place? You told me that your background and degree are in finance. I know of your family's company since they sign my checks." Evan asked as we sat in his boring office.

I resisted the urge to clam up and told him honestly, "The clubs had kinda fallen into my lap." I smiled at the memory. "It wasn't like I'd left my family's finance company. I told you that Alex forced me out. I won the first one, one of the clubs that are now being sold, and then loved the buzz that I got from it all and was hooked. I'd been in Vegas a couple of weeks after getting my inheritance and was living it up with drinks and gambling for a weekend." I gave Evan a wry grin. I was sure he could picture it. A young guy, loaded and troubled, going wild in the gambling capital of the world.

"Max and I were letting our hair down, so to speak, before he opened Books & Biscuits, the business that I'd insisted on investing in." Thinking of Max made me smile. "Well, he'd demanded that I become a partner when I just wanted to give him the money to get his dream going." I shrugged. I really would have been happy just to give him the money, but Max wouldn't have it.

"So we'd been letting loose when this guy put the deeds to his club on the table and I'd won the pot." Evan watched me carefully. "Later, maybe a few months after Vegas, he'd come to me with a request that I buy another of his clubs, at a cut-price since he was hemorrhaging money, and I bought it with what I had left after tucking some safely away."

Evan nodded and noted something down. "Good, so at that point, would you say that your drinking was under control for the most part?"

"It was just before the Ethan stuff." At his quizzical look, I clarified. "My brother's boyfriend. I spoke about that before."

"That's right. Thank you for the reminder. So how did you end up with three clubs?"

"Well, I'd quickly turned both clubs around and within a year I had enough cash, so I bought my pride and joy." My smile dimmed. It was the one club that I was getting to keep. I'd worked hard, day and night, to pull them up from the money pits that they had been. From the start, I'd been written off by other club owners in the area because I didn't have the network they did, didn't have the knowledge and experience. I'd poured blood, sweat, and tears into making them the safe spaces that they were now.

Just a couple of years later and here I was. The loss of the clubs felt like a failure despite the profit I was making from them. It stung.

I shrugged it off, hoping that Evan wouldn't dig too deep today. I felt raw and flayed open.

What little of my pride was stripped away at the twice-weekly piss tests and therapy. I was being treated like I'd committed a crime instead of being the victim of a mugging.

The assault that I'd suffered was in the back of everyone's minds. There was CCTV footage of the attack but the quality was shit and the cops didn't seem to care. Giving a statement from a hospital bed had been the cherry on the shit sundae of my week. At least they'd waited a couple of days to come and had accepted the photos Alex had emailed to them since some of the bruising was starting to fade. To the cops, it was clear I was just another drunk rich boy in the wrong part of town, so I probably deserved it. Mom had talked about hiring a private investigator to find the culprits but I just wanted to let it go. With my luck, looking for them would bring more hassle to my doorstep. So I'd given up on any chance of getting the watch back, the only thing that I'd cared about being taken that night. My father had gifted that to me when I'd graduated college, the first and only time he'd been proud of me.

Immediately after leaving the hospital, I started intensive therapy. My therapist was an older man who'd had an addiction problem himself for years before retraining to help sufferers, even going so far as getting his doctorate.

I'd gone into our first meeting expecting some fancy woman in a stuffy office. My therapist, Evan, was the opposite. Fully covered in tattoos and piercings, gray hair in a man bun, the guy was a walking Daddy fantasy if you liked that kind of thing. Max was never meeting him. We'd never discussed the particulars in what we wanted in a guy. Max had a varied dating history. Some of his boyfriends had been hot but shallow, only wanting a cutie like Max as arm candy. Others had been smart but dull. All had used Max in some way or another. He had the unfortunate ability to attract weirdos. Though I never really saw him that broken up about a guy, never seeming that emotionally invested in the relationship. Evan though, a man this hot and with his life together, would be anyone's type and I worried about the two of them in the same place.

Evan and I got on well and though I wasn't as open as I maybe could be, he cut me a lot of slack since I was still suffering from my injuries. Evan had assigned me work to do in rehab. I had a list of people to apologize to and I planned on writing a lot of letters since I wouldn't have my phone a lot, especially in the first week.

In my last call to Max, I'd told him that I'd been informed by the facility doctors that there would be no outside contact for the first week. This was to allow me a chance to adapt to the program. Though I had a good head start since I'd been dry since the mugging.

Eventually, I'd be allowed visitors, but it'd been recommended that we keep to a small list of permitted guests and short periods for the visits, so only Mom and Matty were allowed to come to the facility. Theirs were the only relationships I hadn't managed to completely fuck up and wouldn't cause me stress by visiting. Well, mostly. I'd rather Matty come on her own but there was no way Mom would allow that.

When I was told that I'd be going to rehab, I'd imagined weeks without contact with anyone, and though they recommended that for the first few weeks, it helped work out any issues by allowing calls and visits. Given that information, I felt my spirits raise a fraction. Maybe rehab was worth doing if it could get me out of this mess.

Rehab was almost a joke. The place I'd been sent to was so far from looking like a hospital, it couldn't be believed. It felt and looked like an upscale spa and wellness center.

My room was cozy, just enough room for a queen bed and dresser, with a small bathroom attached. The shower was over the bath, the water kept off of the floor by a clear curtain.

Being unable to lock the doors was the only visible sign at first that this wasn't a spa. The search of my belongings and having to submit to a pat-down were the next signs.

We had therapy alone and in groups. I had mixed results with both, having never been much of a sharer. Coping strategies were great and all, but I didn't appreciate having to practice them with role-play. Not the kind of role play I liked, though there was no chance of the good kind with the people there. We were told not to get too friendly, to not become codependent on each other. It was fine to make friends, but we had to remember at all times why we were here and instead focus on our journey to good health and habits.

I spent a lot of my time outside in the extensive gardens with my camera or in the gym. The doctors on staff had cleared me to use the gym after my first week there, which was great because the continued forced group therapy had my temper flaring. I tried not to let it show but I often had to visit the gym after a session just to calm down by forcing my body into exhaustion.

After so many benders and a lack of decent nutrition, I was thinner and weaker than I'd realized. It took a few weeks of fresh air, good food, and exercise before I began to look anything like my former self.

I'd gotten permission from the staff and fellow patients to chart my rehab journey with my camera. It'd been a suggestion from an in-house therapist, but I think that they'd meant a bunch of selfies or something. I became fascinated by all the changes in the people around me as they came back to being healthy.

The slow pace and steady routines quickly became reassuring, but the outside world didn't slow. All too soon I was faced with the reality of leaving the comfort and safety of the center for the outside world.

Part of the process of rehab was tallying up all the progress that had been made towards our goals, and even I had to admit that I'd done a lot to work through some of the issues that had been plaguing me.

I'd written all my letters and surprisingly had gotten some replies. After one very awkward call with Will, I was passed on to Andy, and we struck up an unlikely friendship. I wondered if it would continue on the outside.

The manager that I'd hurt and offended accepted my apology on the provision that I stay away from the club. It was a relief, and I knew my family was glad to have the threat of a lawsuit gone from hanging over my head.

The letters and replies really got to the heart of some of my issues, highlighting a lack of support system other than Max, which was unhealthy. I had targets and had identified future issues as part of my preparation for leaving rehab as the days there ticked down. Evan had been making trips to the center to keep up with my progress and make sure that he was aware of any treatment plans that were needed when I got out.

I officially had a clean slate when I rejoined the outside world at the end of my sixty days, but there was a large part of me that wondered if I was ready. Rehab was safe. The people there could be annoying, but they meant well. My family paid a lot to have me stay there and I could grudgingly admit that it'd helped, but going home meant seeing the faces of people that I'd hurt. The letters kept them at a distance and it was all too easy to accept an apology when the person wasn't in your face.

There was also the fact that I was going home to no job and no place to live. I couldn't stay with Mom for long without wanting to escape, and I had no idea how to fill my days. I'd have to find a job eventually, though the club's sale had made a decent profit so it wasn't like I needed the money. Filling my days with something other than partying was going to be my biggest problem. I didn't want to work in finance. It was too high pressure, and was what had started the heavy drinking in the first place. There wasn't much else that I was trained for and nothing that interested me enough to want to go back to college, though I could afford to do that if I found something I wanted.

It made me think about what I could do. Maybe I could buy an apartment and just get a job in a kitchen or something. I could cook, except chefs didn't have the greatest reputation when it came to drinking, so unless it was a café, then that was a bad idea. I wasn't the greatest with people, so retail and food service were probably out. Plus I didn't want to be around alcohol a lot if there were stressors that could cause a relapse.

My options were limited and it was beyond frustrating to hit thirty and have to start over. I mean, thirty wasn't old but most people my age seemed to have their shit together, right?

I spent the ride back into the city dwelling on what was ahead. Tomorrow I'd look for somewhere else to live and do what Will did. When our father died, he invested the inheritance we'd gotten on a property. Then I'd look for a job that I wouldn't mind doing, reminding myself that I was lucky and privileged to have money and not have to worry about making rent.

Mom met the town car when it pulled up in front of the main entrance of her house. The sprawling mansion didn't suit her. It was ostentatious and gaudy. If Dad hadn't been so proud of it, I'm sure she would have sold it by now and moved to the lake cabin that suited her better.

"Hello darling," she said, pulling me into a hug as soon as I was free of the car. Holding me at arm's length after our brief embrace, she ran an assessing eye over me. "The gym seems to be working wonders on you, sweetheart. You look so well!"

"You saw me two weeks ago at your last visit, Mom."

"And in that time, you look different. I do hope you aren't overdoing it. Too muscly isn't attractive." She looked up at the gathering clouds. "It looks like rain, let's go inside and..."

Already I felt trapped and wanted something to shut off the noise in my head. I cut her off. "Could we start looking at properties? I'd like to buy a house and you helped so much with Will and Alex's places."

She smiled at me but her eyes were sad. "Of course!"

I hated to hurt her, but this house held too many memories for it to be a place where I could have the clean slate that rehab had promoted. The sooner I was in my own space, the better.

Chapter Seven

Charlie

Despite spending two months in rehab, I was still expected to turn up to my therapy appointment the morning after I'd gotten home.

Mom had gotten snippy at the suggestion that I might like a few days to reconnect with everyone. I don't know if it was the idea that I'd be out of her sight somewhere unknown, or if it was the idea of my old friends, but she had quickly shot the idea down and all but demanded I go to my appointment with Evan.

I'd endured a slightly hostile family dinner with Mom, Matty, Alex, and Joe later that evening. Will and Andy had been slammed with work, the company in the process of expanding and hiring, so they had been taking work home with them and eating while they worked. They couldn't spare the time for a welcome home dinner and their absence was keenly felt. I understood that they were busy, though it stung that they couldn't make time for me.

My phone had rung with a video call and I'd picked up the call to an exhausted Will and Andy.

"Hey," came my brother's voice. "Sorry, we couldn't make it. Work is a nightmare just now."

"Show him the table!" Andy called and Will panned the camera to the dining table they seemed to be working at. The surface was littered with samples and papers, seemingly with no real order to it. Andy sat at the end, his hair rumpled from running his hands through it probably. He looked up with a smile for me as he pulled at a notebook in the pile and scribbled something on a page.

"Yikes!" I said, taking it all in. "Are you guys okay? Do you need anything?"

"Nah," Andy assured me. "Just wanted you to see that we aren't blowing you off. We're crazy busy, but by the end of the week this will all be done and we'll do dinner properly okay?"

I nodded. "If you're sure. I won't be offended if you can't make it, or just want to chill out."

"I've already told work I'm still going to my support meeting, though I'll have to buy cookies this time. I don't have time to make any."

"I'll make them for you. Just tell me how many and what kind." I was at a bit of a loose end and it would help them out.

"Really?" Andy's eyes went wide.

I nodded. "Sure. I'd be happy to help you out."

"That'd be amazing! Thanks, Charlie! I'll send you a text with the recipes I use, okay?"

"Sure."

"Okay, we better get back to it. You're a lifesaver! Thanks!" Andy said enthusiastically.

"Bye Charlie," Will said with a proud smile.

It took me a minute to recover from the call and even as I got ready for bed hours later, I still recalled the way that smile had made me feel.

It buoyed me through a quiet breakfast and during the short walk to the car. I'd gotten into the town car with reluctance. I wanted a couple of days at home to process before I started back up with therapy. I'd seen Evan the day before I'd left, so I had little to tell him.

The office building that held his office was a short drive from Books & Biscuits, Max's café-bookstore. The driver that had taken me to my appointment had driven by it on our way and I'd found myself looking out the window, attempting to get a glimpse of Max.

There were three other therapists in the building, each with their own specialty, but I hadn't seen into their rooms to see if theirs matched them better than Evan's did. Evan's office didn't suit the tatted-up man at all. It lacked the personality that oozed out of him, often shown in the way he wore his shirts with suspenders, well-cut slacks with heavy biker boots.

The walls were painted a washed-out green that was supposed to be soothing but reminded me of the hospital and often had my pulse rocketing at the memories. The longer I was sober, the more I remembered about that time and I often woke in a cold sweat, panting and shaking. Not that I'd told him that.

Bookshelves lined the walls with an assortment of journals and heavy-looking tomes adorning the shelves. There were comfortable chairs rather than the obligatory sofa to recline on. I'd asked Evan about the lack of a couch once and he'd chuckled and said he didn't often counsel couples since addiction was what he dealt with mostly. Romantic relationships often suffered as a result of addiction and only once that was under control could the couple attend the correct type of therapy.

I think it was the lack of personal touches that made the office seem cold and unwelcoming. Evan needed photos of his beloved Harley, the bike he'd restored after the crash that'd started him on the path to addiction to pain medication. I often thought about offering to take some decent photos for him, as some sort of thank you for all the advice he'd given me, but wondered if that was overstepping. I knew he was being paid to put up with my shit, but I was sure that I wasn't the easiest of patients to deal with.

"Charlie?" Evan's low voice broke through my reverie.

"Hey, Doc."

Evan beckoned me into his office from the small waiting room and gestured at the comfortable armchair that I favored. The beige suede fabric was soft against my hands as I rubbed the arms nervously.

"Let me start by saying that I advised against this session today," Evan said quietly.

My head shot up and I looked at him in question as he sat back in his seat.

"You did?"

"Yes. As I said to your mother, I felt it was more appropriate to allow you a couple of days to adjust to being back in the family home. I wanted to give you the space that you wouldn't have had at the facility and see how you felt then. This is a key juncture in your recovery." He paused assessing me. "A lot of people return to using, being unable to cope with reality. It isn't that I wanted you to sink, I just wanted you to show that you could swim."

The room fell silent while I processed his words.

"Mom and I argued about the session since we're being honest."

Evan nodded as if he had expected that. "You have a difficult relationship. One that I see being a lot of stress for you in the coming months."

"What do I do then?"

"It isn't my place to advise you, Charlie, remember that. I'm only here to give you the tools to deal with your addiction and help you stay sober."

My heart sank even though I knew that was what he was going to say. He'd said it before, after all.

"That being said, I can help you work through it. Tell me, what would you say to someone who had a difficult family relationship like yours?"

We sat quietly while I thought about what I would say to someone in the same situation as me.

"I'd say that they need their own space and boundaries." I received an approving nod. "If they wanted to work on the relationship, that was fine as long as both knew where they stood and that both sides made the effort."

"Right. Anything else?"

"I'd remind them that although they'd messed up before, they had the right support and tools to do better and that they would only know their progress if they actually tried. Get rid of the armbands."

Evan nodded at me. "Have you contacted any of your friends? Made any plans?"

I shook my head. "Most of them haven't contacted me since I was in the hospital. Only Max really bothers with me now."

"And what about Max? Do you have plans to see him? It's been months, right? I believe that a condition of your friendship resuming was that you got help."

"Yes."

"But?"

"Well... He's wanted to see me but I've been vague."

"Why is that?"

"I'm nervous."

He looked at me and I could see the unasked question.

"I'm worried that there's too much hurt there." I paused and he waited for me to continue. "Whatever I did must have been something big for him to cut me off like that."

"It's not just that though, is it?"

"No."

"Charlie?"

"What if I've changed too much, or even not enough, and I lose him? What happens when I meet him again and it's all weird and uncomfortable? Max got me through rehab."

"How so?"

"Just the thought of him being out there waiting for me to do the program and get well....It was the only thing keeping me going some days. When shit got hard or when they hit a nerve."

"Could you tell me when you fell in love with Max?"

It felt like my heart had stopped. The whole world stopped.

Love?

In love with Max?

Was that what that feeling was?

"Ah, I apologize. I assumed that your feelings for Max were romantic. Some of what you've said in our sessions gave me a different impression of the situation. I apologize, I seem to have spoken out of turn." Evan looked contrite.

I reached for the bottle of water on the side table next to me, opening it and gulping down almost half of it, trying to get myself together.

Evan waited patiently for me.

"I didn't realize." The words escaped me without permission.

Evan allowed me to sit and think for the rest of the session, breaking me out of my thoughts just before the end of the hour to check in with me. Did I feel like drinking? Was I going to be okay? Did I want a session sooner than the start of next week? A phone call check-in later? No answered just about all of those questions. I was not okay, but I didn't want to drink and just needed time to work through my feelings.

Outwardly I assured him that while I was shocked, the last thing I wanted to do was drink. If I did that, I had no hope of a second chance at friendship with Max, and not a single chance of anything more.

Did I want anything more?

I think that I did, but did Max feel the same? Was I willing to risk everything to find out?

Chapter Eight

Charlie

Days had passed since I'd come home and I was still avoiding people. I'd sent Max a couple of texts asking if our weekly call was on and he'd asked again to meet up instead. I'd sent another vague reply agreeing without setting something up, and felt shitty about it. It wasn't that I didn't want to see him, I did, but my worries about the changes between us festered and ruled my thoughts. There was a strange distance in his voice in the calls and I worried that we were going to drift apart.

My mind was twisted up and I missed the routines of rehab and the time alone. Twice weekly therapy wasn't enough to fill my week. I was still putting off AA meetings and I was sure that Evan agreed that they wouldn't suit me. The type of alcoholism was rooted in my mental health it seemed, and escape from my issues more than an addiction, or so my research had suggested. It made me work harder in my sessions with Evan, with me finally offering up events that had triggered a binge.

Therapy was a strange experience and I couldn't decide if I tolerated it or loathed it. Allowing myself to be vulnerable and open with anyone that wasn't Max went against the grain. Except Evan had a soothing aura of calm and a lack of judgment that slipped under my defenses and had me sharing things I wouldn't have shared, especially before rehab.

With energy to burn since it had been days since my last workout, I texted Andy:

Charlie: What gym do you guys go to? The one you're always talking about?

Andy was at work and the office was still crazy busy with the new team and big client they'd landed so I didn't expect a reply to come so soon.

Andy: Henry's gym? It's this one...

There was a website attached and I clicked the link, opening up my phone's browser and looking at the well-designed website. Without thinking too much about it, I clicked to sign up and book an orientation with Henry for later that day.

Charlie: Thanks man, just signed up. Hope that's okay

Andy: NP why wouldn't it be? You and Will are putting stuff behind you. It's all good. Might be nice to work out together

Charlie: Cool

While Andy said it would be cool, I didn't want to assume that he was right and I fired a text off to Will checking, fully prepared to cancel my appointment with Henry.

Will quickly called me back. "Hey, look there's no need to check with me. I thought maybe we were making progress."

"We are. I just didn't want to assume. It's your space with Andy and your friends." I paused. "It's just Andy told me so much about it the other day at dinner and it sounds like a cool place." They'd managed to fit in the dinner even with work still cutting into their home life. Andy had told me how much they'd hated taking things home with them but it felt great that they'd made time for me.

We'd talked around discussions of the custody battle Alex was in with Helena over Joe. Will had passed around some photos they'd had taken at their engagement party informing us that they wouldn't be using the guy for their wedding, whenever they could set a date. Their engagement hadn't come as a surprise to me and I felt a tiny trickle of guilt at missing the party to be in rehab. I'd arranged for flowers to be sent as soon as I'd been told by Andy. Just a small way to congratulate them, but I wished I'd been there. The feeling of being on the outside looking in at the tight group my family had forged themselves into had hit me hard then.

"It is, and you'll probably get a lot out of it. If you can get Henry to do your induction that'd be best." Will's tone turned disapproving as he said Henry's name and I recalled all the stuff Andy had told me when we'd broken away from the dinner table.

"Look, I need to get back to it, but let me know how things go, okay?" Will said.

"Sure. Thanks."

The call ended and I smiled. He could have texted, but he'd made the effort to call, so that was great progress.

Will's assurance shouldn't have felt as good as it did. Like maybe it was all genuine that he'd accepted my apologies and was willing to start fresh like he'd promised me. Something warmed in my chest at Will's encouragement, and for the first time in a long time, I felt real hope that it would work out.

We hadn't talked much at the dinner; the only time I'd talked were the moments with Andy and briefly when I asked my brothers their opinions on properties that Mom and I had looked at. It was strange. I wanted my family's attention, but not all at once. I wasn't used to being the center of attention and deflected it off me as much as possible.

My property hunt wasn't going well. I didn't need a lot out of where I lived, but the options were pretty dismal. I just wanted some space of my own that wasn't haunted by my past mistakes. Something central so that I didn't have to drive a lot, or at all if possible since I'd hated driving after an accident in college. Not alcohol-related, and not my fault, but I'd been punished by Father for it. That punishment had given me Max though, so I couldn't complain too much about it.

Instead of taking the car service Mom said I could use, I walked a couple of miles to the gym. I'd take a rideshare home if I didn't feel up to walking back. I needed the time alone and the fresh spring air to process that first post-rehab session that I'd had with Evan.

"Could you tell me when you fell in love with Max?"

No lie, that question had rocked me. I didn't think there was a specific moment that I fell in love with Max. I think that part of me always had been in love with him since the very second that I walked into that dorm room and the fading autumn light had lit up his blond head like he had a halo.

Inch by inch, he'd wormed his way into my heart until he owned the thing, as useless as it was.

It seemed like everyone knew it before me, too. I wasn't completely oblivious to how other people saw my relationship with Max. There had been comments from my brothers before our family went to shit. Snide remarks from my father who didn't think Max was good enough for me like I gave a shit about his opinion. Even Ethan had thrown it in my face when we'd broken up, though I'd brushed it off at the time. "I can't believe I gave up Will for someone who's in love with someone else. He'll never want you now. Not now that he sees how toxic you are. You ruin everything!"

I'll admit I'd thought that Ethan was hilarious for making out that he'd left Will for me when he'd been sleeping his way through the city while the man he lived with grieved for his father.

Unfortunately, Max had been with someone at that point, even if I had been able to clearly see my feelings. The guy's name escaped me, and I was too messed up when he was single again to do anything about it.

Just thinking back on that time and all the support that Max had given me struck me hard. That what I'd been looking for, I could have found in Max. He was the only person that really allowed me to be myself. That just a second of his attention was worth days of anyone else's.

Of course, when Evan asked the question, he'd knocked me off-kilter and I'd spent half the session dwelling on it. He'd wrapped up with going over what we'd covered and asked me to think about my relationship with Max as "homework."

The guy was a great therapist, much better than the first one I'd been handed over to in rehab (not that they lasted long), but I hated the tasks he would set me. Still, after a few disappointing sessions in rehab, I'd gotten Evan to agree to do a once-a-week sit-in with another therapist. One that didn't make me want to escape and hit up Vegas on a bender just to forget the sound of their voice. We all got much more out of it then, and it helped not to have to go over everything again when I was released back into Evan's care.

Over the next hour, as I walked to Henry's gym, the words ran through my head on repeat.

When had I fallen in love with him? Was it when Max stood by me even when I was making things fall down around me? Was it when I noticed he was missing that night I'd left him and panic clawed at me until I knew he was safely passed out in his bed? Put there by my brother, no less.

That was when I knew that he was more important than anything else in my life, but I didn't know what to do with that information. I was stuck in a cycle and couldn't see a way out.

I was pretty sure that if Evan hadn't asked me that question, I wouldn't have picked up on the fact that I'd been in love with my best friend since I'd met him.

Chapter Nine

Max

I was pretty sure that Charlie was avoiding me. Scratch that, I was positive that he was. I'd messaged him countless times in the days since he got home, and aside from an invite to Andy's birthday party next month, he hadn't made any sort of plans that involved us being in the same building in the near future. There was no way I was waiting a month to see him.

Had our months apart caused irreparable damage to our friendship? I found it hard to believe that it would all fall apart now after having survived the fall out of Ethan, the death of his father, and the countless other problems we'd overcome in the past.

If I had more time, I'd chase the idiot down, but things at work had been crazy since a barista quit and another was off sick. Meaning that Kristen and I had been pulling double shifts over the last few weeks. Calling in a ton of favors, I even managed to rope Rachele, Kristen's wife, into helping us out in the bookstore portion of the café, but she had to put her job first. She'd worked on her days off so that I could cover the bookstore and do inventory. There'd been a big book launch and the author signed quite a few copies for us to sell, so I'd been swamped. The only reason Rachele agreed to help out was that she hadn't seen Kristen for a few days. I swear that she would've been asking Kristen to quit if it wasn't for the pile of free books I bribed the pair with, including one of the signed copies that I'd wanted for myself.

We were stuck in a difficult position. We needed to hire more staff, but I had no time to do the hiring. With Charlie home though, hiring a few more employees had become the most important task for the week. I needed a day off to track down my wayward best friend and Kristen's usual sunny attitude was dimming under the pressure of all the hours we were putting in.

With Charlie away in rehab and the weekly calls, I thought I'd be more focused and productive. I'd seen the staffing issue coming. Josie was graduating and had job offers, so I knew she was going to leave, but it happened when Denver was off sick, and all the busy days got to Molly, making her quit in tears...and, well, a shitty chain of events left me with a skeleton staff for a busy café-bookstore in an up and coming part of town.

While I knew that I should be grateful that my business was doing so well, it didn't keep me warm at night. I was overworked and lonely. It'd been months since I'd hooked up with anyone. I needed a vacation and someone to cuddle with so badly.

Charlie and I hadn't taken any time away since his father died and we set up our businesses. Before then we used to go away any chance that we got, even if it was just to his family's beach house. Before befriending him, I'd never been to the beach or even seen the ocean. We used to go on a long weekend, Charlie making me drive his car since he'd lost his confidence. He'd ended up giving me the car after his dad had died and I loved it. That car was the nicest thing I'd owned before my business.

Charlie loaned me some of the start-up cash for Books & Biscuits, and though I'd attempted to pay it back a bunch of times, he wouldn't take the money. One of the many things I loved about him was how generous he could be. He never used to let me pay for our vacations or meals but I was never made to feel like the poor friend. I'd cook for him or do his laundry to make up for it, just my small way of paying him back. He often said he was paying for the privilege of my company, which was sweet. That was a side of Charlie that not a lot of other people saw. I loved that I got that part of him to myself.

Books & Biscuits had been a dream project for me since my college days. My freshman roommate had been a British guy, Eddie, on a year exchange. We'd spent so many nights holed up in our room discussing everything. One night, we'd spent two hours arguing about the difference between biscuits and cookies. He made me laugh so much when his face had reddened with frustration over it all. He'd shown me endless photos he'd searched for online. "No, this is a biscuit!" He'd shouted, brandishing a photo of a cookie. "And this is a cookie!" He'd thrust his phone with a picture of a chocolate chip cookie in front of me. When I'd asked what our biscuits were, I'd thought he'd burst a blood vessel and I'd cried with laughter. We'd kept in touch after he'd moved back for a couple of months. The distance hadn't changed our friendship any.

Sadly, Eddie died in a car accident one icy December morning, so I'd named the shop after him in a roundabout way. My small way of remembering my friend.

A clattering noise from the café made my head pop up from where I'd been resting it in my hands at the book counter while I'd been pretending to do paperwork. The trainee, with a name I hadn't had the energy to remember, flushed and stooped to pick up the smashed pieces of the plate and muffin they'd dropped on the floor while Kristen swooped in to reassure them and give the waiting customer a fresh order.

I rolled my eyes while hoping that the girl didn't notice even if it was the third plate she'd broken in the last two hours. I sighed, deciding to ask Kris what the problem was because she had been lovely and competent sounding in the interview, but it had gone to shit as soon as the girl had been put in front of a customer. It made zero sense to me, because she had café experience, too.

While the girl's back was turned, Kris took the chance and turned to me, shaking her head. Well, fuck.

Unfortunately, that completely unoriginal and undecipherable - insert sarcasm here - signal meant she didn't think the girl was cut out for it. I was inclined to agree based on what I'd seen from where I'd been observing, but letting her know that we wouldn't be keeping her on was the worst part of hiring.

Getting up from the desk, I made my way over to the café portion of the building to get some cash out of the register before asking the girl to meet me in the office.

Books & Biscuits was two units that had been combined. The bookstore and café each had windows facing the busy street and had separate entrances. Sofas were set up in both areas to enjoy a coffee while the customer read their newest purchase. There were tables dotted around the café for people to enjoy sandwiches and snacks made in the tiny kitchen. Beneath the long counter were display cases of cookies and cakes. Behind the service station and coffee machine were doors to the kitchen and office, which is where I led the worried-looking girl.

After a short talk and thankfully, no tears, I paid her for the hours that she'd worked, but let her know that she didn't have a job with us. My heart broke for how disappointed she was, but she seemed to know it was coming because she didn't seem surprised.

If I was honest, I was glad she wasn't staying because she gave off a weird vibe while we were alone in the office and I felt distinctly uncomfortable at the way she had stared at me and asked some questions that bordered on personal and downright inappropriate. It felt like maybe she was hitting on me, which had never happened to me with a female before. She also had this weirdo air about her, a total bunny boiler vibe that had me running for the safety of other people.

"What are we going to do?" Kristen asked when I returned to the coffee counter to help with the orders coming in. One of our part-timers was sent to watch the book shop counter instead of helping Kristen. The coffee machine was temperamental at the best of times and required a real knack for it, especially for the milk frother, so it tended to be one of the baristas that used it. Kristen and I had taken some special training that was given when I bought it and hired her on. The old machine had given up the ghost and totally died on me, so I'd invested in this behemoth and regretted it every time that it needed servicing. I'd figured that an Italian machine would be great, and the coffee it made was worth the cost alone, but it was a pain in the ass to use.

"I dunno, she was the best of the applicants and seemed so capable in the interview." Stopping to consider for a second as I finished the cappuccino I was making, I said, "I think we'll just have to work our way through the rest of them and see how it goes." I shrugged and pushed on with getting through the orders that were piling up.

Kristen was silent on the subject for a bit as she and I worked to get through the rush. "Maybe we should just put the sign up again or put an ad in at the university or something?" She sounded skeptical that we would get anyone decent and I tended to agree with her judgment.

"Yeah maybe... None of the other people gave me the right vibe. Maybe I'm being too picky." I let out a frustrated sigh. I'd really hoped that we'd be done with hiring already.

"I don't think that you are, but we do need people. That guy seems to be doing okay, Finn was it?"

"Yeah, Finn's cool. He's worked in a café before so he didn't need much training, which is handy." Picking up a rag and cleaner, I started to clean down the counter now that the rush had passed while I thought about how to get some staff.

My phone buzzed in my pocket and I made a wish for good news and not a sick call.

Charlie: I'm so bored that I signed up for the gym just so I can leave the house.

Max: I've been asking to meet you for days. If you're that bored, come help us out at work, we need the staff. I'll show you how to use the coffee machine and you can be useful.

My stomach fluttered with butterflies at the thought of Charlie helping us out before the idea settled and I realized that it was the perfect solution. I wanted to see more of him. He needed a job that wasn't around temptation. We needed at least one more staff member.

Before I could put that into a text, Charlie called me. I moved away from the counter into the bookstore so I could hear him better.

"I have a crazy idea," he said before I could even say hello. "Why don't you hire me?"

I let out a laugh, startling an older couple browsing, and Charlie took it the wrong way, his tone gruff and mildly affronted. "I mean, it'd help you out..."

"Charlie, wait. I was laughing because I literally just thought the same thing."

"Seriously?" Doubt was heavy in his tone.

"Sure. You want a job? Because there's one here for you if you do."

There was a pause at the end of the line, and when he spoke I could hear the smile in his voice. "Yeah, that'd be great. Just what I need. You're a lifesaver, Max. Thanks."

"Nah, you're saving us." There was a slightly awkward pause. "Okay then. Let me look at the roster and I'll text you when to come in, okay?"

"Sounds good. Are you sure?"

I hated the thread of worry in his voice. He'd done his time in rehab, he'd more than fulfilled our little bargain, so as far as I was concerned, it was back to normal for us. What was he worried about? That I'd reject him again? Deciding not to tease, and reassure him instead, I told him in a firm voice, "I'm sure. I'd love nothing better than to work with you." Then, more gently, "I've missed your face."

"Missed you, too."

Was it just me or was there more weight to the words there? A depth of feeling in his tone that hadn't been there before? I shook that idea off, I had to be thinking more of it than was there...right?

We hung up and I turned to give Kristen the great news but she'd obviously been listening in. "You sure that's a good idea? Thought you said he wasn't that great with people."

I brushed that aside since she was right. Charlie had a short fuse at times. "He'll be fine. He's smart and will pick up stuff quickly. He's helped clean the coffee machine before so he knows how to treat it nicely so it behaves." Thinking of other plus points in his favor, "He helped set this place up so he knows where everything is, too."

Kristen looked at me thoughtfully. "I guess we can always stick him on coffee making and have someone who smiles on orders."

I laughed, imagining Charlie dealing with some of our regulars, the sound bubbling out of me while Kristen gaped at me.

"You know, that's the first laugh I've heard in ages, so Charlie's already helping."

Smiling at her because I knew she had a point, I went to head back to the office since it was quiet and picked up the roster for us to work on before the next rush.

The bell rang over the door as another customer came in and I flushed when I recognized him. Dr. Daddy, as I'm sure he'd heard me call him last time he was here, was one of our regular customers. He was always polite and tipped well. He didn't go out of his way to chat, being more of a listener than a talker, but he was in Books & Biscuits five days a week, so I couldn't ask for a better customer. He didn't just come in for coffee, he asked for us to order in books for him, which is how I'd found out that he was a therapist, having gotten his doctorate a couple of years before.

He was taller than me, which wasn't hard since I stood at I five-eight. Muscular, with gray hair in a bun and a beard. Tattoos ran up his arms, disappearing into the rolled cuffs of his white button-down shirt. He wore black jeans and biker boots, a strange mix of formal and casual that worked for him. He was beyond hot, and gave off an authoritarian vibe. I wasn't sure if I had a crush on him, but something about him drew me in, enough that I wouldn't mind getting to know him better.

When he came over to order he would spare a little time for conversation, giving a hundred percent of his focus to you while he talked. At times I found it unnerving to have all of his attention like he knew more about me than what I'd shared.

There was no way I could cope with trying to talk to him while wondering if I'd let his nickname slip since I'd likely do it again. It was Denver who had coined the name and it had stuck to the point that I hardly remembered his actual name.

Kristen looked at me as if asking, "Do you want to serve him?" and I answered by heading out back to the office, throwing him a wave. Not before I heard her ask, "How are you today, Dr. Cross?" and not Dr. Daddy as I'm sure slipped out when I'd spoken to him. My cheeks burned with mortification and I pressed my hands against them to cool them down. My gut churned at the thought of my slip up. Kristen hadn't heard me, so I couldn't be sure, and it wasn't like I could ask him.

While it wasn't the first time I'd possibly used a nickname for a customer instead of their real name, it was the first time I'd done it to one I wouldn't mind seeing out of my work environment.

My plan was just to avoid him as best as I could until he'd forgotten all about it or decided to go somewhere else for his daily coffee. I was screwed if he wanted something specially ordered because I usually dealt with that myself since no one else knew the system as well as I did. Kristen had resisted my efforts to teach her, not wanting to take on the responsibility.

I waited in the tiny office until I was sure he was sitting comfortably with his coffee and whatever pastry he'd decided on for the day. He was a creature of habit and absolutely stunning to look at. Kristen teased me mercilessly about it, but I think she was pleased that I'd noticed anyone that wasn't Charlie since he'd been on my mind so often over the last few months.

When Charlie had been doing better, it was easier to hide my feelings for him. There were clear lines when he'd been in control of his life. When that control had slipped, my worry for him had been unbearable and had bled over into other areas of my life. I'd let things slip, like paying vendors or making up schedules, to check up on him. It'd been obvious to anyone that wasn't Charlie that I'd acted out of love rather than friendship.

I'd been in love with him for as long as we'd been friends, probably from our first day at school together, but I had no reason to hope that we would ever be more than that.

Over the years I'd tried to have serious relationships and had thought I'd felt something for each of those guys, but I think I'd subconsciously held parts back from them since they weren't Charlie.

Books & Biscuits had kept me pretty busy, so it'd been a while since I'd had a relationship, my last one having ended just after I'd opened. The stress and long hours had pulled us apart and he claimed I wasn't fully emotionally invested in him or making things work. It didn't take me long to pick myself up, so I guess he had a point. Since then I'd been sticking to quick flings or one-nighters to take the edge off. Not very satisfying, but it did the job.

Noticing the doctor was a great first step, though I doubted that someone that hot, with the tattoos, piercings, the silky soft looking hair, wouldn't already have someone at home. I wasn't even sure he was gay, I just had a feeling. I bet that if he had someone they were totally spoiled. He looked like the type to need a partner to care for and cherish.

Just thinking about it caused a pang in my chest. A longing to have someone. I got the appeal of the Daddy/boy thing. The idea of having a Daddy to take care of me was lovely, but I wasn't sure it was the right lifestyle for me. I was pretty independent after being on my own for so long and didn't think that I'd be able to give over control easily. I didn't think I could be the caregiver either, needing not to be depended on constantly.

My previous relationships had all been complicated, not just because of my feelings for my best friend but because of my preferences in the bedroom. With usually being the shorter partner, it was always assumed that I would bottom, and yeah, that was great, but I loved the control that topping gave me. I loved to take control and have them follow my lead. There were a few other quirks that partners weren't keen on too, a certain fastidiousness with condoms that pissed off some guys. I was expected to be a little more passive than I could manage convincingly. Partners never considered that though, and I bottomed and bit my tongue rather than argue about what I liked. I'd learned that bringing it up would prematurely end something before it got going. This answered the question of why a lot of my sex life was dull and left me wanting. I'd never met anyone that I properly clicked with in bed.

A good fifteen minutes had passed so I decided to head back out and sure enough, Dr. Cross was at his usual table with a cookie instead of a pastry today. He preferred the teas that we stocked over coffee, so his orders were always easy to do.

"Got it," I said to Kristen brandishing the folder as I rejoined her at the counter. She gave me a meaningful look which I ignored. "When do you think is best to get Charlie in?"

We took a few minutes to go over the schedule, resting the book in between us so we could keep an eye on our customers, before deciding that since Tuesday mornings were usually slow going, we'd have him come in then. It meant that Kristen could have the day off since we had a couple of part-time staff over the day. Easy, a quiet day to settle him in a bit and for us to get time to catch up.

Max: Can you come in tomorrow? Tuesdays are usually quiet.

Together, Kristen and I worked on the line that was forming before I had the chance to see if he had replied.

Charlie: Sure, I have a therapist appointment in the afternoon though, sorry I should've said.

Max: You can just do the morning or have a couple hours off and help in the afternoon. See what you make of it first. You might hate it lol

Charlie: Cool. Will do

My head snapped up as Dr. Cross walked by the counter, saying goodbye to Kristen before offering me a smile and a light, "See you tomorrow, Max."

Face heating at the twinkle in those light blue eyes of his that were perfectly framed by black-rimmed glasses, I managed to stutter out a quick, "Bye!"

"So," Kristen said as she sidled up to me, "You want a Daddy, do ya?" She gave me a cheeky wink and laughed before going to clear Dr. Cross' table.

"Not my kink!" I called after her and she just snorted in reply. I blushed as a couple looked at me questioningly and I gave them a quick smile before making myself busy to stifle my nerves. I couldn't wait to see Charlie.

Chapter Ten

Charlie

W as I doing the right thing by working with Max? Would Evan's words change the way I acted around him?

Keeping away from Max until I had my head sorted out had been my only plan, but out of habit, I'd found myself texting him. I hadn't meant to offer to come and work for him but Max needed the help and as usual, I just had to be the one to do it. There was no way that I could see him needing something without stepping up to help him out. We'd always been like that. In fact, it would be out of the ordinary if I hadn't volunteered, or at least that was how I was going to justify my impulsive actions. I could have at least waited until he'd asked for help.

Would it be weird between us, though? Had things changed? We hadn't been in the same room for three months, since I'd been in the hospital, and that visit had been slightly strained.

Though physically I was now pretty much fully healed, there were mental scars I hadn't taken into account.

Walking the city had been no problem to me before, but now I was more cautious. I found myself flinching at noises that probably wouldn't have bothered me before. Instead of putting my earphones in and listening to something as I walked, they were tucked away in my gym bag and I stayed alert. Scanning faces had become a habit when previously, they'd have blurred together. I was fearful where I'd been confident before. Evan had explained that this was a natural reaction to trauma, but I hated it.

Life was separated into before and after, and I knew I had to be grateful that there was an after. I'd nearly been denied that. It didn't stop me from feeling angry at having my feeling of safety taken away from me.

Forcing my thoughts away from morbid subjects with the notification on maps announcing that I was nearly there, I noticed that I was coming up to the building that housed Henry's gym that he ran with his sister, Holly. I'd heard some stuff about him and Andy's other friends in our calls while I was away, but had never had the chance to meet any of them.

The calls with Andy were a real surprise. He was acting as a bridge between me and my brother, but I honestly felt like I could count him as one of my own friends. I had so few decent ones these days, so God knew I could do with more, especially ones who were as sweet as Andy.

Now that he and Will were engaged, I knew that Andy had asked Pete, another of his gym friends, to be his best man. There'd be no chance of meeting Pete soon since he was away traveling. I recalled that there had been some sort of issue between him and Henry after the engagement party and decided to keep my nose out of that. My life had enough drama without borrowing someone else's.

Andy still went to the gym, and as far as I knew, the issue between Pete and Henry hadn't moved into the other friendships in the group aside from some minor tension.

There'd been a bio about the trainers at Henry's place, Farmer's Fitness, and I'd read about Henry being in the army and losing half his leg. Due to that, they had focused programs on rehabilitation after injury, which was ideal for me. While the wound was closed, the muscle around it wasn't quite finished healing. I'd thought that I'd brush it off after a week and be done, but apparently, stab wounds took longer than that to properly heal. Plus, I'd had cracked ribs to baby. Recovery had been hampered by my malnutrition and blood loss which also took time to get over.

Months in the center, decent food and light exercise had done wonders, but I was sure I'd pulled something or just not been ready when I'd used their gym facilities, because even though I'd had visible changes, I had aches and pains that I didn't think I should have.

Approaching the reception desk, I caught the attention of the woman there. Objectively, she was beautiful, all dark curls and tawny skin with stunning warm brown eyes and a dusting of freckles over her nose, though she did nothing for me. Women, in general, didn't. She must have caught my lack of interest and she gave me a pleasant, welcoming smile as she flipped her braids of dark hair over her shoulders, her long bangs were unbraided, leaving some curls to frame her face.

"Welcome to Farmer's Fitness. I'm Holly, how can I help you today?"

"Hey Holly, I'm Charlie, Will's brother. I think there should be a booking in the system for an orientation with Henry for me."

"Will's brother? Yeah, he called to say you'd be coming in. He wanted to check that you'd noted the recent injury on your application." Holly looked at the screen in front of her, clicking away and then scanning the information there. "I see that you did note it, that's great." She gave me an approving smile. "It's not just for insurance reasons. We can't do too much with you at first if there's still healing going on. It could set you back otherwise." Her explanation made sense and was probably the reason that I was feeling achy after the center's facilities. No one had been on hand to make up programs. I'd learned how to use the machines by using YouTube on my phone once it had been returned to me.

I wondered vaguely if they had a feedback process because someone needed to monitor their gym there, ideally someone that knew their shit.

Movement from the gym floor caught my attention. A man with similar golden brown skin to Holly approached and I guessed that he was Henry. He wore his hair close-cropped, similar to what it would have been like in the military. His uniform was a black tank and shorts with the gym's logo on, his gait slightly off with the prosthesis that replaced his lower right leg. I noticed some scarring on his right side, along his arm and hand. When his tank gaped open, I could see some tattoos going up along his ribs and I wondered if those were to cover more marks from his injury.

It was pretty cool to me that he had an air of confidence about his leg and scars and didn't seem to care if anyone was looking at him. I wasn't sure how much of that was bravado; it must have bothered him at some point if he'd gone to the trouble of covering some of the scars with tattoos. Still, though, I respected the hell out of him for it.

As a teen, I'd had a teacher that had lost his arm and I'd been fascinated with the different options he had as a replacement. The prosthesis that he'd favored hadn't been nearly as cool as Henry's leg. It had been heavy and uncomfortable with how it attached to what was left of his arm, he'd admitted. Taking it off was similar to taking off an ill-fitting bra, he'd joked to our class. We'd laughed at the time, not knowing much better, but I could see how he had put up with it to attempt to look "normal" in passing as parents and classmates had made comments about his other, lighter, prosthetics. He had probably put up with a lot of discomfort and some pain in order to keep his job.

Henry caught the direction of my stare and frowned. Shit. Hardly the impression I wanted to be making. I decided just to own it. "Sorry man," I shrugged. "I think your leg is cool is all. I had a teacher with a prosthesis and it wasn't nearly as badass looking as that."

My words must have caught Henry off guard as he seemed to be ready to go on the defensive. He stuttered for a second, chuckling briefly, and gave me a "Thanks?" before pasting on a professional smile. "You Charlie?"

"Yeah, that's me."

"Great, let's go get you through the paperwork, and then we'll go over some of the equipment and some useful exercises for you."

Holly handed him over a folder with the freshly printed documents I'd filled in online. It didn't take us long to go through them with Henry warming up to me as we chatted. He took me through some stretches before starting a basic routine that he thought would suit me well.

I laughed at his stories of Will and Andy, even when I didn't need to know the details of my brother's sex life, and soon I felt at ease with Henry, like I'd known him a long time.

My muscles burned by the time we'd finished up and Henry encouraged me to make use of the steam room and sauna at the back of the building. The place was pretty well kitted out with a wide variety of machines and a separate area for women to work out. I was more than a little impressed and a tad intimidated by the guy with such a great setup.

Taking him up on his suggestion, I found myself sitting surrounded by steam, letting the warmth soak into me. It was relaxing for sure but it was also giving me too much time with my thoughts. I wondered how the next day was going to go with working for Max. I knew he was an easy-going boss, one of those that wouldn't ask anyone to do anything he wouldn't do himself. He hated to be stuck in the office, opting to do paperwork at the book counter or taking it home.

His only downfall was that he needed everything in order and was obsessed with cleaning. It served him well when the Health Department came to give his certification, though.

It was useful that I already knew the place. I'd helped set it up, so it wasn't a strange environment that I was worried about. It was more that I was anxious that our time apart had changed us. Could we settle back into friendship after the enforced break? My thoughts kept circling those questions, to the point that it was giving me a headache.

There was also the issue of not knowing exactly what I'd done to Max to make him press pause on being friends. He'd stuck by me even after I'd left him a couple of times so I was sure it wasn't that. I regretted those times so much and still felt sick at the idea of Max's drink being spiked because I wasn't there to protect him.

The idea that I'd hurt him had rattled around in my mind for weeks in rehab until I'd finally addressed it in one of our calls. His quiet, "No, you didn't hurt me," had tears of relief running down my cheeks. That would have been something that we couldn't ever truly come back from. It would have sat between us, festering.

The first thing that I needed to do was to appear early and apologize to Max for avoiding him these last few days. I should have gone to see him as soon as I was out and instead I hid away at my mom's. We hadn't even gone looking at properties, so that meant I was stuck living with her for longer than I wanted to. Fan-fricken-tastic. I loved my mom, but she was worse now that I'd been in rehab. I think there was some guilt there for not seeing my problems sooner, so she was overcompensating.

In truth, if I looked really hard at the situation, I hadn't given my mom or any of my family a chance to see how bad things had gotten. After I'd met Max, we'd formed our own family and I'd stopped pushing as hard to be a part of their lives. There were occasions that I'd stuck my neck out and risked the hurt of rejection. Over the years though, they became fewer and fewer.

For all too long, it had just been me and Max. He was the only family that I wanted and he needed to be told how important he was to me.

Chapter Eleven

Charlie

Cracking open my gritty eyes at the break of dawn was not how I wanted to start my day, especially after fuck all sleep. My body was a heavy weight, exhaustion pulling at my sore limbs.

With how gentle we were in the gym yesterday and the steam session after, I thought I'd have escaped that feeling, but nope, there was a ton of pain. It was a good hurt though, how my muscles should have been feeling, instead of the aches that had plagued me in rehab.

Despite being tired, I couldn't sleep with the worry about seeing Max after months.

We'd texted back and forth a little last night and something like our usual dynamic was there, but we didn't joke around quite the same. We were restrained in the way that messages came across. The whole thing was odd. My anxiety rocketed all over with thoughts of what could happen. I imagined like Evan suggested, taking all of my worries, everything I couldn't change, and turning them into a ball. Then I picked up the ball of anxiety and instead of letting it sit on my chest where it could suffocate me, I threw it away.

There was a point when I contemplated calling Evan out of hours. He'd said I could before and I'd just be billed an extra fee, but I thought back to some of the techniques that I'd learned between him and the center, and calmed myself down. The anxiety didn't let me get any real sleep, but at least I could take a full breath with no issues. I assumed I dozed in snatches of stolen sleep which were full of nightmares or weird-ass scenarios that just wouldn't happen. Like Max kicking me out of Books & Biscuits as soon as I appeared and laughing in my face for being so dumb that I thought he needed my help, or just closing the door in my face.

Those were the ones that hurt the most. I guess I'd never really thought about my place in Max's life now. He had it all going for him. Did he really need a recovering alcoholic best friend dragging him down? I had no place of my own. For fuck's sake, I was thirty and living with my mom and sister. Sure, they'd basically forced me to give up my apartment, but no one was going to listen to that excuse. I didn't even have a job since I wasn't allowed near my club.

I couldn't go back to working for the family's company even if I wanted to, since Alex ran that and he was still acting like a dick to me. At the welcome home dinner, it was obvious that any headway we'd made in fixing our relationship had been undone. Things with Will were so much better, and it had taken Andy to offer up the reason for Alex's cold behavior towards me. Apparently, Alex had seen how close we were and had pulled him aside and warned him away from me because I was a "snake." Charming.

Will, to his benefit, had assured me and his fiancé that he had no worries on that score, that he liked that we were getting to be good friends. He even ended the night by hugging me. I couldn't remember the last hug we shared. He'd whispered in my ear, "I trust you." My throat had been too clogged with sudden tears and I could only offer him a watery smile in reply.

Instead of dwelling on shit I couldn't do anything about at that moment, I got myself ready for the day ahead.

There was no real dress code for Books & Biscuits, with Max providing t-shirts with a logo he'd designed on it, so I threw on some comfortable black jeans and a forest green t-shirt and called it good enough.

I spent far too long messing with my hair in my bathroom mirror before giving up and cursing myself for not getting it cut since I'd gotten home. I could do with a shave too, a good close one, as a few days' worth of stubble covered my face but I'd left it too late to do anything about that. There was no time to do it myself if I wanted to get to the café early so I could talk to Max.

My stomach was in knots, so breakfast was out.

After a lecture from Mom about not eating, I accepted the protein shake she handed me, kissed her cheek, snagged a light jacket, and headed out to the car that was waiting.

The city sped by and it seemed like no time had passed before we were pulling up to the store.

Books & Biscuits was dark, the blinds down, and showed no signs of life. Unsure what to do, I had the driver park and wait for a few minutes as I sent Max a text letting him know I was there.

After a minute, the blinds in the bookstore were raised and I saw Max standing, lit up and looking as angelic as he had the first time that I'd seen him all those years ago.

Getting out of the car and thanking the driver, I couldn't help but return the grin that Max gave me. Maybe things would be okay with us after all.

Before I could get there, Max hurried to the door and yanked it open, rushing over to me. He slammed into me, wrapping his arms around my middle and squeezing tightly.

"Ouch! Careful. I'm a bit sore still." I said reluctantly. I wanted to keep holding him, but I should have done some stretches or something because I suddenly felt worn and achy. Relief at his greeting carried my worries away and the weight on my shoulders lessened.

Max didn't let go, but his hug did gentle, holding me like I was made of glass. It made me regret saying anything.

Settling my chin on his white-blond head, I inhaled the scent of him, the familiar shampoo and smell of my Max. He tried to pull away but I held on firmly. "In a sec."

I felt more than I heard his chuckle, and his arms tightened briefly around me before he grabbed handfuls of my t-shirt, settled his face against the base of my neck, and sighed.

This was what peace felt like. Better than any medicine. More healing than all my hours of therapy. Exactly where I needed to be.

"I'm sorry, Max. Whatever I did. I'll fix it if I can. I'll be better. I promise."

Max sighed again but made no effort to move away from me. His hands gripped tighter at my shirt. "I know. I believe in you."

I let out a shuddering breath at the sincerity in his voice.

"You ready to tell me what I did?"

"Not yet, but soon Charlie. Come on, we need to get inside. The bakery will be in soon with the delivery."

We broke apart and headed inside wordlessly. There was no point in pushing him for answers if he wasn't ready, but my mind was spinning with possible scenarios.

Max led me to the office so I could hang up my jacket and then started my training. I quickly recalled how the coffee machine worked; I'd watched Max use it enough times that I could have figured it out without him taking me through it again. I was grateful that there weren't many other changes for me to worry about and I soon got into the rhythm of things.

I helped him put out all the pastries and cakes from the bakery delivery, being careful to keep apart the different types because of allergens. Max was gluten intolerant and had found it hard to find cafes and restaurants with a good gluten-free selection, so that had been his first priority when he'd opened his own place.

The café opened at seven. The bookstore wasn't staffed until nine so the screen between them was pulled down until then. Max had talked about opening both parts earlier but saw so little trade before nine that it made no sense financially. Plus, he'd burnt out pretty quickly after trying it. They didn't close until seven in the evening, and when he started out he was doing that six days a week since they were only closed on Tuesdays. Once they found their niche, they opened seven days and Max had more staff so he could have days off. He still worked too much, and I worried about that a lot. Often he could be found taking meetings or doing paperwork on days he was supposed to be chilling out. Since he'd taken Kristen on, and she had gotten more comfortable in her role, she had pushed him to actually use his time off for what it was intended for— relaxing. Gradually she had taken on more tasks for him and I'd seen the weight drop off his shoulders.

If we had been our usual selves, this was the time that I would suggest that we take some time off and go somewhere even if it was just to the beach house. We were far from back to normal, though. I caught Max watching me a lot, just silently observing me as I made up coffee orders and plated pastries. Sometimes he looked worried if I stretched too far and tried to curb a wince at the ache in my muscles.

"I'm okay, Max."

"You sure?"

"Yeah, just overdid it at the gym yesterday. I'll just make sure to go a bit easier next time."

"You're going back?"

"Yeah, I like the feeling that working out gives me."

He looked me over consideringly, and I shivered at the brief flash of heat in his eyes before he turned away. "It's working for you."

My mouth dropped open and it took a couple of seconds for me to recover my wits.

I stewed over his comment for the next couple of hours as I served customers, wondering what he meant by it. Did he mean it as it had sounded like he was flirting with me? It was still on my mind as I took a break in the bookstore section, where I got caught up reading a photography book that I eventually realized I just had to buy.

Max was in the office when I went in to stash the book until I finished for the day. "You getting back into photography?"

Rubbing a hand over the back of my neck, I considered his words. I didn't feel embarrassed, but I'd lost a lot of confidence in my abilities since I'd been forced to give it up. "Uh, yeah. You know how I took photos at Christmas?" He nodded. "Well I took my camera to rehab, thinking I'd take shots of the gardens and stuff, but I received a special dispensation to take some of the people. I thought about doing something with them, but I'm not sure."

"Can I see them?"

The photos had been taken with the idea of documenting my journey and all the subjects in them had their identities obscured, a condition of permission being granted.

I could feel my cheeks flushing. "Uh, I think so. I think I'll have to show the ones I want to use to the facility management first to get approval. I can ask for permission to show you them. Maybe tell them you're giving me advice or something."

"Sounds good. I'd be happy to give you an outsider's perspective, you know that. Anything you need and I'm there."

"Thanks. Well, I have to head out soon for therapy. Do you want me back later or...?" Evan's office wasn't far from here, so I could walk over, or maybe eat something here first. Now that my nerves had settled, I was starving.

"Nah, that's too long for a first day. I'm not even in all day today. I have a supervisor in soon to close, so I'll be finished, too." He checked the clock on the wall and moved some papers about on his desk. "I've got a lead on another member of staff so that will make things a lot easier on all of us."

I followed Max back through to the counter so he could quickly grab the scheduling folder he'd tucked next to the register to have a look at when I was needed. He stopped quickly and I bumped into him. I dropped my hands to his waist to stop him toppling over and we both flushed.

"When do you have therapy next?" He asked around our awkwardness.

I didn't even need to think about it, since there were so few things to occupy my days just now. "Friday afternoon. All my appointments are in the afternoon, so I can do any opening shifts you need me to do. I should've said that before."

He studied the roster for a minute, absentmindedly chewing on his lip and tapping his pen on the counter. I watched his mouth. Had it always looked so soft and tempting? The bottom lip was fuller than the top, lips rosy pink. Max spent a lot of time indoors so his skin was pale, but I knew he was prone to freckles along his nose. I could remember the path they'd take along his cheeks.

"Charlie?"

"Hmm?" I blushed when I realized that I'd been staring at his mouth. "Sorry, what were you saying?"

"It's all good." He seemed distracted too. Was he still thinking about what he'd said earlier, the gym thing? He cleared his throat. "Okay...so tomorrow with me. I'm off Thursday, do you want off then, too? We're okay for staff then, so it'd be better than Friday." He scanned the sheet focused on working out when I was needed. "What time's your appointment?"

"Noon. Sorry, it's an awkward time."

"No, that works better actually. Can you start at two?"

"Yeah, that's no problem."

We finished going over the roster, adding in my shifts for the weekend and the following week and I promised to move my therapy to slightly later if I could.

Max made sure to fix me up a quick lunch after hearing my stomach rumbling, and I left my first shift there happy that I could help him and do something useful.

Chapter Twelve

Max

It only took a week to realize that having Charlie working with me was going to be torture. We hadn't spent much time together; our coinciding shifts were short and we didn't see each other afterwards, but I could see the changes. He was different from how he used to be, but in a good way. Less hectic energy and more introspective calmness.

I hadn't meant for the comment about the gym working for him to slip out, but it was an honest observation. To be fair, it wasn't hard for him to look better than the last time that I'd seen him in the hospital months ago. The image of him in the hospital bed would haunt me for a long time.

My supervisor Heather and I did the handover and I wrote some checks before I left for the day. If I didn't need my car for work the next day, I'd have taken a cab home. I hated driving tired. As usual, I'd slept terribly and was paying for it now.

During the night, sick of tossing and turning, I'd gotten up and folded laundry and done some dishes, working through my cleaning routine. My roommate was staying with his girlfriend again since her apartment was closer to his work, so I didn't have to worry about disturbing him. After catching up with the laundry, I put on the TV, turned it down low, and watched it until I'd fallen asleep.

Getting home mid-afternoon with no real plans, I ate and sat myself back in front of the TV to pick up where I'd left off before I fell asleep.

I needed to get my mind off Charlie. Off how he looked on his first day working, filling out the dark green tee he wore that showed every line of muscle. Off how he smelled, clean and fresh without a hint of booze. The feel of that hug, how tightly we'd clung to each other, refusing to let go. I remembered all of it later that night in bed when I found myself jerking off to the memory of his body against mine.

I'd offered to pick Charlie up for work on Wednesday, but his mom's house was out of my way, so he refused politely. There was still a strange undercurrent between us and I wanted to try and recover the same closeness we had before everything went to shit.

Our calls during rehab had been hellish. I often regretted allowing him to call me since we had so little to talk about. I couldn't tell him a lot of things over the phone and it had hurt to have this gulf open up between us.

With him back, I tried to bridge the gap. Encouraging Charlie to let me in was harder than it used to be though, but after some coaxing, he told me about how he'd finally told Will some of the Ethan stuff. Alex was being a dick to him and I was more than sure that Charlie was being made into the scapegoat for all the other crap Alex had going on. I felt bad that he was getting divorced and that his ex was already pregnant by someone else, but none of that was Charlie's fault. I'm sure that he loved Helena in some way still, but if Will was over stuff then Alex had to work it out with Charlie, too. It wasn't fair to keep treating him like dirt because of some misplaced grudge. Anger flared, sharp and insistent, as I thought of Alex, but I pushed it away. I'd always fight in Charlie's corner when it was needed, but we weren't anywhere near that yet.

Charlie was frustrated with living at home. His mom was constantly on top of him about his sobriety, eating, and therapy. She was worried about the stress of him working, even though it was with me and he badly needed to be out of the house on a regular basis before he snapped.

When we hit a lull at work, I pulled up a property website on my phone and Charlie and I browsed for a bit until he got despondent over the lack of anything good being available.

Though there were times that we could chat, I knew I needed to see him outside of work to clear the air over what had happened so we could move on from it. I could feel it hanging between us in the way that he was hesitant with me. Before we would casually touch each other and now I didn't know if that had stopped because he wanted to appear professional, or if he was just unsure over our whole friendship. The whole thing had been playing on my mind and I just needed to purge it, just get it out so we could talk it over.

Since we had the day off together, I suggested we meet up for lunch and maybe go to a movie and Charlie accepted quickly, which was a huge relief. Part of me wondered if he would make an excuse to get out of it.

"I wasn't sure where we stood. If we could hang out outside of work," he said softly. I wasn't used to this quieter version of Charlie. The version that thought before he spoke, who didn't push for what he wanted all the time.

I picked him up for lunch and was grateful that his mom was out and his sister was at school, so we didn't have to make small talk and explain why I hadn't been around as much. I felt kinda shitty that I'd left Charlie to explain my absence over the weeks he'd been home recovering. Alice had been nothing but kind to me, but her priority was Charlie and that was fair. I wasn't anyone to them. They'd had enough to contend with recently without dealing with my stuff, too.

We decided not to eat out, so I drove us to the grocery store so we could pick up the ingredients to make lunch at my place, where we could talk without being overheard. I got the feeling that Charlie was feeling nervous being around a bunch of people and wondered if the attack was on his mind more often than he let on.

Charlie quickly took over making us a pasta dish that I loved, with the special gluten-free pasta I liked, and I watched him move competently around the small kitchen serving us the food from my place at the sink. My job was going to be cleaning up after him. He wasn't the cleanest cook and seemed to use every pot and dish that I owned. My fingers twitched every time that he made a spill or didn't put something in the correct place, but I willed myself to calm down.

Settling on the couch, we didn't speak much while we ate and the tension ratcheted up the longer that the silence sat between us.

Taking a deep breath, I set my plate down and started the speech I'd been rehearsing. "I need you not to interrupt for a minute while I get this all out, okay?"

Waiting for him to agree, I paused. He nodded, looking concerned, and put his plate on the table.

"You're my best friend and we've been through so much together. So I know that you know, what went down was something big." Not the greatest opening line, you sound like you're breaking up with him. I mentally rolled my eyes at myself. I'd practiced my speech and already it was off the rails.

Another nod. His eyes scanned my face. Sweat broke out on my forehead as my heart started hammering in my chest. I hated the words that I was working up to speak.

"It wasn't that you left me, Charlie. I knew that you didn't mean to, and really, you shouldn't have to watch over me all the time."

Another deep breath. My fingers trembled as I ran a hand through my hair.

"You got aggressive with me a couple of times when I tried to curb your drinking," I finally blurted.

Charlie inhaled sharply. Shock spread all over that handsome face before tears filled his eyes and he tried to speak.

"No. You didn't hurt me. I swear." I had to stop for a second to hold back my tears. I grabbed at his hand, needing to touch him, soothe him somehow. "But I did get scared and I've never been scared of you before. I'd always felt safe and suddenly that was gone." The words kept spilling from me. "You would loom over me, or growl at me and you just....you just weren't you." The words faded out.

He took a sharp breath and seemed to push back tears. "Why don't I remember that? I don't blackout." His voice was firm, completely sure of himself.

"I think you were blacking out more than you realized," I said gently. "Can you look back and see any missing spots?"

He didn't immediately dismiss my words as he would have in the past. While Charlie trusted me, sometimes he didn't fully listen, but this was proof that he was different now. He stopped to consider that what I'd said had merit.

I let him think about it for a few minutes and digest what I was telling him.

"I can't think of it, but that doesn't mean that you're not right." He shrugged, clearly devastated but trying just to pass it off. "There must be stuff that's gone. You wouldn't lie about this and I just don't remember anything like that...there are times I remember feeling angry at you and

I don't even want to remember them." Tears spilled down his cheeks and I wrapped my arms around him. Immediately he leaned into me, taking comfort from the embrace. With a shuddering breath he said, "Max, I don't want to remember scaring you."

That right there was why I'd already forgiven him.

"I know, sweetheart."

We sat with me holding him for a while as he came to terms with just how bad things had gotten.

Eventually, he spoke, the words warm against my neck where he had his head tucked. "Knowing I did that to you, giving you a moment's fear of me, is worse than anything else I did. I don't know what I'd do if I hurt you. If you gave up on me forever, I'd have no one."

"You'd have your family," I reminded him.

"Not the same. No one knows me like you do."

I couldn't help but bask in the warm feeling of pride that knowledge gave me. I mean, I knew that already but we'd been apart for so long I wasn't sure that someone hadn't come along and taken my place. The number of times that thought had woken me in a cold sweat was scary.

We were on such rocky ground when he went to rehab. Our calls had shrunk to quick check-ins from our hours-long conversations when he'd first entered the facility. Part of it, I knew, was that Charlie was only going to therapy or for walks around the family home. He wasn't able to go anywhere without supervision and didn't meet any old friends. He hadn't talked about how it made him feel but he was basically on house arrest.

After holding him for a bit longer, I felt my arm going numb. "Charlie?"

"Hmm?"

"I need you to move. My arm's dead." I let out a little laugh to show it wasn't a big deal. I didn't want him to think that I was pushing him away. I'd have stayed wrapped around him all day if I could've.

"Oh! Sorry." Charlie pulled back and I immediately missed the warmth of his body and shivered.

Charlie picked up my hand, the fingers tingling from the blood flowing back in. He moved each finger, in turn, to help lessen the pain and I watched him silently as he focused on his task. My stomach swooped with how close we were. I could see the shadows on his cheeks from his eyelashes and his breath puffed onto the skin of my neck.

"Better?" He whispered.

"Much." I managed to croak out.

"Good." He dropped my hand and moved away, putting distance between us. He picked up his plate and dug into the food, keeping his face turned from me. I left him to get control of his emotions for a second and picked up my plate, too.

Lunch after that was easy and light and it was only when we settled on what movie to watch that the tension washed back in between us.

"You want some popcorn?" I called to him.

"Sure." He said from directly behind me, making me start. "I'll put it on while you finish the dishes." Charlie put his hands on my waist as he moved around me in the tiny kitchen. Awareness of him, of how close we were, rushed through me. His touch felt like it burned through my t-shirt, branding my skin. I felt the echo of it for long moments after.

He found some microwaveable popcorn in a cabinet and I passed him the bowl. Our fingers brushed, a prickle of electricity passing between us, the current holding a promise of something more there. His eyes held mine for a second and I thought I saw them darken with heat before he looked away.

Settling on the sofa, we placed the bowl between us as a sort of barrier as we tried to pretend the tension wasn't there.

"Sorry," I said as our fingers brushed for the fifth time as we both reached for a handful of popcorn.

He let out a strained chuckle, "It's fine. Are you okay?"

"I'm fine." I was not fine, but I didn't have a good excuse for how strange I was acting. "Are you okay?"

"Me? Yeah, I'm okay." His voice wavered with the lie, one of his tiny tells, but I didn't call him on it.

We finished the bowl and set it on the table. Neither of us moved closer, though. Usually, we would sit close with the easy affection of people who'd been friends for years. While I'd always wanted more from Charlie, there'd never been the right opportunity to make a move in the beginning. After a few years, there was too much history between us to risk damaging it for something uncertain. Now we were sitting with a careful distance set between us.

The movie ended and we tried to act normally. "The book was better," I said firmly.

"You would say that," he shot back.

"So would you if you'd actually read the book. You've still got my copy!"

He held his hands up. "I might have let Matty borrow it," he said sheepishly.

I slapped his arm but laughed. Just like that, we settled back into something more like a normal us.

I wasn't ready to confess how I felt. The break had been good for me in some ways. It'd given my feelings perspective, and if I was sure that he felt the same, I would make a move, ask him on a date, or even kiss him to see if we have the explosive chemistry I think we could have. Except it wasn't the right time. Charlie was still fragile, still finding his feet in his new normal.

He just needed time to see that I was who he really needed, as his best friend and his lover. I wanted to be everything to him like no one else had been before. He needed to trust that I knew what he needed to be happy and healthy, but we weren't there yet.

The break brought out some side of me I hadn't known was there. There was this urge to protect Charlie that was stronger than I'd ever felt before.

"Want to put on the sequel?"

"Sure."

As I watched him pretend to focus on the film on the screen out of the corner of my eye, I made a silent promise to him to be what he needed as soon as he was ready.

Chapter Thirteen

Charlie

Something wordless was different between me and Max. I'd felt it that day a few weeks back when we'd had lunch and hung out at his place. Things had been strange. There had been a weird need to be closer to him, but I couldn't make myself move any closer. I knew that he caught me looking at him more than once since he was always looking back at me. We danced around the new tension and awareness of each other, pretending that everything was cool.

Working with each other after our talk became easier, probably because we weren't alone often so there was a lack of opportunity for something to flare up. I found myself enjoying the job more than I thought.

Part of the new tension between us was probably me just overreacting to the revelation of my feelings for Max and him being weird because I couldn't help acting differently around him. At least that's what I was attempting to pass it off as.

Max had changed, though. There was a new confidence in him that had him standing taller. Not all the time, though. There were moments that his old self-consciousness slipped in and took over, but as he served customers, he was all sweetness and smiles.

He had this glow; his pale skin was luminous and my fingers itched for my camera when the light would hit him just right. He looked angelic but had a devilish smile that he only used for me. He had begun touching me more since we cleared the air. Putting a hand on my lower back, just above my ass, as he moved past me behind the counter. Standing just a little bit closer than he used to. I got the feeling that he'd be open to more than we were, but not being sure had me drawing back just in case I was wrong.

Clearing the air had been good for us, but I didn't want to go back into the best friend box. I just didn't know how to navigate the move to boyfriends.

Being able to help Max out, to be useful instead of having him look after me, was my way of working to make up for what I put him through. My way of repairing our friendship. He insisted that it wasn't what my working there was about. He just wanted me around and did need me for the first week at least, since he was in the middle of taking more staff on since the place was busier than ever.

"Charlie, could you help me with this?" Heather, one of the supervisors I worked with asked.

"Sure," I went over to the bookstore to the new LGBTQIA literature section that she was setting up. There was everything from fiction to self-help. "Where d'you want these?" I indicated to the box of fiction paperbacks I'd just opened.

Heather scanned the titles. "In the fiction section, in alphabetical order by author's last name please."

We worked side by side until I unearthed one particular title that caught her eye. "Ooh, I'll have to tell my son about this one. It has a trans character with an enby partner."

I must have given her a questioning look and she passed me the book so I could look at it and read the blurb.

"These characters are like my son; he's trans and his partner is non-binary. He loves seeing himself represented in books. It's part of the reason I campaigned to Max to get this section up and running. The ones that we'd had in before sold well so really it was just good business sense to expand it to a full section.

"Yeah, that's a great idea. D'you want to go message your son about the book?"

"Nah, I'll just use my staff discount and get it for him later."

I'd thought she was cool before, but the way that she talked about her son really did it for me. Nothing but true love and support for them both, unlike my father. Will had thought Father was being progressive with his attitude, but it was nothing but paying lip service to calls for diversity. I'd heard some of the things he'd come out with. Maybe it was his old-fashioned Greek upbringing, but he was happier when Will was with Helena than with Ethan and it had nothing to do with their personalities. He tolerated me being gay, but it wasn't at all the same as the way Heather supported her son.

Since I was only helping out Max part-time, I'd had a lot of time to work out. I practically lived at Farmer's Fitness, so much so that Andy had asked me a couple of times to join their Friday group for their gym trips. He even offered to move their hang out afterward to some other place instead of the bar that they liked, which was pretty cool of him, but unnecessary. Things with Will weren't there yet, and I always declined. I knew I needed to make more of an effort for us to be okay, but there was just too much going on for me.

Sobriety was harder than I thought. It wasn't that I craved the alcohol, just the way it took me away, softened the hard edges of my reality. With the work I was putting in with Evan, still visiting his office twice a week, I'd identified some emotional triggers. Mom was one of them that I had not seen coming. I loved her, but I'd never noticed the way she treated us all differently, and how that affected my self-confidence. As expected, I'd identified some daddy issues too, more with how he bulldozed me into following him into the crazy pressured world of finance. He'd gotten me to give up photography, the one thing that I'd loved, and it was only with Evan's prompting that I'd seen how much of a soul wound that was. It was the turning point for me with no outlet for my feelings and a whole lot of stress to manage.

Weekly family dinners at the insistence of Mom were uncomfortable but I saw the value in them. Will and I were slowly working on our relationship, which was more than could be said for Alex. With him, there was more and more of a gulf between us. Evan had stressed time and time again that the issue belonged to Alex, not to me. It still stung.

With being at Farmer's Fitness a lot, I'd been spending a lot of time with Henry and he ended up asking me to watch the reception desk once a week, and monitor the gym floor another day in exchange for a paid membership of his gym. It was a sweet deal and it felt good to have someone trust me with something important like that. I loved being there and under his watchful eye, I began to notice some significant changes to my body and I felt good about my shape for the first time in a long time.

It was my day on the desk and Holly was on the floor. If I wasn't gay, she'd be my type. Whip-smart and wicked funny, always cracking me and clients up, I loved working with her almost as much as working with Max.

The phone rang and I answered, "Hello, Farmer's Fitness, how can I help you?"

"Charlie it's me, Henry."

"Oh hey man, how's it going?"

"It's going."

"Like that, huh?"

"Pretty much. You busy?"

"Nah, it's pretty quiet just now. I was looking through your invoices like you asked."

"Cool, thanks for that dude, the accountant's really been slipping and I know you and Will both did finance but..."

"Still strained with Will?"

"Yeah, I don't get it." Henry wasn't that dense. He knew exactly why Will was being a bit of a dick to him.

"Look, my brother holds grudges like nobody's business." Understatement.

He chuckled down the line, "I hear ya."

"He's just being loyal to Pete because of Andy."

"Andy isn't acting that way!"

It was my turn to laugh. "That's because he has Will to do it for him."

He was silent for a second, considering my words. "How long do you think they'll punish me for my fight with Pete?"

I made an unusual attempt to be gentle when I said, "Until he comes home, I'm afraid." Sugar-coating my words wasn't really my thing.

I didn't know much about what had happened between them all but I knew something went down at the engagement party and Pete abruptly picked up and went traveling after that. I figured that Andy blamed Henry for something, but Andy wouldn't give me the details, not that I'd asked, though I was sure he'd give in if I pressed him on it. At the end of the day, it was none of my business since I wasn't there.

Pete, Brad, and Dylan were all Andy and Will's friends. Henry, though, often voiced that he felt on the outside of that group. Especially just now with all the stuff with Pete and the way that he acted at the cabin. I didn't know the full story of what went on when Will took his friends to the lake cabin our family-owned, just that Henry and Gemma broke up the day they all returned from there and that Brad wasn't happy with Henry. Seemed like Pete was getting the blame for the breakup because Pete had feelings for Henry. I'd never met Pete, so I couldn't say if that was true.

Henry felt like he was my friend now and I hated seeing him so cut up about what was going on with his group.

The line had gone quiet and I considered putting the phone down and sending him a text when he spoke again.

"Guessed as much," he finally said. "Hey, you still looking for somewhere to stay?"

A guy came up to the counter so I told Henry to hang on a second while I booked the client in.

"Sorry, what did you say?" I asked him.

"You still looking for a place to live?"

It took me a second to pivot, the abrupt change of subject catching me off guard. "Yeah, there's not much out there, though. Not sure I want to commit to buying just yet since nothing is grabbing me. Might rent again." I shrugged even though he couldn't see me.

"Look, I haven't known you long, but you're cool. We get along and most importantly my sister trusts you with the books. So...um...I have a room if you want. Just for a share of the mortgage and bills like Pete did."

The idea caught me completely by surprise. I'd shot the shit with Henry a few times while he spotted me and vice versa, complaining about things like being back home, but I'd never expected this. Realizing I'd been quiet for too long I asked, "You're offering me Pete's old room?" I wanted to take the offer but was torn over it being Pete's. What if he came back and wanted it?

"Yeah, it was his, but he moved out nearly a year ago because of shit with my ex-girlfriend, Gemma."

"Shit, sorry, I forgot."

"Nah, it's cool. I kept it open for him in case he wanted to move back in after Gem and I split but he didn't. And, well, shit went down and here we are. I can manage without a roommate, but I know you need to be away from your mom."

Did I ever. Alice Petraki was a fantastic mother, despite her faults, and I adored her. I was thankful for all she had done for me, but she was smothering me, constantly hovering and checking up on me. I needed some space in a bad way.

"You sure you want me as a roommate?" I tried to tease, but it fell flat. I wanted to move out of my house so bad that it hurt. This was the fresh start that I needed, I could feel it.

Mom couldn't take any issue with Henry as my roommate. He was thirty-eight, a veteran, straight, and ran his own business with his sister. She'd really love how close he was to his family. Her main issue with me moving out was that I'd be on my own with no one to check up on me. Living with Henry, hopefully still working with him too, then also working with Max, gave me plenty of support.

"Yeah man, to be honest, I'm sick of going home to an empty apartment. I even thought about getting a dog."

"A dog would be great for you," I burst in. "You could take it to work. Like a support animal. Not that you need a support animal..." I trailed off. Slapping my hand to my head, I silently cursed myself.

"When I first lost my leg, the therapists suggested one and I was gonna take them up on it, but my now ex-wife was allergic."

Relief flooded me that Henry wasn't offended.

"Maybe we can see how we get on living together and see about a dog later? Not that we'll be together as a couple, but like two guys who might want a pet to keep them company," Henry rushed to say.

I laughed as Henry started to ramble. "I get what you're saying man, chill a sec. Have you run this by Will?" I wanted to be sure that this wasn't going to be crossing any lines. Henry was, after all, Will's friend first, no matter how well Henry and I got along.

"Why would I need to?"

"He was your friend first. That sounds so kindergarten, but y'know what I mean." I wasn't getting into the middle of friendships. I'd run me working at the gym by Will and he'd loved the idea, or more likely, Andy had loved it, and he'd been made to agree.

There was a pause on the line. "Look, I've got something to confess." Henry sounded strained like he was worried he was about to offend me.

"If you are about to confess to keeping an eye on me for my brother, I already know about that."

"You do?"

"Yeah, Andy told me that Will had asked you to when we had a family dinner the other night."

There was a relieved breath on the line. "Okay, cool. So Will knows how much your mom has been on your case and he suggested it. Said it'd be good for us both."

"He did, huh?"

"Yeah. So...you're at Books & Biscuits tomorrow, aren't you?" I let him turn the subject away from that uncomfortable subject.

"Yeah, therapy in the morning and then an afternoon shift with Max."

"I've never been, so I thought I could come in and give you the keys and address, maybe get a coffee and meet Max since I'm sure I'll see more of him with us being roommates."

"Sounds good to me. Max has been wanting to meet you but he'll never set foot in a gym by choice."

As expected, Henry laughed, and the deep chuckle made me smile.

Chapter Fourteen

Max

Charlie texted me after his shift last night to tell me that Henry had asked him to move in and that I'd get to meet him since he was coming by during our shift with the keys.

Unused to sharing Charlie's attention, I had to admit that I'd felt a few prickles of jealousy when he talked about Henry over the last few weeks. It was all "Henry this," and "Henry that," which was fine, totally fine, but the photos on social media...weren't. Henry was hot, and together they looked great, striking even, which left me feeling insecure and needy.

It seemed like they'd really hit it off, and I was grateful to Henry for giving Charlie work to do since I hired some more staff and couldn't give him a ton of hours. I felt like maybe I was taking advantage of our friendship by hiring him, and then not being able to give him more hours once everything stabilized. But when I voiced that with him, he insisted that while he was happy to help out, he wanted flexibility around therapy appointments and working out at the gym. He'd been spending more time exploring the city taking photos, too.

We texted back and forth about him moving out. Charlie didn't think that his mom would take the news well. Her worry over him put a lot of pressure on Charlie to act a certain way. The typing soon got exhausting, so I called him instead.

Deciding on a video call rather than just voice, I got myself comfortable and angled my phone to look half decent. Why did front-facing cameras always make me look like shit? Charlie quickly picked up the call, his hair a disheveled mess from running his hands through it. Stress pinched at his mouth and his eyes were dull.

"Hey, look, take me with you and I'll help you talk her down."

"You sure?"

"Of course. I'll be the voice of reason or something." I gave him a quick grin and he chuckled.

"Okay," the screen blurred with movement and I heard the sound of footsteps on the stairs. "Mom?"

"In the kitchen."

Charlie came into view as he settled his phone on the kitchen island where I could see them both as they sat on the bar stools.

"Hey, so I've got something to tell you and Max is here to explain it better than I could."

She turned to look at me on the screen. "Hey, Alice... look..."

An hour later, Charlie was back in his room taking time out from the stress that was his mom. She had not taken the news well. "It'll be okay. Just let her get used to the idea."

"I know, I'm just going to hit the treadmill for a bit, okay? Thanks for trying."

He disconnected the call once I'd said goodbye and I couldn't help but worry about him.

Alice's anxiety over Charlie's well-being and about everything that had happened to him was understandable, but instead of feeling cared for, all Charlie felt was smothered. It was all he'd complained about recently, even though he was seemingly happy in every other part of his life. For both our benefits, I'd stepped back a bit with him because I'd sensed some frustration at how little freedom he had. My ability to read him well had come in handy more than once. Feeling trapped and suffocated was the last thing I wanted for him. It could've undone all his progress if he had snapped under the pressure and returned to drinking.

I got why it was so hard for him to adjust to the attention; he'd never had this sort of watchfulness from his family so he didn't know what to do with it. His mom expected him, as a grown man who'd been on his own since college, to report his every move and it chafed at him on the regular. She was constantly texting him when he was with me, not that he was with me often outside of work. Charlie hadn't felt free enough to hang out on my evenings or days off much, which sucked because things were so good with us now.

Since we cleared the air weeks ago, I'd tried to focus on this new Charlie. The one that thought before he spoke, was better with people in general, showing more patience and understanding. There was an empathy in him that he didn't have before, and like an unused muscle, it'd grown the more he'd used it. A few of my more vulnerable customers had taken to him and it was sweet the way he lit up when they gifted him with smiles.

I just wished that I could move things forward with us. We flirted constantly and I used every opportunity to get into his space, to touch him casually. There was no mistaking the heat, the interest that I'd seen there in Charlie, but something was in the way, some sort of hidden barrier to us taking our friendship into more.

The bell above the door rang, breaking me from my thoughts, and as I noticed the time on the clock above the café counter from a table in the back, I started to tidy up all the paperwork I was getting nowhere with.

"Max. Hey." Charlie blushed as he came over to greet me. That's new.

"I'll just go stow my stuff and be right out. Where do you want me today?"

Home, in my bed. Preferably without clothes.

I coughed and pushed that thought away, "Um...can you do the coffee orders today? Denver struggles with it when it's busy."

"Sure thing."

He headed to the office and the lockers that I'd had to buy. A few things had gone missing recently. Luckily for me, they'd happened on days when Charlie wasn't in, otherwise, there might have been a need to have had an awkward conversation with him. I was a hundred percent sure it wasn't him, just as I was pretty sure he wouldn't cope well with being questioned about the thefts though. It was bad enough for him that his mom was doing weekly alcohol tests.

As it was, I'd had to wire up cameras over both the registers, the bookstore stockroom, and the office, since inventory was missing too, alongside cash from staff members' wallets.

I'd have loved to have a proper staff room since there were so many employees now but there just wasn't space. The lease didn't cover the attached outbuildings in the back of the building. As far as I knew, the landlord used them for the storage of furniture from the two apartments upstairs, which was also not a part of my lease.

When Charlie came out of the office, I took pity on Denver and sent him to the bookstore, taking over his role at the counter so I could chat with Charlie in between serving customers.

"Evan is thinking I can drop to one session a week starting next week." Charlie sounded over the moon. His eyes were lit with genuine happiness.

"Really? That's great news!"

"It is, but I don't think Mom is going to go for it with me moving out, too. She's going to say that it's too soon with such a big change happening."

"What did Evan say?"

"He has no concerns about the move since it's with someone I know."

"Even though you haven't known him long?" The petty jealousy was out in force.

"Will's known him for about a year, Andy a bit longer, I think. Mom has met Henry, at the engagement party, remember?" He reminded me and my stomach swooped. If that feeling of being left out ate at me, I couldn't begin to imagine how Charlie felt.

"I wasn't there, Charlie."

His face fell when he realized his mistake and he moved to wrap me in a hug, his instinct to soothe me, one that I was getting used to. I'd never relied on him like this before and I both loved it and hated it.

Pressed against the firm muscles of his chest, I could tell that the gym was really working for him. I took a breath of Charlie's smell. Laundry detergent, his shower gel, and that warm skin smell all mixed together with that hint of something that was just him.

"Shit, sorry. I hate thinking of the stuff we both missed out on because of my fucked up life," he said into my hair.

I patted his back. "It's okay." I tried to joke with him to lighten the mood. "I'm just worried you're going to try and replace me with Henry."

"Not a chance." His words were firm and there was so much affection in his gaze as he pulled back from the hug. Also a dash of something else, maybe a reluctance to pull away? Likely I was projecting my own need onto him and seeing things that weren't there.

The bell going again had us pulling further apart but not far enough that I didn't feel Charlie going rigid next to me. I flicked a glance at him, noticed his worried look, and glanced at who had walked in.

"Hey, Dr. Cross."

I saw Charlie jerk out of the corner of my eye, having moved forward to greet Dr. Cross.

A look passed between the doctor and my best friend which was loaded.

"Hey Evan, didn't know you came here," Charlie finally said to Dr. Cross, who had stayed silent.

"Hey Charlie, yeah, I'm in here pretty much daily, except this last couple of weeks which have been busy and had me missing a few days here and there. Must have been why I never put two and two together."

My mouth must have been almost on the counter. "Dr. Cross is Evan?" I squeaked out.

Evan laughed, "Back to Dr. Cross, am I?"

God, if you're there, make me invisible right now!

Charlie looked at me, confused, and I knew I'd have to say something so he didn't ask Dr. Cross, no, Evan, what the hell he meant.

"Long story, tell ya later."

Obviously not mollified, but unwilling to push it after the look I gave him, Charlie turned to Evan to take his order.

Evan's light blue eyes were filled with mirth as he observed us.

"How did I not realize the Max that runs this place is your Max?" Dr. Cross mused aloud, delight sparking in those light blue eyes.

"Owns," Charlie corrected firmly at the same time I repeated, "Your Max?"

We looked at each other before turning back to a laughing Dr. Cross, nope, Evan. This was going to take a lot of getting used to.

Looking at Charlie again, I noticed that there was a line of tension running through him and his eyes had shuttered. He seemed to be upset about Dr. Cross being here. Not because I knew that he had a therapist, we'd talked about that before, and he'd told me things from his sessions that he hadn't needed to.

No, there was something else there. He bristled every time that Dr. Evan looked my way.

Jealousy. It had to be.

Joy, pure and simple, filled me at the thought of Charlie being jealous at the way that Dr. Evan was looking at me and the idea that we had some sort of relationship. At least one that was close enough for an in-joke or nicknames.

I didn't know how to play this. On the one hand, I was over the moon to be getting this kind of reaction, even though I was worried about the effect it would have on Charlie. On the other hand, I kinda wanted to flirt a little, but I decided to go with my first instinct, which was to placate Charlie. We were working slowly towards something more. He'd only been home a few days short of a month so I didn't want to rush anything, but I also didn't want to play with his feelings or risk mine being hurt either.

I couldn't seem to put the idea of Dr. Cross, the hot therapist, potential secret daddy, together with the guy, Evan, that Charlie had told me about. Though to be fair, he hadn't told me much about the guy other than he was pretty cool and easy to talk to. I just assumed that since Evan was a former addict, or a recovering addict, himself, (painkillers, not booze), that he was...I dunno what I thought. It wasn't that, anyway.

Dr. Cross had admitted to driving to us since he was at least five blocks away, and at first, I thought it was strange that he would return here, but he confessed to becoming addicted to our treats since he was also gluten-free and we catered so well to those with dietary requirements.

While I'd been thinking, looking off into the bookstore like it had the answers, Charlie had taken Evan's order and quickly turned to start making it. The man in question looked at Charlie's rigid back at the coffee machine and seemed amused.

I moved a couple of steps to put myself next to Charlie and rubbed my hand up his arm gently, wanting to reassure him. He was holding himself stiffly. I wasn't so far away from the counter that I missed the way Evan's eyes tracked the movement before he glanced at me in approval.

Interesting.

"You okay?" I whispered to Charlie.

He glanced quickly at me before returning to the decaf caramel latte he was making with clear skill.

"Yeah. Talk after?" He was careful to talk in a way that he wouldn't be overheard.

I nodded and stepped back to the counter so I could check which pastry Dr. Cross, no, Evan, wanted.

After passing along the treat on one of the plates I'd made with our logo, we both watched Charlie as he pretended to ignore us while he finished up Evan's drink. His movements were quick and efficient and it was clear that he was comfortable with the machine. I was proud of how well he used it now. He'd picked it up again really quickly.

Charlie grabbed a tray, placed the cup carefully on it before scooping up the plate and putting it next to the cup. Competently arranging some sugar packets and a couple of napkins, he settled them on the tray before sliding it carefully closer to Evan.

It was a dismissal more than anything else and Evan noticed it. Charlie wouldn't meet his eyes. I'd say something about Charlie being rude to a customer, but I figured that this was regular behavior in their relationship.

"Thanks, Charlie," he said, picking up the tray and tossing me a wink. "This looks great. I'm expecting someone, can you tell them I'll be up in the back? I need to find a book."

"Sure," I said, confused. Evan had never met anyone here before.

After he picked a table, he took a quick drink of his latte and nodded, clearly satisfied with it without adding any more sugar to the already sweet drink. Then I watched him get up and wander over to the bookstore, greeting Finn as he caught his eye.

"What did Evan mean?" Charlie asked abruptly.

"Can we talk about this later? It's embarrassing." My cheeks flushed at the memory.

Charlie grunted, clearly displeased but willing to wait.

It wasn't long before we had to put the conversation aside, regardless of my feelings, to deal with a group of students from the nearby university campus. I'd made a point in checking out some of the courses offered so we could stock the relevant books. In leaner months when we first opened it kept the lights on without another cash injection from Charlie, so I couldn't complain about them frequenting the café.

A beautiful bronze-skinned man approached the counter after the group dispersed and I was struck with how delicate his features were. He was smaller than me and his hair was blue, giving him an ethereal quality. He wore a natural pout as he placed an order, looking between me and Charlie before his eyes narrowed on my name badge.

"Excuse me," he directed this at me, "Do you know where Dr. Daddy is?" His tone was snide. He smirked, "Sorry I mean, Dr. Cross." in a faux apologetic voice.

Well, fuck.

Confirmation if I needed it that not only did I call Dr. Cross - Evan! - Dr. Daddy, but he heard me and told this person.

We didn't get a chance to point out his table before Evan reappeared and called to the newcomer, "Elias, love, I'm here."

"Hey, Daddy," Elias called back.

Nailed it.

Chapter Fifteen

Charlie

I'm not ashamed of needing to have therapy. I was with Will, and now Andy, when it came to this; it was a useful tool to have in order to deal with some of life's shit. Mentally healthy people have had it or are having it. There was no shame there.

Ordinarily, I'd have had no problem with Max meeting my therapist...if my therapist looked like anything other than Evan.

The man was cool, effortlessly so. Smart and empathetic, too. Mom did a great job when she not only found a gay therapist, not that his sexuality really counted, but one that was a recovering addict himself. He got me, and it made everything so much easier. I honestly had come to enjoy our sessions.

The only problem that I had was that he was a gorgeous man and he'd wanted to meet Max since I started working at Books & Biscuits.

Evan claimed it was to understand my support system and since technically Max was my boss, we had that dynamic to deal with, too. I'd set up a session with Will, which had been strangely easy to do, and I'd already had a few with Mom and one with Matty.

Alex, though, wouldn't even consider it. I was given a flat no and he hung up on me. Even Evan frowned when I related the conversation, which was a rare facial expression to see on his too handsome face.

I'd put off asking Max several times. I knew he'd make the time for me. Work had calmed down with the addition of a few more employees, but I just didn't want Max and Evan in the same room.

I must have put that thought out into the universe because not only had it happened, Evan was a Books & Biscuits regular, and Max had some sort of nickname for him.

Initially, everything in me flared with a sudden feeling of panic. The sensation was so alien and familiar at once that it made me want to run. My two worlds collided and the pain at knowing that I was once again the outsider had flared brightly. They had history and I didn't belong.

Then Evan was looking at my Max too much and the green-eyed monster was on my shoulder, wanting me to do something before Max wasn't mine any longer. Not that he was mine really, but the caveman side of me had claimed him.

While I brewed coffee I rubbed absently at my chest at the thought of Max not being mine, of him belonging to someone else, and I knew beyond certainty that I had to do something before that nightmare became reality.

As I worked up the courage to suggest we talk, not just about Evan but more than that, Elias appeared and that went out of the window.

Later, after Evan and Elias had left, Max explained the whole Dr. Daddy thing and I tried to laugh convincingly while my worst fears were realized. Max had been interested in Evan.

Did that mean that I didn't have a chance? That I'd missed my chance, even if there had been one in the first place?

Evan had discussed my relationship with Max a few times, leading me to talk about the things my family had said about us in the past and the proprietary feelings I'd had about him. Matty had told me recently that she thought Max was in love with me, and I had mentioned this to Evan.

If Max was looking at other guys, taken or not, did that mean he was over whatever feelings he'd had for me? If he showed me any sign that he was interested then I...I would have to go with my heart. I needed Max in whatever form our relationship came in.

My mind was still spinning when Henry came in to meet Max and give me a key to his apartment.

"Hey Charlie, you okay?"

It took me a second to get the words out and sound halfway convincing about it. "Yeah, I'm good." Gesturing to Max I said, "Henry, this is Max," and then to Henry, "Max, this is Henry."

"Have we met before?" Henry asked Max.

"Um...no? I don't think so." Max looked confused.

"Oh! I know what it is. You're the guy Will took home. Man, Andy was so mad about that. He thought you guys were hooking up."

Silence hung thick in the air and Henry looked like he wanted to tug the words back at the way Max stiffened.

The color drained from Max's face and I instinctively went to hug him. He settled immediately into my arms and we both sighed at the contact.

Just the motion, the way that he came to me so easily when he was embarrassed and upset, said more to me than I could understand.

It felt right.

Henry looked shame-faced, "Sorry, I forgot the after bit of that. Will said you'd maybe been slipped something?"

Max nodded into my chest and my heart sunk because I knew he'd been in that situation alone because of me. Would I ever be able to make up for all the trouble I'd caused?

Max must have felt me tense because he began to rub my back even as he turned to look at Henry, his face now flushed.

"All in the past. It's great to meet you officially, Henry. Thanks for giving Charlie somewhere to stay." He'd pasted a fake smile on his face and the color was still high on his cheeks, the red contrasting starkly with his creamy skin. "Can I get you something to drink? On the house, of course." Max was working hard to push the mortification aside and make a good impression on my new roommate.

"Yeah, that'd be great. Do you guys use oat milk at all?"

Talking about his business was a great way to break the ice with Max, and I gave Henry a smile over Max's head that he caught and returned with a quick lift of his lips.

Max insisted I have a break and go and sit with Henry, so I grabbed a cookie and a bottle of water and slumped down in a seat opposite him.

"I put my foot in my mouth there, didn't I?" Henry immediately said.

"Nah, he's just a little sensitive about things like that. Even though it wasn't his fault, he was drugged for God's sake! He still feels like he made an idiot of himself. He gets very anxious about shit like that."

Henry considered this for a second. "Okay, noted. I want him to like me since I know how important he is to you. Even if you don't end up living with me long, I consider you my friend and I want Max to be comfortable around me."

"I promise he likes you already. You're doing me a huge favor getting me out of my mom's, and Max is sick of me complaining about my living situation."

"That bad?"

My phone chose that second to chime with a text.

"Five bucks says that's my mom now, checking to see if Max and I are hanging out after we close."

He laughs, "I'm not taking that bet after some of the crap you've told me. She still trying to get you to agree to random alcohol checks?"

Rolling my eyes, I huffed out a breath. "That and keeping my sessions at twice a week. She doesn't want me working here so much, but with Easter and spring break at the university coming up, it's all hands on deck."

"Will you be okay doing both? I can check with some of the others for coverage if I need to?"

"Nah, if it does get to be too much, Max will step in. He'll likely know before I do."

"He's watching you just now, you know. Is there something there?"

"I think maybe we're building to something."

"What d'you mean?" Henry tilted his head slightly as he tried to understand.

"Well, how much do you know about me and Max?" I asked him, not wanting to repeat the whole deal unless it was necessary.

He thought for a second and must have recalled something because he nodded. "You guys had to make up after rehab, right?"

"Yeah, we did. And I realized how much he means to me," I said in a quiet voice, "And that I want to be more, but we just aren't ready."

"Don't think it'll be long, judging by how you are with each other."

"Hope so." Even to my own ears, it came out wistful.

Chapter Sixteen

Charlie

Although I wanted to be out of Mom's house and into Henry's apartment as soon as possible, I was working too much over the next few days to do anything about it.

We sat on Max's slightly lumpy sofa, letting our food settle a bit before we decided what we were going to do with our day off. Max was still scheduling our days off together so we could try and hang out. Our shifts either had us working at the same time or overlapping, so we'd at least see each other.

"D'you want a hand picking up some stuff for the apartment? We could go shopping and get stuff if you want," Max asked.

I'd gone over to his place after my therapy session, the last of the twice-weekly sessions, and he'd made us brunch.

"Would you mind?"

"Wouldn't ask if I did," he said, giving me a nudge. "What all do you need?"

"Henry said I could borrow some of his bedding." I saw Max make a face. "Yeah, I'm not really into that idea either. So my own stuff is a must."

"You don't have any from your last apartment?"

"No, I gave it all away, remember?"

He nodded before jumping up. "Hold on a sec, I'll get some paper and make a list."

I waited for him to be ready and tried not to be distracted by staring at him again. "So bedding and towels, stuff like that."

"Sure."

"Oh, and Henry said the mattress was cheap shit so probably a new one. He couldn't afford much when he moved in and Pete complained about it." He noted that down.

"Anything else?"

"I'll text him now and let you know what he says."

"Sounds good to me."

There hadn't been a lot of time for us to hang out with Mom on my case so much. I felt fifteen and not thirty. Part of me thought that she blamed Max for abandoning me and getting myself mugged, or for enabling my behavior to the point I ended up in a mess I couldn't get out of. Not that I could tell Max that, but I think he knew something was up.

"What else do you need to get?" Max's voice broke through my thoughts.

"Henry said there's just the bed with the crappy mattress and a built-in closet in the room. So a dresser and a couple of nightstands."

"At least one lamp too," he interjected. "D'you know if there's carpet or wood flooring?"

"I have no idea." It hadn't occurred to me to ask.

"Maybe just get a rug just in case. You could always take it back if you don't need it." Max was always the more practical of us. He wouldn't have forgotten to ask these things. I'd been sure he was going to complain that I hadn't even seen the place before I agreed to move out. Maybe all the hassle with my mom had him cutting me some slack.

"True. Good idea. Where should we start?"

"There's a furniture store not far from here if I drive us. A family-run place." I nodded in approval, preferring those kinds of stores over chains. "Then we can hit up a department store for towels and bedding. After that, dinner out somewhere and we can drop your purchases at Henry's, sorry, your place. Once your furniture is delivered you can move in but there's no point in upsetting your mom by taking stuff there to store it." He shot me a concerned glance. "Is she okay with you moving out?"

"Not really, but she knows she can't stop me. I think Evan is going to call her and arrange a few sessions for her."

At the mention of Evan, Max's cheeks heated and it was so adorable I couldn't help reaching over and running a finger over the blushing skin. "Or do you prefer to call him Dr. Daddy?" I teased.

He caught my finger, looking me in the eyes, searching for something. I held my breath as the tension ignited between us, the swarm of butterflies in my stomach bursting free and prompting me into action. We leaned in and the moment stretched between us, snapping at the sound of my phone. I groaned when I saw who was calling but still answered since the mood was already broken.

"Hey Mom, yeah, I'm okay."

Max drove us the short distance to the furniture store, insisting that we would need the car to transport our purchases. I couldn't fault his logic and was grateful that he wanted to drive so I didn't have to use the car service.

My thoughts were spinning at that near kiss. It was going to be a kiss, wasn't it? Had he meant to lean into me like that? Had he felt the electricity between us?

Up ahead, I could see the sprawling modern building of the store Max had recommended. Lots of light brick and windows made up half of the bottom floor. Max had explained that the bedroom furniture was on the second floor, along with a pretty decent café that stocked the same beans that he'd used. In fact, he told me, that was who had connected him to the supplier when he'd been buying sofas for Books & Biscuits.

I'd been on a few of those shopping trips but didn't remember coming to this store. I wanted to ask him but was worried that one of my binges had stolen the memory for me.

"The building looks great. I haven't had a chance to visit it since they reopened."

"Reopened?"

"Oh, they had a store a few streets away and they outgrew it, so had this custom-built. I've been following them on social media since I opened my place. They found this unit, knocked it down, and rebuilt something to their specifications. It was really cool, they did polls on cladding and stuff. When they finally opened a couple of weeks ago, they did a video tour."

"Cladding?"

"The...uh...outside of the building. Like the wood details." I explained.

"Ah, right. So that's why I don't remember this place, then."

Max reached over and patted my thigh. "You were never drunk when we went shopping to furnish my place. Stop second-guessing yourself. You weren't nearly as bad as everyone is making out."

I put my hand over his and squeezed. His faith in me had gotten me through so much. I didn't deserve him and I knew he wasn't lying. If Max believed that I hadn't been that bad, then I wasn't. He grew up with an addict so he would know; his mom had liked to hit the bottle.

My words, when they finally came out, were choked with emotion, "Thanks, I needed to hear that." I took a minute to think about what I wanted to say, but then it just burst from me. "It's like everyone is blaming the attack on me. Yes I was drunk, and yes I'd been thrown out of that club, but it doesn't mean it's right that I got mugged. I didn't ask for it. Maybe I shouldn't have fought back, but I just wanted the watch. They had everything else." A sob choked me and I was unable to swallow it down.

Max pulled over just a street away from our destination, quickly switched off the engine, and crawled into my lap.

His movements shocked me into stillness and he wrapped himself around me, muttering soft words I couldn't catch into my neck.

Hesitating for another moment, I broke out of my confusion and wrapped him up tightly against me.

This is what I want, for always.

A knock on the window startled us both and we pulled apart, though Max was still in my lap.

A parking enforcement officer was pointing at the No Parking sign with a no-nonsense look on her face. "Sorry, I'm just moving. Don't give me a ticket, please!" Max shouted, his voice becoming higher pitched with panic, as he moved back into the driver's seat, quickly snapping on his seatbelt and starting up the car.

The woman moved on and I couldn't help but catch the humored look on her face. Max was the color of a tomato and it was so adorable I couldn't help but laugh the rest of the way to the store as he barked at me to stop. Before long, he was laughing with me.

The store didn't seem busy from the look of the half-empty parking lot, but during the workday on a Thursday was likely to be quiet, I guessed.

Max looked like he wanted to say something as he parked and switched off the car. He started to speak, but another tap on the window interrupted us again.

"Max! Hey." The guy at the window was young-looking, likely just out of high school.

Max unbuckled his belt and opened the door, motioning for me to do the same. Okay then, guess we will talk about this later.

"Hey, Noah." Max greeted the young guy with a fist pump and a laugh. "This is Charlie, I don't think he was here last time I was. Charlie, Noah is the owner's grandson." Giving Noah his full attention, he asked, "You here full time now?"

"Yeah, graduated high school last year and deferred for a year to travel but didn't get far." He laughed, turning to include me in the conversation. "Turns out I'm the worst flier. Ever." He shrugged casually. "So I came home and Grandpa put me to work."

The kid seemed okay, down to earth, and there was a real affection when he mentioned his grandpa.

"Let's get out of the sun," Noah suggested. The April sun was beating down on us, making me long for air conditioning. Noah led us into the blissfully cool building. The interior was set out in mock rooms to display the furniture as if it was in your home, and it was tastefully done in a variety of styles.

"I was just helping a customer with a rug. Didn't think it would fit in her car but we managed. You here for stuff for the café?" Noah asked Max.

"We're here for me," I cut in. "I need bedroom stuff."

"Cool, well that stuff is on the next floor and there are a couple of assistants up there that can help you out. Nice to see you Max, and to meet you, Charlie. Hope you get what you need." With that, Noah headed back to the main reception area where a couple was waiting with some purchases.

"Was I rude?" I ask Max quietly.

"Nah, he probably would've gotten into trouble for making those people wait."

I moved over to a sofa that caught my eye and dropped down into it, tipping my head back to watch the light travel over the ceiling. I was suddenly exhausted. Just completely done. I wanted to get the furniture and stuff I needed but I didn't want to pick it all. I just wanted to be somewhere quiet and calm.

Max stood watching me for a second before sitting next to me, our bodies aligned from knee to shoulder. "What's going on, Charlie? I haven't seen you like that in a long time." He leaned further into me, reassuring me with his presence.

"I..." I sighed and ran a hand through my hair, still not used to the shorter cut that Mom insisted I get. I felt frustration bubble up. "I just feel like I've had control of my life stolen from me. Like Mom and Alex took the mugging as an excuse to take it all away. Mom doesn't like me working. She doesn't think I'm ready for it even when I was going out of my mind at home within just a few days after getting out. She doesn't want me to move out because she doesn't trust Henry to keep an eye on me. It's ridiculous!"

Max wrapped an arm around me, pulling my head down to rest on his shoulder.

"You are more than ready. Okay, so you didn't wait long to get a job, but you don't work full time, you are doing therapy and are home most evenings. She can't fault you. You have to do these things eventually and I think doing them now while you have Evan to support you is the best thing for you." Max stroked his hand through my hair and I melted into the touch. It was perfect to be like that with him, letting him look after me and soaking up the warm affection.

"I honestly think that moving out is the best thing for you both," he went on. "You've been home a month and I can see the cracks forming. One of you is bound to say something they regret. You're too alike for you not to. You'll get the blame though because Alex is a dick."

I couldn't help the chuckle I let loose. "Fair and true."

"Let's just focus on problems as they come, okay? This move is going to be great and Henry knows what's happened and still wants you to move in, so he must trust you not to throw it in his face by getting wasted, right?"

I gave a shrug. "I guess. The last thing I want to do right now is get drunk. I honestly don't miss the constant buzz of anxiety from the day after a bender. Booze isn't worth the hassle it causes."

"See? Growth. Let's go get you moved out."

An hour later I was ready to hand over all decisions to Max because I was utterly done with shopping. We'd lain on what felt like a hundred mattresses before Max found the one he thought was best. The sales assistant looked at me like I had a screw loose for letting Max dictate what I spent my cash on, but she didn't know how well Max understood me and my personal tastes. I had to admit that I spent most of the time we were shopping completely distracted by him. Each time that we lay down together, I couldn't help picturing us doing this all the time. Climbing into our bed at the end of a long day and curling up together. Nights twisted around each other, sweat-covered skin. Panted moans and breathy gasps.

There was something in his eyes whenever they caught mine that made me think perhaps he was thinking something similar.

Surrounded by people, it wasn't the time to do anything about the feelings surging within me.

My phone buzzed with a text.

Will: Where is that animal shelter you helped out at? I want to get Andy a cat for his birthday.

Taking a second to draw up the shelter's website on my phone, I shot the info back to him.

Will: Thanks.

A smile played on my lips at Will casually reaching out to me like that. Progress. Then it fell as I remembered how much shopping we still had to do.

I caught Max observing me as we neared the end of mattresses and I gave him a questioning look.

"You're done, aren't you?"

"Yeah. I really don't care now. I just want something comfortable to sleep on." I cast a look around me. "This is too much. I can't choose."

Max moved closer and wrapped an arm around me, pulling me into his side.

"Why don't you head over to the café and order us something? I can pick up stuff you'll like. I've seen a couple of things already."

"Really? You'd do that?"

"Sure. You can have the final say if you want. I can send you some pics."

"Nah, I trust you." I handed him my credit card and from the corner of my eye, I saw the assistant's eyes bug out. She didn't know us though and I trusted Max and knew our tastes were similar.

We should have done it this way from the start. I sat in the café with an iced coffee for Max and a fruity iced drink for me. There hadn't been much that was gluten-free, so I decided that we'd just get something to eat elsewhere.

Less than twenty minutes later, Max returned to my side, plopping down in the seat next to me.

"Done. They'll be delivered tomorrow. I paid extra for that. Hope that's okay."

Shocked, I stared at him for a minute. "Seriously? That's great. I thought I'd have to wait a while."

"They'd have done it today since they're just using the display stock. I got you a discount for that. A driver is out sick today so they don't have time."

"Thanks, Max, you've really come through for me. Gone above and beyond, really." I thought for a minute. "I think I might just get stuff and sleep at my new place tonight. It's only one night on that old mattress. I can get most of my stuff today while Mom is still at the lake and go see her tomorrow for the rest of it." I wanted to avoid a confrontation with Mom. She'd spent the last few days trying to convince me that moving out was a bad idea and trying to guilt me into staying.

Max looked thoughtful. "Are you and your Mom going to be okay after this?"

I shrugged, the movement jostling him slightly, so I dropped a hand to his thigh, quickly removing it when we both colored.

"Um," I cleared my throat and tried to calm myself. "I'm working on it with Dr. Daddy." I teased.

I wanted to bring us back to the mood that we had going on in the car. What would have happened if that meter maid hadn't interrupted us? Just the memory of Max in my lap, wrapped around me, had my dick twitching in my jeans and butterflies trying to escape my stomach.

Over the years I'd had crushes, I even thought I was in love with a couple of my boyfriends. Yet nothing that I'd felt before managed to come close to what I felt for Max.

When I thought of a future, years down the line, it was one with Max by my side. He was there for every part of my life. We would have a home, one cluttered and full of joy, so far removed from my family's one. We'd have animals of all descriptions. And there were kids. Lots of kids. We'd help out those that need someone for just a short time, just a landing spot before moving on to better things. We'd have ones that were with us for years and we'd watch them grow together, supporting them when they fell and cheering when they flew. The only thing that was crystal clear about that dream was that Max was there, my constant through it all. With him next to me I didn't need anything else.

I came back to the moment when Max squirmed in his seat. As expected, Max blushed again and we shared a laugh but the mood between us was lighter.

After we finished up our drinks, Max took me shopping to get sheets and stuff before taking me to my mom's house. I didn't pay much attention to things in the department store, just picked up a few sets of sheets in darker colors and some matching towels. Now that I'd decided to stay in the new place for the night, I was itching to get moving so I could drop off my things and take Max out for a well-earned dinner.

Our footsteps echoed in the hallway as we entered and the place felt hollow, so I was sure that no one was home. It was rare that Matty went to the lake, but since she informed us of her choice of school after summer, Mom had kept her close. Calling it bonding time before Matty moved to study across the country from her family. Not that I blamed her.

In my room, I picked up discarded clothing and shoved it into the bags I'd stashed there when I'd moved into Mom's from my apartment.

Max was subdued, looking around my room before making his way over to my desk. He picked up my camera and looked at me for permission before switching it on and flicking through the shots there.

"Charlie! These are amazing! I'd forgotten how good you were."

His praise soothed something in me. It reminded me that I'd forgotten to show the pictures I'd taken in rehab to him. I'd gotten them printed after emailing them to the center for approval.

"Here," I pick up the envelope on the desk. "These are the ones from my time at the facility." I handed them over carefully, my movements belying my casual words. "They've checked them and there is nothing that really identifies these people, and the ones in the photos have seen them and okayed them for use."

"What are you going to use them for?" He asked as he studied one photo of the back of a woman while leaning against my desk.

I'd spliced two images together. One from the start of her time there, which was the week after I started. The other from the week I left. It was still startling for me to see the images together. The contrast between them was what appealed to me about them, and it took me hours to sew the images together to really highlight the difference.

In the before pictures, the patients were often hollow looking, frail, with an unkempt look. They would stand slightly hunched like they were afraid to take up space.

After, they stood with pride, and it was possible to feel their hope in the way that they held themselves. In appearance, they often looked like they cared about what they saw in the mirror. In the women, their hair shone with health. Some of the men had asked for haircuts.

I ran my hand over the back of my neck nervously. The idea that had been rattling around my head was approved by all the involved parties, but it still made me worry.

"Uh, well...I want to write a book. Or, rather, have the images tell the story." My voice fell away at the look on Max's face.

He rushed me, wrapping himself around me in a tight hug, pulling back only to speak. "That's perfect, Charlie! I could sell them in the bookstore when you're ready."

His enthusiasm was so infectious that I revealed my other news. "A publisher is willing to print it. I just need to write a few pages about what I want to say and give them the finished images."

"Are you serious? That's amazing! I'm so proud of you!" His eyes filled with tears so I pulled him closer and muttered into his hair. "It's not that big of a deal, just a small indie press, and they've started formatting what I've given them already."

He pulled back again to scold me, "It is a big deal. You are going to be a published photographer and author! I think it's amazing that you're making something positive out of what was a dark time for you."

I wiped the tears from his eyes and the mood between us shifted again. An awareness of how close we were. The tension from the car seeped back in, crackling between us, but I felt in my gut that this wasn't our moment. I wanted us to start out better so when we looked back we had a better beginning story. I stepped back, watching Max's face fall a little.

"Would you...would you help me write the introduction?" I paused and let that idea sink in for a second. Worrying that he needed encouragement, I continued, "I have some of it but you've always been better with words. I'll credit you, of course."

He hesitated for a second. A blink and you'll miss it expression of frustration played across his face. "I'll be happy to help, but it has to come from you." His tone was gentle. "I think it's more genuine if it's you that writes it."

I knew that he was right, but the deadline was looming, having been put off by me more than once. The press had a slot free and if I missed this one then it would be months before I could get published.

"Does anyone else know?"

Outside of Evan and the center, Max was the only person that understood the part of my soul that needed expression. My mom should, with her art, but I'd repressed that part of myself so fully that she didn't see it in me compared to Will.

"Aside from the necessary people? Just you and Evan."

He nodded. "Let's get your stuff to Henry's, then we can take a look at what you've got."

Chapter Seventeen

Max

We pulled up to the building where Henry had his apartment and I surveyed the area. Some of the blocks were newer and there were a number of local businesses. It wasn't actually that far from Books & Biscuits or Henry's gym—one place I had yet to set foot in. Out of all the places that we had looked at online, this was already shaping up to beat them.

There was resident parking in the rear and I pulled into a guest spot and parked. Next to me in the passenger seat, I felt Charlie tense. Clicking off my seatbelt, I shifted to face him, giving him my whole attention.

"What's up?"

He was silent for a moment while his gaze wandered the area. "Uh, nervous I guess. It's been a long time since I lived with someone that wasn't you or family."

I rubbed his arm gently. "It's not like Henry is a stranger though and it doesn't have to be long term. You can keep looking for somewhere if it isn't a good fit for either of you."

Charlie digested this before shrugging. "Yeah, I know, it's just a lot of change."

"And you don't do well with change. I know." I smiled at him to let him know that I didn't mean anything by my remark.

He gave me a quick grin and moved to get out of the car. I needed to have a proper talk with him because his emotions were giving me whiplash with how quickly they were shifting.

We gathered up the bags, attempting to make just one trip to the fourth-floor apartment. I was happy to see that they had an elevator and that it was working. An elderly lady was exiting as we waited by the doors to get in, the bags strewn around us.

"Handsome boys," she cooed. "Do you live here?"

"I'm just moving in, ma'am. I'm Charlie, this is Max." Charlie told her politely. He had such a sweet way with old ladies and they adored him, like he was catnip with kittens. They flocked to him constantly.

I smothered a laugh as she gravitated towards him and set a wrinkled hand on his arm.

"Which floor, sweetie?" She asked.

"Fourth, ma'am."

"Ma'am nothing, you call me Lily y'hear?" She demanded in her sweet southern accent, as she continued to pat his arm. "I'm in 502, an' it gets lonely on my own sometimes, so don' be a stranger." She gave his arm a final squeeze and let go.

"Well, I'm in 402, so if you ever need anything, pop down to my apartment, okay?"

"Oh you're Henry's new roomie! I just love that boy," she gushed, her eyes practically filled with cartoon hearts. "Always helps with my groceries an' I make him these protein balls my grandson loves. My grandson, Kelly, just started going to his gym. I was telling him about Henry's pretty sister an' he said, 'Nana, you know I don't date girls,' an' I told him it was a shame that Henry didn't date men because he's so handsome an' kind."

I stifled a laugh and Charlie sent me a look, a sort of panicked expression that had my shoulders shuddering with the effort it took to keep quiet.

"Oh, I... uh, work there, too." Charlie finally managed to get out.

"Have you met my Kelly?"

"Um, I dunno. What's he look like?"

I didn't think we were ever getting away from Ms. Lily as she gave us a detailed description of her red-haired grandson, even looking through her phone for photos of him.

"Um, no Lily, I haven't met him but he probably works out in the evenings with his job."

"Of course! That'll be it." I got the feeling that Lily was lonely and I felt bad for her. I hoped that Kelly visited often.

I decided to step in before she tried to set Charlie up with Kelly. "It's been lovely to meet you Lily, but we better get Charlie moved in. He promised me dinner."

"Oh, of course! I need to get goin' before I miss the ladies. We're getting cocktails! You boys have a lovely dinner. What a handsome couple you make!"

I glanced at Charlie, but neither of us made any move to correct her and that hopeful feeling rose in me again. This was progress. Of course, we'd played the fake boyfriends game to deter unwanted attention before, but Lily's assumption had been something different. In situations like that before we would have immediately rushed to ensure that it was clear that we were just best friends.

We said our goodbyes to Lily and headed up to the fourth floor and the well-appointed two-bedroom where Charlie would be living for the foreseeable future.

"The rug was a good idea," Charlie remarked, breaking the silence. He gestured to the hardwood floors of the almost empty bedroom that now belonged to him.

"It should be here tomorrow with the rest of your furniture. Probably not worth unpacking until then, is it?"

He shrugged. "Nowhere to put anything, since the closet isn't that big. I'll just get my toiletries and a couple of changes of clothes out for now."

"I'll help you make up the bed."

Together, we got the room set up quickly. We worked so easily with each other and I couldn't help imagining that this was our apartment and that Charlie was just helping me with the regular chores. I felt my face heat as I thought about waking up with Charlie in this bed after a night of amazing sex. In my dream world, it was perfect and he woke me with gentle nose kisses because morning breath was yucky.

Before my body betrayed me with its reaction to being in such a small space with Charlie, I returned to the living room to wait for him to wash up before heading out to dinner.

During dinner at a great Thai restaurant, I contemplated saying something about what was happening between us. I tried to find the right words. While I tried to speak, Charlie's phone rang.

"Sorry," he said as he looked at the screen, "I better take this." He answered the call, "Hello?"

The restaurant was quiet enough that I could hear the other side of the call and heard the police officer introduce himself. Charlie could see that I was listening and put the call on speaker so I could hear better.

"I'm just calling to tell you that an item of yours has reappeared. There was an inspection at a pawn shop and your watch turned up as stolen goods," the bored-sounding man said.

Charlie gasped, "You have my watch?"

"We do, but unfortunately, since the pawnbroker didn't keep records, we don't know who brought it in, so we aren't any closer to the culprit of your mugging." I could see Charlie bristle at the dismissive way the man broke the news.

"So I can come and collect it?" I could see his struggle to brush off thoughts of his attackers.

"You can during business hours, yes. It's been processed and is ready to be returned. Have a nice evening, Mr. Petraki."

The officer hung up, leaving us both staring at the phone. I was simultaneously furious and relieved. While I was grateful that Charlie was getting back the item that he cherished, I was horrified at the way that the police were treating him. Charlie had been a victim of a crime and didn't deserve the lack of respect he'd been given.

"Want me to come with you to pick it up?" I asked carefully, aware that this was a big deal to him and he was already going through a massive upheaval with the move.

"Hmm? Oh, no. I'll manage, but thanks." He gave me a soft smile and we slipped into silence for a while, each of us picking at our food.

"Max?" Charlie's voice broke me from my thoughts.

"Yeah?"

"I don't know what's happening with us, but let's not force it, okay?" He looked worried about my reaction.

I frowned and he rushed to explain. "I can feel something changing between us, and it's as exciting as it is terrifying, but I don't want to rush it, or force something to happen before we're both ready. D'you know what I mean?" His voice was imploring, begging me to understand where he was coming from.

After thinking for a minute, I nodded. I didn't have the words to explain my feelings. I knew that this wasn't a rejection and I also knew that I'd pushed a lot today and Charlie had a lot of changes to deal with. Only this morning I'd been in Charlie's lap and goodness only knew what would have happened if the officer hadn't interrupted. It was out of character for me to be so forward with someone that I was interested in romantically.

This new Charlie seemed to bring something out in me. When it was just us, I could stand taller. I felt stronger. It went against past history to rely on him but he gave me such a feeling of safety, that I knew that I could let this new part of myself unfurl and stretch when I was with him.

We were heading for a major change in our relationship and I could stand to be a little more patient with him. He'd only been out of rehab for just a few weeks and was having to wrestle with a lot. He admitted to being excited about it, so that was progress at least. Now our feelings were sort of out in the open. We were acknowledging that things were different, that there was something more on the horizon.

"Okay, I can wait."

Chapter Eighteen

Charlie

Over the following week, Max and I danced around this new awareness of our feelings.

I was glad that I'd spoken up, although I'd been terrified that I'd hurt Max. For all his bluster and bravado, he was sensitive. He didn't allow people in often so they couldn't hurt him.

It was important to me that we started off well, and my head had been spinning from everything that had been happening.

The apartment offer, Mom's reaction to me leaving and settling into a new place with my sort of friend/boss was a lot to deal with before adding a new, probably serious relationship into the mix.

Max was going to be the most serious and important relationship I ever had. He was endgame for me. If I believed in marriage as an institution, then he would be my future husband. Hell, if he wanted to get married, despite my feelings on it, then that was what we would do. Anything for him.

The afternoon after moving, I'd gone back to my mom's house to explain that I'd moved and she had cried. It broke my heart to hurt her and I tried to explain the damage that living in such close proximity was causing to our relationship.

We ended up talking for a long time and I hoped that it had done a lot to clear the air. I'd sent Evan a message explaining the situation and he'd offered to set up an appointment with me and Mom so we could work it through together, with professional supervision. When I floated the idea to Mom, she'd agreed, which I took to be progress.

She even came back to my new place to meet Henry and see where I would be living. I took her around the neighborhood, pointing out Farmer's Fitness and even Books & Biscuits when we wandered that far. We had to stop and have a drink and wait for the car to collect us since Mom had worn the wrong shoes for so much walking, and ended up with a blister. Heather was on shift as a supervisor in the bookstore. I'd introduced her to Mom and she had given Mom a bandaid. They seemed to hit it off and they chatted as we waited. I left them to it and jumped up to make up orders when needed.

By the time we'd finished dinner back at my apartment, with Henry joining us, I felt like Mom and I were in a better place. Just having that off my shoulders made everything feel so much better.

I went alone to pick up my stolen watch and hadn't mentioned it to Mom even though the thought of it weighed on my mind. I was grateful to have something so important to me returned, but I felt humiliated over the way that the officer had spoken to me in front of Max. I hated that the police didn't care about what had happened to me. Being drunk wasn't a free pass to be mugged. It made me wonder what would have happened if I'd died. Would they have left me in a morgue for days as a John Doe before impassively telling my family how I'd died?

Realizing that the watch was a trigger, or at least my complicated feelings attached to it were a catalyst, I called to get an appointment with Evan after I picked it up.

I walked into Evan's office later that day with the metal band strapped to my wrist, the once familiar weight feeling so foreign after all these months. I sat pondering my feelings as I ran my fingers over it and tried to work out how I felt.

"Charlie?" came Evan's voice. I must have stopped talking after a while and he'd let me sit and stew.

"I'm okay. Really, I am. It's just it's been a big week, with the move and things with Max."

Evan looked like he wanted to ask, but kept quiet.

"We've both got feelings for each other, but my head is spinning with everything. So I asked him to let things just develop naturally. I just needed the breathing room with everything going on."

"I have to say that it shows a lot of growth," Evan said evenly, "to know that you are reaching a limit and to ask for that space to process. This is a real improvement and you should be proud. How did Max take it?"

"He understood, actually."

"Good, that's really good. Are you feeling okay about the watch now that you've had the opportunity to discuss it?"

"I am, yeah. Sorry, I just needed to get it out. I'm grateful to have it back. It's the one thing that is just mine from my father. The one time he said he was proud of me, so I guess it's a symbol of that feeling. I just wish that the police wanted to catch the people that hurt me."

Evan sympathized with me, but ultimately there was nothing that could be done and I had to let it go. It had happened and my life had changed because of it. I could either dwell on it or be grateful something good had come of the whole experience.

After all, nearly dying had probably saved my life.

Over the next few days, I settled into the apartment. Henry was easy to live with and was so busy that I didn't see him all that much. His need for order was similar to Max and so I adapted to that easily. The familiar ways they lived often had me smiling but it helped me relax.

I'd worried that things between Max and I would be strained with me asking him to wait, but if anything, the conversation had helped. Perhaps it was just admitting that there was something there, acknowledging that it was a mutual feeling, that had us relaxing into what was happening.

Over the course of the week after, we carried on as normal, or a new normal. We touched often, sharing secret smiles, and I'd noticed the other staff and some of the customers at Books & Biscuits watching us a lot.

We spent more time together outside of work too, with Max coming over to my apartment a lot since it was closer to the shop. We hung out, watching movies and cuddling but taking it no further.

Each night after he left, I'd find myself jerking off to the memory of him up against me in the car. The heat of his perfect body, all lean lines pressed against me as he leaned in, the near kiss that we missed and I still ached for. The times I'd spent looking at his mouth, imagining him swallowing down my dick.

Spending so much time with him was torture and it was clear he wanted me to know he just needed a green light. He would sit against me, cuddling in close, while we watched T.V. Often looking up at me with those pale blue eyes, biting his lip. We'd hold hands, or he'd stroke my arm affectionately. He'd say goodnight with a kiss on the cheek, so close to the corner of my mouth that it was a whisper away from where we both wanted it. Just one tease after another.

It was then that I wondered why I was teasing him, and myself, by dragging it out. It was clear that we both wanted more, and everything else had settled down, so I was out of excuses.

It was time to go after what we both clearly wanted.

Chapter Nineteen

Max

Maverick Kane was a pain in my ass. Not literally, though I'm sure that he wanted to be. The guy had been trying to get his coffee into my café, and himself into my pants since I'd met him about a year ago.

While attractive and arguably my type, being tall, dark and some might say, handsome, he did nothing for me.

Actually, he set off every warning bell I had developed over the years from dealing with creeps. This guy set off my creep meter to a red alert, but I had no reason for why I acted so defensive around him. He'd never given me a reason to think that he was anything but a rep from one of the coffee bean suppliers in the city. This one was far more persistent though and was trying to poach my business from the fair trade supplier that I'd used since I'd opened.

I'd been brought up to always trust my gut, so I worked hard to keep polite but firm, never showing any sort of weakness or doubt since I could guarantee that Maverick would be all over that if he thought he had a chance with me.

"How've you been?" he asked as we sat down at our usual table. I always picked this one because of its proximity to the counter. Usually so that Kristen or one of my other employees could come up to me with an emergency that I just had to handle right then, if they saw me struggling or if Maverick was coming on too strong.

"Busy, so busy, thanks, you?" It was always a good idea to keep Maverick talking. I wasn't interested in listening to his answers, distracted with Charlie handling the counter himself, looking like a black cloud had settled overhead. He'd been doing so well with the customers, giving out sweet smiles to old ladies with cups of tea, and quick quips to the university students loading up with caffeine before lectures.

Maverick rambled on and on, with the expected humble brags and flirt routine that I was used to, and I tuned out briefly as I watched the muscles of Charlie's back flex as he ground beans confidently for his latest order. "What do you think?"

"Sorry?"

"What do you think about me taking you out for dinner?"

There was a clatter from the counter and a muffled curse. Charlie bent to pick up the milk jug and shot me an apologetic look.

"Excuse me for a second," I said to Maverick as I got up to help Charlie clean up, but Finn got there first and quickly cleared the spill, handing a fresh jug to Charlie to use instead.

Shrugging, I sat back down.

"So sorry. What did you say again?"

"I'd like to take you out to dinner. Look, I'm sure it's not a surprise that I'm interested in you. I wouldn't be nearly as persistent about coming here otherwise. I know as well as you do that you aren't changing suppliers. Your current one must either love you, or you managed to con them into giving you a fantastic price. I can't do those numbers without being fired and I happen to like my job."

I shuffled in my seat a bit, uncomfortable and unsure how to let the guy down gently. The ones that were confident enough to just straight out ask me out were always the ones liable to make a scene when they didn't get what they wanted.

Instinctively, I looked up and caught Charlie watching me. It was impossible to know what he saw in my expression but he rounded the counter and came to my side.

"Babe, I need you to come look at the schedule for the week after next. You promised me a date night and it's been a month since we've had one." He settled his expression into a faux pout, teasing me with a sly twinkle in his eyes.

I stiffened briefly as Charlie ran his hand up and down my back gently, not expecting the gesture, but thankful that Maverick was too busy reacting to Charlie's interruption to notice me. Just having him beside me, touching me, filled me with relief, though there was a touch of melancholy since I wanted this to be real. This was the ultimate tease. Acting the part of my boyfriend when he knew I wanted the act to be real.

"Oh. Oh! I'm sorry. I thought you were single."

I didn't even manage to speak up before Charlie cut in and answered for me.

"It's new." His tone was short, not inviting any comment and I saw Maverick measuring Charlie up.

"Right, well I'll let you get back to work, Max. You have my number so if things change with your supplier, or your man here, gimme a call okay?"

Charlie tensed and I could almost hear him growl at Maverick as he gathered up his things and left.

Moving to get up, I noticed that Charlie was still tense and wondered if he was okay. He wouldn't look me in the eye.

"Everything okay?"

"Hmm." He muttered, the rest of the sentence was too low for me to hear as we made our way behind the safety of the counter.

"Thanks for stepping in."

His eyes shot up to my face as if he was looking for a lie.

"Maverick doesn't know when to take no for an answer," I pressed, wanting Charlie to talk to me.

He offered a grunt but there was a smile playing on his lips, and I knew what he wanted to say. He wanted to tell me I was trouble. That I could get into all sorts of situations without even trying. That I'd be lost without him. He'd be right.

What he didn't say were the words that I wanted to hear. That he didn't want to pretend to be dating, that we should be planning dates for real. That we belonged with each other because no one else got him like I do. No one would ever know me like he does. That I own his heart as much as he owns mine.

I wanted him to tell me that he was ready for the next step. That the week of ignoring the elephant in the room was over with. Even if he couldn't say the words, some sort of sign would do.

Charlie slung an arm around my shoulders and in a move that he'd never done before, he pulled me in close and pressed a kiss to my temple before moving away and leaving me struck dumb.

Chapter Twenty

Charlie

I didn't mean to kiss him and it wasn't the kiss that I wanted to give him. I wanted to pull him into me and claim his mouth so he wouldn't even think of another guy. That casual sign of affection was something a boyfriend would do; what I would do if I was more to him than his best friend.

Was this our moment? The time that I'd been waiting for to move things forward with Max? I'd asked for him to let things happen naturally, and this felt as natural as breathing.

Watching Max sit with that smarmy guy and have coffee was torture. He'd been sitting close enough that I could hear almost all of what was said, and Maverick... who calls their kid Maverick? The name was ridiculous. The guy was oily and intense. He kept looking at Max like he wanted to eat him right then and there and it turned my stomach.

I had wanted nothing more than to go over and stake my claim. Except I had no right to do that without talking with Max first. My mind had been spinning. Random thoughts, like maybe he'd changed his mind, went through my head.

I was spiraling a little and making more of what had probably been an innocent supplier meeting and not a coffee date. So I'd taken some deep breaths and kept an eye on them while Finn and I worked through the line that had formed in my distraction.

When I'd heard Maverick ask Max out to dinner, I nearly jumped over the counter in my haste to stop it happening, but Max had looked over to me, and he'd seemed so worried that I knew that he hadn't wanted the attention. He hadn't wanted to have to turn the guy down in case that set him off. With Max's track record, that was a possibility.

It surprised me how quickly I'd settled back into the role of protector. How easily the responsibility dropped onto me. The pride that filled me at doing something so familiar, so necessary.

That kiss, though? Not something I usually did. Sure, Max had been gifting me small kisses this past week, but everything was instigated by him.

Letting it happen naturally was dumb. It wouldn't happen at all if one of us didn't make some sort of move. One of us had to take that leap of faith that it wasn't going to go to shit and that we could recover our friendship if it all went down in flames.

What I knew for sure though, was that we couldn't keep treading so carefully around what we both felt.

I watched Max out of the corner of my eye as he recovered from the tiny kiss while I was left still filled with the need to pull him to me and kiss him properly.

Not that I was going to do that. Not here in front of his customers and staff.

We needed to have a date. I just needed to have the courage to ask him.

―――――――――――――――

For the rest of the afternoon, we worked alongside each other with our usual ease. I wondered if Max had just brushed the kiss off as playing the part, even if Maverick had already left. The idea that he might think that caused a physical pain in my chest.

I tossed that thought aside because that sort of negative mental talk led to bad places. It didn't matter because I was done waiting to see if Max would make a move and take the responsibility away from me. I was going to do it and hopefully put us both out of our misery.

Waiting until everyone else had gone and just the two of us were left locking up was excruciating. I tried several times to decide on the right words.

The minutes stretched out while I played out scenario after scenario in my head.

"You okay? You're more quiet than usual." Max put a hand on my shoulder and squeezed. The worry in his expression had me blurting out the words instead of carefully thinking of how to say them.

"I want us to date."

Max stilled as the words hung heavy between us.

"You want us to date?" He repeated.

"Yes." I didn't say anything more, wanting him to get used to the idea, except he didn't think.

He launched himself at me, wrapping me in a fierce hug. "I want that, too."

The relief was staggering and I had to lock my knees to stay on my feet when all I wanted to do was sink to the floor and thank whatever force was out there for giving me this man.

We stood just hugging for a little while, my chin resting on his head, the scent of his coconut shampoo tickling my nose.

"Tomorrow?" he asked hopefully.

"Brunch, tomorrow? Then I'll figure out a plan for us."

It was funny, I could almost feel him thinking over what he wanted to do.

"That sounds perfect. Nothing too stressful. Just us hanging out."

"But not as friends this time. Something more than that. I'm done waiting for it to happen," I stressed. I wanted it to be perfectly clear.

"Something more. Yes."

Max surprised me then. He pulled back a little before both hands came up to my face. He pulled me down and his lips met mine for the first time.

Maybe I was already biased to anything relating to Max, but the kiss rocked my world.

It was utterly perfect.

His lips were slightly damp and warm against mine. The pressure was firm but not hard. Like he wanted me to be sure that he wanted this, that this wasn't a mistake.

Before long the kiss became something more as need took over and his mouth opened to my tongue.

Time stretched on as we explored each other's mouths. Max's grip on my face moved to the back of my head, fingers running through the dark strands. My hands dropped to his waist and I pulled him firmly against me as my cock began to thicken at the feel of his compact body against mine.

After a few long moments, Max let out a sigh and began to withdraw, but not before I pulled him back to me and placed a firm but chaste kiss on his slightly swollen lips.

He took a step back and grinned at me and I couldn't help but grin back at him. There was a feeling of rightness in my chest that I couldn't explain.

"I didn't want to wait to do that," he said, his voice husky. "Better to find out before we date if we have any chemistry."

"Well, you answered that question," I said, adjusting my dick in my jeans, the thick material strangling it painfully.

Max laughed, a sound so full of joy that I couldn't help my smile widening.

"Let's get out of here. I don't think I'll be able to sleep tonight. This is just so unbelievable, y'know?"

I did know. Even though we'd sort of talked about it, there had always been room for doubt or Max changing his mind. The idea that we wouldn't be compatible as a couple had never occurred to me.

We finished locking up and I waited for Max as he made sure both the café and the bookstore entrances were secure and the alarm system was on before taking his hand and walking him to his car.

"You want a ride home?"

"Nah, it's still early. I'm going to head to the gym for a bit and then go home."

"Okay. Text me about tomorrow. Do you want to meet somewhere or d'you want me to pick you up?"

"I'll think of something when I'm getting some miles in at the gym and text you, okay?"

"Okay."

I couldn't help pulling him back in for another long hug and kiss before we parted ways.

Chapter Twenty One

Charlie

Before I realized it, I was standing in front of Farmer's Fitness. The blocks I'd walked to get here hadn't even registered, my thoughts still tied up in Max, our kisses, and the fact that in less than twenty-four hours we would be going on our first date.

When I had monumental news like this before I would turn to Max, but now I wasn't sure who I should talk to.

I paused outside and sent Will and Andy a text in the group that I'd set up the previous week. Sometimes I felt awkward talking to Andy without Will, so it was easier to have Will included so he could see there was nothing underhanded going on. I knew that he trusted Andy implicitly, but me, not so much. And that was okay. We were a work in progress and with every uncomfortable family dinner we endured, we got a little bit further down the road to making it work for real.

Alex was a different situation, but I'd work on that once everything just slowed down a bit. I didn't have the spoons for his drama.

Charlie: I have a date tomorrow! Freaking out
Andy: Max? Please say Max.
Will: Better be Max *angry emoji*

I let out a snort at their replies but realized with a start that they already knew about my feelings for Max.

Charlie: Yes Max. How?

Waiting for their replies, I paced outside for a minute and caught a glimpse of Henry watching me as I moved back and forth in front of the automatic door.

"Knock that shit off, Charlie!" he bellowed at me and several people inside were startled. One woman let out a yelp and then laughed at herself.

I stopped and gestured that I'd just be a minute as my phone vibrated in my hand. I'd taken to putting it on silent, or at least vibrate since Mom had kept blowing up my phone while I was working and hadn't changed it back.

Andy: About freaking time!
Will: You've been into him forever. He's just as bad.
Andy: He really is from what I've heard.

I laughed at our transparent behavior. I hadn't realized I'd been so obvious.

Charlie: Well I'm freaking out about it. What do I do? Where can I take him?

Another few minutes passed as the little dots showed that both my brother and Andy were typing and I smiled at the thought that they were probably sitting on their couch together, sniping at each other's suggestions and blurting out ideas.

Andy: Lunch, walk in the park or go to an art gallery or something Max is interested in. Movie. Early dinner.

I thought that through. The plan was decent. I could take Max to the Botanical Gardens and then maybe he could help me find something for Andy's birthday, which was soon.

Charlie: Sounds good. Low key. Thanks.

Stowing my phone in my pocket, I turned to head inside when it vibrated again. Opening the message from Will, I was met with a picture of Andy sitting on a blue couch with a glossy black cat in his arms. The cat was resting its head on Andy's shoulder and I could hear the contented purr through the image. Its eyes were closed in a blissful expression.

Will: Lucifer joined the family today.

I choked on air. Who the fuck called their cat Lucifer?

Charlie: Seriously????

Will: Unfortunate name but he's a great cat. He loves Andy and the feeling is mutual.

Looking at the photo again, I noted Andy's serene expression and decided that a name was irrelevant when the cat was capable of making Andy that happy.

Charlie: Yeah I see that. The cat is cute.

Pocketing my phone again despite the buzzing, I went inside to tell Henry my news and hopefully burn off some of this nervous energy.

An hour later, I'd gotten in five miles on the treadmill and was lifting some smaller weights as Henry hovered over me.

He'd been ecstatic over my date news and had hooted with laughter over the Lucifer pic that I'd gotten permission to show him. Our family chat was still going insane over Andy's present, with his twin, Abby, cooing over all the pictures Andy kept sending of the slightest thing that Lucifer did as he settled into his new home. The guy was gaga over his pet. Will had knocked that out of the park.

Will had messaged again to ask me to cat sit so he could take Andy out of town after Andy's birthday party so they could have a proper break. They weren't coming to family dinner this week so the cat could adjust to the apartment and Andy was even working part of his week at home so Lucifer wouldn't be alone.

The pride at being asked burned hot inside me since it showed so much trust in me that I wasn't sure that I'd earned. I'd said yes and made a mental note to discuss it with Evan at our next appointment.

"Charlie?" Henry asked, breaking into my thoughts. My eyes swung to his. "How did you know you were into guys?"

His question was so abrupt that my grip slipped on the weight and it thudded onto the mat-covered floor, thankfully missing my feet as I jumped out of the way.

Henry looked anxious and his personal question had thrown me for a loop. We got on great as roommates and as boss-employee, but we didn't do personal things like this. I'd hesitated to tell him my date news since I wasn't sure that we were the type of friends that discussed feelings like that.

"I, uh..." I rubbed the back of my neck nervously. There were too many things to explain to him if he was questioning. "You know it's a spectrum, right?"

"What d'you mean?"

"Well, take Will for example. He's pan. It's the person, not their parts, that he's into but sometimes he will be more into guys, other times women, y'know?"

Henry nodded, but didn't look completely certain.

"I've always been into men. I've never had a crush on a woman."

"Never?"

I shook my head. "Never. Max did, though. Only certain types of women and very rarely. He'd never do anything about it, I don't think. But it's okay to discover this about yourself. You're questioning stuff?"

Henry pondered this for a moment before flushing and nodding, "So it's normal to find a guy attractive after never being into guys before?"

Placing a hand on his shoulder, I tried to reassure him. "It might just be the person. It could be that type of guy. Could be all guys, and you've just become open to it. People change all the time. Can you honestly say you are the same person you were at twenty compared to now?"

Henry smiled. "Yeah, you're right. I'm not the same. Been through too much shit not to have changed."

"Exactly. So what does this mean? Are you going to try and date a guy? Go for a hook-up or something?"

"I dunno, I think I just need to sit with this a bit. I thought it was just one guy, but I've noticed others since then, so maybe he woke something up in me?"

"Possible. Just be careful okay, there are a lot of weirdos out there. I know you have a ton of gay friends but if you need someone to talk to...." I trailed off.

"Thanks, man. Means a lot."

After finishing up my workout, I headed home, texting with Max the whole way about our plans.

I didn't think that sleep would find me as I lay in bed that night, but exhaustion from the work day, all the emotions I'd gone through, and a heavy workout had me falling asleep in seconds with a smile on my face.

Chapter Twenty Two

Max

Charlie wanted us to date! Okay, so I knew it might happen soon after our discussion the week before but I'd figured it was this abstract thing that would never come into fruition. That we'd dance around the something that was building until it fizzled out between us.

That wasn't what happened though. That meeting with Maverick seemed to have unlocked something in Charlie.

I couldn't believe that he'd asked me on a date! And I'd kissed him.

He'd kissed me back! And enjoyed it. There was no hiding how much he'd enjoyed it.

Sleep was eluding me. I'd been in bed for at least an hour and couldn't slow my brain down enough to drift off.

When something this big happened, it was usually Charlie that I turned to and we'd talk, or I'd talk his ear off and he'd listen in his stoic way, but I couldn't talk to Charlie about himself.

I'd always dreamt that he'd feel for me even a fraction of what I felt for him, and over the last couple of weeks, it'd been hard to keep my feelings to myself.

Charlie had needed to adapt to his new life after rehab. Then there'd been him working for me and there just never seemed to be a right time to drop that bombshell on him.

The idea that Charlie would come to me and tell me that he wanted to date had never entered my mind. In all the scenarios I'd dreamt up, it'd been me that had taken all the risks. Countless daydreams that had had him rejecting me or laughing it off as a joke. The ones that ended well were always too easy and felt almost abstract. I couldn't hold onto the details after waking up, since they had no substance.

He had come to me, though. My heart had nearly stopped when he'd said those oh so special words, "I want us to date." No question. No room for doubt, even though I'd dumbly repeated what he'd said. He was firm, a hundred percent certain at what he wanted us to be, and the joy that had filled me nearly had me floating.

Our first kiss had been everything, so perfect for us and how I hoped we could be.

There was no way that I was sleeping if I didn't try and calm down. I was practically buzzing out of my skin and all we'd done was kiss.

Since it was Charlie, someone so very dear and precious to me, I was determined to take things slowly, so I was going to have to be content with my own hand for a bit longer.

I didn't want us to rush things and jump into bed. I wanted us to be long haul and not a fling, plus there was the added complication of Charlie's sexual history to consider.

Charlie would love to have everyone believe that he wasn't prone to getting blackout drunk on occasion, but that wasn't the case. He was also a bit of a whore when he was drunk, too.

Simply put, I couldn't trust that he'd been safe with the random guys that he'd picked up, I'd been bitten with an STD before and wasn't doing that again.

Somewhere over our next few dates, I'd have to break it to him that I wanted to be extra careful with using condoms even for blow jobs until he'd gotten to the six-month mark and been fully tested again.

Finding out I'd gotten chlamydia during college had left me with an icky feeling that I couldn't shake for a long time, much longer than the actual infection had lasted. It had been easily treated with a round of antibiotics, but the memory of the shame had lasted for a long time. In fact, it had taken nearly a year before I'd been willing to be with anyone.

Since then, I'd been religious about testing and condoms to the point it had affected a couple of relationships. Not that I'd had many. I was too busy to deal with a boyfriend and Charlie always came first.

My heart stuttered at the thought of calling Charlie my boyfriend, bringing my thoughts back to how it had felt to hold him and kiss that perfect mouth. Electricity had sparked between us at the first brush of our lips and I still felt the ghost of the touch. The memory of his hands holding me close had me reaching into my boxer briefs and tugging on my hardening cock.

Reaching over to the nightstand, I grabbed the lube there, some tissues for after, and slicked myself up. Stroking fast, I worked myself over quickly, unwilling to draw this out. I needed to get off and get some rest for my date with Charlie.

Replaying the kiss again, the feel of his firm muscles under my hands, his dick pressed into my stomach had me reaching my climax quickly. I shot over my stomach with a loud groan, thankful once again my roommate was out.

After a cursory wipe down, I slipped into sleep with a smile on my face.

Despite the orgasm, I slept like shit, waking an hour before my alarm went off with a mild headache.

After taking some aspirin with a coffee and eating some gluten-free toast, I headed into the shower. I'd take the time to primp and preen since I had nothing else to do. The apartment was sparkling and I wouldn't want to get all sweaty with cleaning before my date.

My phone buzzed as I got out of the shower.

Charlie: Can't wait for our date. Can I pick you up in an hour? Don't think I can wait much longer.

I gave out a little squeal, thankful I was alone when I followed it with a happy dance. My towel loosened and I grabbed at it, perching on my bed, so I could reply.

Max: Sounds good. Can't wait either!

A single heart emoji was the reply. My stomach swooped with nerves and excitement. Actually going on a date with Charlie was like all my Christmases and birthdays coming at once.

Charlie had said we might be walking a bit so I wanted to wear something that wasn't too tight. I had a black pair of cargos that managed to look smart, ideal for eating out, but were stretchy for all-day wear.

I'd set out what I wanted to wear after considering my options. I liked to be prepared and the late April weather was unpredictable, so I'd settled on a dark blue button-down over a lighter blue tee. Charlie had once said that darker blues made my eyes pop, so it was perfect for our date.

My hair was a nightmare. I'd been distracted with Charlie so it needed cutting. Covering the top of my ears with small waves, it wouldn't sit right, so I worked a little product into it to tease it into curls. It gave me a messy bedhead look that wasn't too much with the smart casual clothing I'd picked.

Alice had bought me a really nice cologne that I spritzed on sparingly since it had clearly been expensive. It had a lovely honey and citrus scent that made me think of summer at the beach house with Charlie and the first time he took me there. Our first summer as friends, he'd taken me to their beach house for a week. I'd never seen the ocean before, and that week I practically lived on the sand. It was a piece of heaven that he never shared with anyone else. Just me.

The bell rang five minutes before Charlie was due to arrive and I smiled at the idea that he was as eager for this as I was.

When I opened the door, Charlie held out a bunch of tulips to me. They'd been my favorite flower since he'd taken me to Amsterdam on our post-graduation trip across Europe. The small bouquet was filled with reds, pinks, and purples and I felt tears welling at the thoughtfulness of the gesture. Not only was he the first person to ever buy me flowers, but he'd remembered such an obscure fact as my favorite type.

"Oh! They're lovely! Thank you." I reached up to kiss his cheek. "I'll just put these in water and then we can go."

Charlie followed me into the kitchen. His nerves were apparently stealing his words. I found a pitcher that would work since I didn't have a vase and let him work through whatever he needed to.

Finally losing patience I broke the silence. "Charlie, it's just you and me. There's no need to make this a huge thing." I was a total hypocrite but one of us needed to take charge or we were getting nowhere. "The only thing that has changed is instead of calling me your best friend, you'll say boyfriend instead."

"Boyfriend, huh?" He smirked and I smiled at him.

"Yes, boyfriend. I know we're supposed to be taking it slow, but if we're doing this, we are doing it properly. So where's my boyfriend taking me on our first date?" I moved over to him and put my arms around his neck. He looked down at me with a private smile. It suggested feelings and intimacy, and I wanted to pinch myself that it was leveled at me.

He leaned down, pressing a kiss on my lips. "I would like to take my boyfriend to the botanical gardens, then to lunch. I thought we could shop for a gift for Andy's birthday then."

"Abby's too," I cut in.

"Shit, yeah. Abby, too. Then we'd maybe see a movie and go out for dinner?"

"Oh, so you want my whole day?"

"I want it all day every day. I can't see me getting sick of you."

I flushed with pleasure at his words and pulled him into a kiss.

"Sweet talker."

"Probably not very romantic, getting the bus on a date," Charlie muttered.

"Not having to drive and worry about parking is great. Traffic is crazy, so a bus is smart."

Charlie squeezed my hand. I still couldn't get over how easy it was to be openly affectionate with him. He'd held my hand on our walk to the bus stop and all the way around the botanical gardens.

As first dates went, it was amazing so far. He'd been so patient with me as I'd studied all the plants and flowers, reading over descriptions and asking questions of the workers. We'd wandered the grounds for a couple of hours until my stomach was trying to claw its way out of me and we'd decided to go and get some food.

Lunch was equally as good and easy. We talked in between bites of tasty food. Charlie seemed to have knowledge of all the best places that were safe for me to eat at. If I didn't already think I loved him, it would have helped me fall in love with him for sure.

I leaned into Charlie, basking in his solid presence and easy affection as we waited for the bus to travel the busy streets to the mall we'd chosen to look for gifts at.

"Do you have any gift ideas?" I asked him.

"Not really. I thought we could look around a bit and see if anything catches our attention."

Shrugging, I said, "sounds like a plan."

We wandered the mall, stopping for a snack but not seeing anything until we left the mall and roamed the streets a little. It was then I spotted a craft store with a bright display with various knick-knacks.

"Let's go in here," I said, pulling Charlie behind me.

He turned up his nose. "I'm not sure it'll have something for either of them here."

The store was small but well-appointed, the shelves artfully crammed with trinkets for sale. What caught my attention were the photographs that were mounted tastefully and available to buy.

I nudged Charlie. "Yours are better," I whispered.

He blushed. "You're biased. Mine aren't nearly as good as these."

"You're being too modest. You have a book coming out of your photos, Charlie!"

The woman behind the counter must have heard at least part of our conversation because she asked, "You're a photographer?" to Charlie.

"Um, kinda. I have a book coming out that's a series of photos surrounding rehab. It shows the journey that each person goes on. The difficulties that they face and the celebrations of their successes." He started quietly, quickly becoming earnest in his wish for her to understand his reasoning behind the book.

What I'd seen of it had been beautiful in its honesty. I was so proud of him for taking the chance to finally use his talent.

"Do you have any samples of your work on you?" she asked. "We are always looking for new photographers. Art like that always sells well."

Charlie drew his phone out of his pocket. "You won't be able to see it that well on this screen, but I've emailed some of my stuff to people so I should be able to show you something."

He fiddled with the device for a bit before pulling up several images. Including one of me in our university days. I was lying in a pile of fall leaves, my breath fogging the air and the fading light turning everything to gold and silver.

"This is one of my favorites."

"Oh!" She let out a tiny gasp as she examined the image, comparing it to me as I flushed bright red and tried not to squirm. "Wow! That's just beautiful. Do you just do portraits? Because there isn't demand here for that, but if you had your own studio you'd be in high demand, I'm sure."

"Do you think so?"

"I do!" She said honestly. "I mean, your model is very pretty," she said as she cast a glance at me, giving me a smile. "But you've turned him into something else. I just don't have the words."

"Ethereal," Charlie said simply, looking me in the eyes. My breath was knocked from my body with what I saw there. It wasn't just affection, it was more than that. I wanted to label it as love, but it was far too soon for that.

"Yes! That's the word," the woman said, grabbing our attention again.

I had to move, so I left them to chat about Charlie's work while I looked at the other merchandise that was sold. It took me a few minutes to get myself together again. I'd always thought that my feelings for Charlie were entirely one-sided, which was stupid considering we were on a date, but then I hadn't had much time to get used to the idea of dating him. The idea that he saw beauty in me just didn't compute.

Charlie gave me the time to collect myself before returning to my side. I picked up a frame. "This would be a good gift for Andy. You took pictures of him with Will, didn't you?"

"I did. Actually, I think I have the perfect one for them. I'd just have to get it printed." He thought for a second. "Monica," he indicated the woman who was now behind the counter, "said that if I wanted to supply them, she'd sell some of my photos. For a commission, of course."

"How would you print them?"

"There's a printer that I'd looked at getting. Cheaper long-term to print my own images. I could get it and do Andy's gift. Maybe print off some for Mom, from Christmas."

"I think that's a great idea. Do you have to pick it up somewhere?"

"Nah, I'll get it delivered." He clicked on a few things on his phone. "It'll be a couple of days. If it gets tight, there are always those photo booths to print the gift."

"Just Abby to go then?"

"I have an idea for that."

Chapter Twenty Three

Charlie

By the end of our date, we were both exhausted, but it'd given me a real insight into what a relationship with Max would be like. In all honesty, it wasn't that different. It was just now I could hold him close, walk holding hands, and stop to kiss him whenever the mood struck, as it did often throughout the day.

I was already addicted to the way that his mouth felt against mine and his soft sighs as our lips reconnected. It was difficult to keep things PG in public when he felt so good with his tongue in my mouth. My body reacted to him like he controlled it now, and I had no problem with that at all.

"Do you want to come back to my place for a bit?" I asked when we left the restaurant after dinner. We'd spent so much time shopping that there hadn't been time for a movie and we had both been starving again. "We could watch something."

Max looked a little reluctant and it had me tensing. He felt my reaction since he had a firm grip on my hand, our fingers laced together. "Sure, it's just...I want to take things slowly."

"Oh!"

He began to pull away.

"No, that's fine. I thought...well, I don't actually know what I thought, but taking it slowly is fine with me. I'm happy to go at whatever pace. Anything you need Max, okay?"

"Really?"

"Yeah. So we'll watch a movie, maybe make out a little. You set the pace."

Max had relaxed some by the time we got back to my apartment. Henry was out with my brother and his other friends since it was their usual Friday night routine. Having the place to ourselves seemed to make Max tense up a little again, so I tried to reassure him. "Max, nothing but kissing unless you initiate more, okay?" He nodded his agreement and settled onto the sectional.

I pulled a couple of bottles of water from the fridge, handing one to him as I sat down beside him.

He held the remote and was flicking through the options on the screen. "Any preference?"

"Nah, just nothing heavy. Maybe a comedy?"

Max eventually settled on a movie, checking for my approval before switching it on.

It took a while for the tension to bleed out of him, for Max to settle back and rest his head on my shoulder. I wrapped an arm around him, pulling away a fraction when he stiffened.

I didn't watch the film on screen, I watched Max gradually lower the walls he'd put up for whatever reason. Not because I wanted to push things further; I'd meant what I'd said. More because I wanted him to relax and trust me.

There was a point that I thought he'd fallen asleep, so I kissed the top of his head and started to pull away. As I shifted away, he put a hand on my thigh to stop me.

"Where are you going?"

I turned so I could face him properly. "I thought you were asleep, I was going to get you a blanket."

He paused the screen. "Are you not watching the movie?"

"Nah, I just wanted to spend time with you."

He blushed, "That's going to take a bit of getting used to, you saying stuff like that."

I lifted a hand to his cheek, he had such sharp features he looked elf-like in the right light. I rubbed a finger over his cheekbone, down along his jaw to his slightly pointed chin. Grasping it lightly, I pulled his face to mine, stopping just shy of our lips meeting. "This okay?"

He didn't answer with words, just closed this distance and brushed soft lips over mine.

Our kiss started out teasing. Just light brushes until need built between us and I used my hold on his chin to open his mouth to my tongue.

He slipped his hands around the back of my neck, holding my head in place, controlling the angle.

I was happy to just explore his mouth with my tongue but before long, the heat had risen between us, and it wasn't enough. He needed to be closer. I ran my hands down to his waist before moving back up into his silky hair. I couldn't get enough of being able to touch him. To taste him on my tongue. Hearing his little gasps and sighs as he reacted to me so beautifully.

Max climbed onto my lap, his knees bracketing my thighs. His tongue battled mine and he bit at my bottom lip as he braced himself with hands on my chest.

I ran my hands down his back, taking a firm grip of his ass and pulling him into me. I loved the weight of him on me. The feel of his firm body against mine. Just knowing that this was Max and he was kissing me back, blew my mind.

In this new position, his ass was on my thighs and he could rock his pelvis to meet mine. We moaned in unison as our hard cocks brushed.

Max undulated in my lap as I kissed along his jaw and down his neck before attacking his mouth again. I couldn't get enough of kissing him.

He grunted as I pulled him tightly against me and bit down on his neck, laving the mark I'd left.

My dick hurt, it was so hard. I mentally cursed my jeans and their stranglehold and wriggled in place making Max moan. Slipping a hand in between us to open them and unzip my fly, I didn't pause kissing Max. I needed him more than air.

He groaned as he felt my movement, my hand brushing his hardness. His movements stuttered, there was a small pause before he came to a decision and swatted my hand away. He pulled my cock free, the tip purple-red and swollen. Running a hand over the hard shaft, he breathed a sigh against my lips.

Using the precum at the tip, he ran his hand up and down my length, giving a twist as he reached the crown.

"Max, so good," I panted against his mouth.

Resting my forehead against his, I watched him work me over until my hands itched to be touching him, too.

I maneuvered my hand into his pants, drew him out, and fused my lips to his as I gripped him firmly. I loved the feel of him in my hand and was desperate to taste him, but didn't want to push it. I settled with getting him off, hopefully erasing the strange tension that I could feel in the way he set his shoulders, the slight frown at the edge of his mouth.

He worked my cock quickly, moaning into my neck when I rubbed my thumb over his crown and pressed slightly into his slit. We both quickly rushed towards our mutual release. The heat between us was undeniable and I felt half outside my body watching as Max took control of our pleasure. He was so sexy that I almost couldn't stand to watch. I wanted to make him feel as good as he was making me feel, every stroke sending me spiraling higher.

I came first, sharp and suddenly, spilling over his hand and crying out his name. I tightened my grip on him and bit down on his shoulder and he followed me. His cum was hot against my fingers, and my name was a moan on his lips.

Instead of basking in the afterglow, Max pulled away and looked around almost frantically, like he was squashing down his reaction. "Tissues?" He kept his face away from me. I narrowed my eyes as I tried to assess the situation

"Charlie?"

I looked at him, confused at the way he was behaving.

"Nevermind," he moved to the hall and entered the bathroom. I heard water and Max returned a minute later, all traces of what we'd done gone.

His hair was back to being artfully tousled, his clothing straight and his eyes shuttered.

"Do you need a cloth?" He asked.

"I'll...uh." Words failed me. "I'll go clean up."

I entered the bathroom, washed up, and tucked my spent dick away. My t-shirt went into the hamper and I contemplated grabbing another before I returned to Max.

Glancing down the hall, I saw him perched on the edge of the sectional worrying his lip and clasping his hands together.

I skipped getting another t-shirt, wanting to check in with him.

"Everything okay?" I asked as I sat down next to him.

"Everything's fine," he lied. I could hear it in his voice.

"I'm sorry if I pushed you." I moved to touch his hand.

He flinched before restraining his reaction.

"You didn't, I did. I got caught up in the moment."

He laughed but there was a hysterical tinge to it. "Should we finish the movie?"

"Sure."

We sat back comfortably on the sofa, though there was a gap between us that hadn't been there before. The tension in the room was suffocating, but I didn't want to say anything and make things worse.

Max turned the movie back on and pretended to watch it for a while. His eyes were glazed like he was lost in thought somewhere I couldn't reach him.

I let him stay lost in his head, hoping he'd come back to me soon while I thought over what we'd done. What I'd done to make him react like that.

After a while, the movie caught my attention and I began to watch it, absorbed in it to the point that I started when Max spoke.

"It's late. I should go."

"Okay, if you're sure."

I wasn't getting answers soon, so I let him go with a promise of dinner the next night. Another date had to be a good thing, right? I couldn't have messed things up that badly if Max would still kiss me goodbye and make another date.

As I lay in bed that night, the worries kept me from sleeping. I turned over the whole day, looking for clues and finding nothing.

Chapter Twenty Four

Charlie

It was late morning by the time I got up from a night of broken sleep. I'd tossed and turned all night as I tried to figure out what had happened with Max.

On the surface, there wasn't anything for me to worry about. Someone who knew Max less well would have thought our date was a resounding success, that maybe he'd just been awkward after his orgasm. I knew differently.

The way that Max had escaped from here last night told a very different tale of our first date. I just wasn't sure what the problem was.

Maybe it was just as simple as he hadn't wanted to go as far as we had, but he'd been the one to initiate things. I'd just been opening my pants before the denim had strangled my dick. There hadn't been any expectations there.

It hit me then, that maybe he didn't know that and he'd felt pressured to take things further than he'd wanted to.

Feeling like scum, I left my bed and hit the shower, wanting to wash away the icky feeling. The water beating down on me eased my tense muscles but did nothing for my conscience.

In between washing and shaving, I thought about how I'd make it up to Max when I saw him later. Henry's kitchen was larger and better equipped than Max's, so he said he would come here for our second date. I'd make dinner and apologize. Making a big deal over it was a bad idea. I didn't want to put Max under any more pressure to behave a certain way. If he wanted to put the brakes on our physical relationship until he was ready, then that was fine with me.

We probably needed to have a proper conversation about what we were to each other, and what we wanted out of a relationship. I had a rough idea from watching Max when he'd dated other guys, but we were older and hopefully wiser. I knew that I wanted something deeper, permanent. So I had to be sure that Max was on the same page.

When I entered the kitchen, Henry was seated at the breakfast bar shoveling granola into his mouth, looking too fresh and alert for a guy that had been out until the early hours. I'd been awake enough to hear him return, though he'd been pretty quiet.

"Morning."

He gave a head nod and continued chewing while I set about making my breakfast of eggs and toast.

Henry was pretty much the ideal roommate. Clean and tidy. Didn't party till late all the time. In deference to my alcohol issues, there was nothing alcoholic in the apartment. He'd shrugged it off casually, saying he wasn't a big drinker anyway. But it'd meant a lot to me that he'd done it so easily. We got along great and I was slowly learning not to trigger his PTSD.

I'd been coached by his sister, Holly, never to approach him from behind and touch him, and to always announce my presence first and come at him from where he could see me. He didn't have massive problems with PTSD but would react badly if caught by surprise.

I opened the butter and realized I didn't have enough for my toast. In fact, I was low on a lot of things, so I'd have to go to the market before I started dinner for Max.

Going along the side of the breakfast bar, I caught Henry's attention. "Can I use your not butter, butter stuff?

I'm out."

"Sure, you don't need to ask. Just replace anything you finish." His voice was always a pleasant rumble.

"Thanks, man. I'll pick up some more of your dairy-free stuff when I go to the store. Is there any particular brand or anything?"

"Oh, um, you don't have to do that." I started to interrupt and he glared at me. "I'll write you a list," he conceded.

We may have only lived together for a week, but Henry had learned early on that some things weren't worth arguing with me over. He vastly undercharged me for my room and utilities, so I made up for it by getting groceries. The first time I'd gotten things that he couldn't eat without realizing it, I'd accidentally made him sick by using dairy in a recipe when I'd cooked for us. I still felt shit about that days later.

"Oh, Max is coming over for dinner. I hope you don't mind."

"Max is welcome here any time. No issues here. I'm glad that you two are taking a shot at things."

"Yeah, it's tricky though. I think I messed up already."

"What d'you mean?"

I explained the situation and Henry frowned in the direction of the couch, making me laugh.

"Don't worry, it's clean and we won't do that again. Anything sexual stays in the bedroom."

"This is your home too, so whatever." He shrugged. "Just don't leave anything that you wouldn't want your mama to see."

There was silence for a moment. "Just talk things through with Max, maybe it isn't as bad as you think. Slowing it down isn't a bad idea, though. I'll be out of your hair since I'm closing at the gym tonight."

"Won't be a late one since Max is opening Books & Biscuits tomorrow, and I don't think he's ready to sleep here."

"Well, I have no issue if he does stay here." I glanced at him and he shrugged. "Pete had a boyfriend stay with him for a couple of weeks and it was no issue."

"Yeah?"

"Yeah, it was fine. They kept to themselves most of the time. The guy didn't like me though, so it didn't last." Another shrug. "I like Max from what little I've seen of him."

"Max is cool, low drama. Always has been." I said loyally.

"You have to say that." Henry smiled. "I've gotta go get showered and ready for work. See you later maybe."

Passing the rest of the morning grocery shopping and cleaning up the apartment, I started to get worried about my date with Max. We'd texted on and off throughout the day, and in the messages, everything had seemed fine. Tone was so hard to get from a text though, and I wished that I had someone else to talk to about this. Max was too important to me to fuck everything up as soon as we started.

I took another shower to wash away all the anxiety sweat after attempting some meditation the rehab center had recommended. I'd have liked to say it had helped, except I knew nothing but seeing Max was going to help me.

He called to say they'd been late getting out of work, so he would be a little late. His calm voice settled me a fraction.

When he finally arrived, I buzzed him up and waited with the door ajar.

"Hey you," he called as he exited the elevator and came into view. He pushed up onto his tiptoes and kissed me quickly, squeezing my arm. "Oh my god, it smells amazing in here!" Max moved towards the kitchen. "What are you making? Is it Indian food?"

I smiled, so far so normal. "It's a vegan curry. There're poppadoms that are gluten-free and I managed to find gluten-free naan bread."

"Seriously? I haven't had curry since we were in the UK!" Max wrapped his arms around me in a tight hug. "You're the best."

I had fond memories of our brief Europe trip just after college, and one was of a little Indian restaurant that we'd happened upon in London.

"I dunno how this recipe will stand up against that place, but it smells great. I promised to leave some for Henry."

Max took a seat at the breakfast bar and chatted about his day while I finished up with the food. Setting out the plates and dishes in front of him, I took a seat. "Help yourself," I told him.

I let him eat for a little while first. He was clearly ravenous as he dug into a little bit of everything, spooning ample amounts onto his plate. His noises as he ate were adorable and I couldn't help but smile at him, pausing in my eating to watch him enjoy what I'd made for him.

As he started to slow I asked. "Are we okay after yesterday? Things were a bit weird when you left."

He picked up a napkin and wiped at his mouth before replying. "Honestly, I think I got in my head about how quickly we jumped into the physical side of stuff. We haven't talked about preferences or anything."

"So you didn't feel pushed into it?"

"What? No! Why'd you say that?"

"I just wondered. I honestly was just opening my pants, it wasn't a hint."

Max held his face in his hands and his shoulders shook with laughter. "I knew that Charlie, honest."

I let out a little chuckle, relieved that things seemed to be on an even keel again. "So should we talk about those preferences?"

He started to say something, reconsidering before shaking his head. "Maybe later, okay? Let's just finish up dinner first."

I was just placing the last dish into the dishwasher when Max came up behind me and encircled me with his arms. He pressed his cheek to my shoulder blade and sighed.

"I can't get used to this. Being able to touch you like this." Max ran his hands over my chest. "Fuck, Charlie," his hand roamed over my abs, "you were always hot to me, but this is just..."

He held me a little tighter as his hands continued to wander. I loved the feel of him plastered against me.

Just under the curve of my ass, I could feel Max's reaction to his exploration, as his cock thickened in his jeans. Unable to stand it, needing to touch him, I turned around, pulling him close to me so I could brush my lips against his.

What was going to be a tender touch sparked to a flame between us. Our movements quickly became frantic. Max pushed me against the counter as his tongue plundered my mouth, his hands moving to the hem of my shirt and pulling it up.

He flung my shirt away and kissed down my throat, along my collarbone, and down to a nipple. He laved at it as his slim fingers tweaked at the other.

I groaned at the sensation and yanked at his shirt, removing it to get at his creamy skin. My hands explored as he kissed and sucked along my chest. I just needed to be touching him.

It became too much and I needed his mouth like I needed air. Grasping at his hips, I pulled him close and took his mouth in a hard kiss.

The angle wasn't right so I turned our positions and lifted him to perch on the counter.

He used his feet to pull me into the gap between his legs.

This was perfect, we fit together better this way and I groaned at the feeling of our bare chests touching.

I lost all sense of time as we made out in the dimly-lit kitchen. All I could feel was Max. The citrus smell of his skin, his hair like silk under my fingers. Pants and moans filled the space. The sense that all was right with the world as our lips continued to press together, his tongue delving into my mouth to meet mine. He groaned as I nipped his bottom lip and I swallowed the sound.

Awareness of how my dick ached had me pulling away a little. We needed to slow this down. I wasn't going to ask Max for more.

Max made a noise of protest as I put some distance between us, his legs around my waist flexing as he tried to pull me back to him. He reached for the button of my jeans, quickly opening them and delving a hand in.

"Max," I choked out his name in a gasp as he took a firm hold of my cock.

Desperate to taste him this time, I unhooked his legs from around me, pulled him from the counter, and went to my knees.

I was just about to take his cock out when he cried out. "No!"

Immediately I shuffled back, thumping against a cabinet in confusion.

Max looked around the room frantically and moved to pick up his shirt.

"I'm sorry, I need to go," he said, his voice wobbling with pent-up tears.

It took a couple of seconds for blood to return to my upper brain as I watched him re-dress from my place on the floor.

"Max? What's going on?"

He gathered up his keys and phone.

"I need to go. I'll explain, but not now. I have to go." A tear escaped and I watched it trail down his cheek, gutting me as it reached his jaw.

Max approached tentatively. Stroked a hand along my jaw, before leaning down and pressing a kiss to my lips.

Then he turned and left.

Chapter Twenty Five

Charlie

I don't know how long I spent sitting on the cold tile of the kitchen floor. Time was pretty meaningless when it felt like the bottom had fallen out of my world.

That had been a pretty hard-core rejection. So where did it leave me and Max? Were we over before we'd started? What the fuck was going on?

Eventually, I got up and dusted myself off, deciding to finish cleaning up the kitchen and switching my brain off with activity. I'd have to wait for him to get in touch.

A drink sounded pretty good, but I wouldn't undo months of progress. I was so close to six months sober.

A text ding sounded and I searched for my phone for a few minutes before giving up and using the function on my watch to find it.

"I'm here," came the robotic-sounding voice as my phone screen lit up between the cushions of the couch.

I picked it up and opened my notifications, my heart leaping at the text from Max.

Max: I'll explain everything tomorrow. Come over around four? We are okay, I promise. I just freaked out. *heart emoji*

It took me a minute to process. He said we were okay, but I still had this prickling feeling, like my skin was too small for my body and every movement I made would have me bursting out all over the place.

I rubbed at my chest absentmindedly, before texting back, looking for reassurance.

Charlie: Are you sure I didn't do something wrong?

He replied immediately.

Max: I'm sure. You're perfect. See you tomorrow? I'll make us dinner after we talk.

Charlie: *thumbs up emoji* See you tomorrow *heart emoji*

Dinner after a talk meant that he wasn't breaking up with me, didn't it?

I sat and stewed in the silence of the apartment until a key in the lock drew my attention.

"Charlie? You okay?"

Relief filled me at seeing Henry's worried face. He came around the sectional to sit next to me. I leaned into him and he slung an arm around my shoulders pulling me close.

The contact was all I needed before the events of the night came spilling out. Although it helped to talk it through, Henry had no advice for me.

"Sounds like there's something going on with Max. Not you though," he consoled me.

"Yeah, I mean I tried to slow it down."

"You did." Henry shuffled back and let out a groan.

"You okay?"

"Yeah, I took a knock to my leg." He indicated his prosthetic. "I just need to take it off. Maybe ice my knee."

Henry reached down to remove the prosthetic, unclipping the suspension that wrapped just above his knee. He slipped the stump of his leg from the socket, the liner flexing with the movement.

I bent to take a hold of the prosthesis and gently laid it on the couch next to him, while he slipped off the sock he wore under the artificial limb to protect his skin. There was a noticeable darkening of the skin around his knee and I knelt to examine it, running a finger around it, careful of the scar tissue.

I glanced up at Henry. "Sorry, I should have asked. Is this okay? Does it hurt?"

"You don't mind touching it?" He asked, his voice coming out gruff.

"Not if it doesn't hurt you."

"It aches a little where I knocked it." He let out a defeated sigh. "I think I'll have to go on crutches for a couple of days."

I backed up and went to the kitchen. "We'll ice it and see what happens. Elevate it."

"Yes sir," he chuckled.

It helped my frame of mind to shove my problems out of the way and care for my friend. I got him the ice pack and then heated up some of the curry for him.

"Here," I said, placing the ice pack on the bruising that was quickly developing. I pushed the coffee table against the sofa and piled it with pillows before indicating Henry should rest his legs on them.

He smiled at my poor nursing skills, shuffling over to elevate his abused limb. Then moaned around his first mouthful of food.

"Goddamn, that's good."

It was my turn to laugh at the sounds Henry made while he devoured the food. I settled next to him and he patted my leg.

"It'll be fine. With Max. You'll see."

"Yeah?"

"Absolutely. You guys are meant to be."

I let out a wistful sigh. "I hope so."

"Bet you fifty dollars I'll be there at your wedding one day."

Laughter bubbled up again. Henry didn't know my thoughts on marriage. "If we aren't married in five years, you owe me fifty."

"Deal."

Chapter Twenty Six

Max

'm not going to self-sabotage this. I'm not giving him up. He'll get it.

Although I repeated this mantra over and over, there were still lingering doubts in my mind. If Charlie didn't accept this part of me, if he couldn't help me get over the feelings that I was often left with after sex, then we were doomed to go the way that all my other relationships went.

Down the toilet.

Taking a fresh cloth, I worked the astringent cleanser over the surfaces of the already gleaming kitchen. The bathroom that I shared with my roommate was sparkling after getting the same treatment earlier.

It soothed me to go about performing these tasks even though they really didn't need to be done. The actions of the routine settled my mind and the knowledge that everything was clean as a whistle squashed some of the panic.

Charlie was due any second and we would have to talk about what happened after our last date. I owed him an explanation at the very least. If he didn't want to date me after I'd laid it all out for him, then hopefully we could salvage our friendship.

A knock came from the door and I went to let him in. It took a second, his hesitation making him question if he should, but he leaned down to hug me and planted a kiss on my lips.

So far so good if he was still affectionate after last night's abrupt ending.

I trailed him to the sofa and sat at an angle to him so I could watch his expressions.

"You had something you wanted to discuss?" he asked nervously.

"Relax, I'm not breaking up with you." I attempted to joke with him but it didn't quite land properly and he flinched before slumping back.

"Thank fuck for that. Jesus, Max! After last night, I was sure I'd done something."

It was then that I noticed the dark shadows under his eyes, his generally rumpled appearance, and realized that he'd probably slept as little as I had. Work had been a great distraction but I'd slept terribly.

"You look about as good as I feel," I said, rubbing his leg. I needed to touch him to reassure myself that he was here and willing to listen. "I, uh, have a few issues."

He shot me a look, a soft one that said, "duh," and I couldn't help my smile.

"I know that you know about the cleaning." He looked around the small apartment and frowned. "I freaked out a little after last night. I guess....I guess I'm worried that you wouldn't accept all of me."

"Max..."

"Just listen a minute, okay? I need to get this out," I cut in. If I didn't do this now, it would fester between us.

"The reason I haven't had a boyfriend in so long is that they don't want to stay after they pick up on how weird I am."

"You're not weird!" Charlie interrupted, looking upset on my behalf and I couldn't help but lean in and kiss him briefly.

"I am, but that's okay. You can decide how weird after I tell you what I need to tell you." Charlie settled back on the sofa and looked at me to continue. "I struggle with sex because I don't like how...messy it gets. Hookups are easy because I can get a guy to wear a condom for blow jobs but a boyfriend doesn't want to do that for long." I assess his response and pause to let him speak.

"So you might never be comfortable with it when it comes to us?"

"I'm not sure." I paused to think for a second. "Look, how do I put this without offending you?" The moment stretched between us. "Um...when you were drinking...we have no idea how safe you were." He looked ready to interject, so I continued "and I know you were tested, but it hasn't been six months yet."

Charlie dropped back again. "Fair point, so would it be until after the six months and re-testing? Or would you want to see how you felt after?"

My mouth dropped open. "That doesn't bother you?"

He considered for a second and then shrugged, "It's reasonable. Safe. Why would that be an issue? It's not like you're asking me to scrub down with bleach or anything before we touch." Another shrug. "Honestly, you have a point." There was a pause. "Not that it doesn't sting, the idea that I might have been reckless and picked something up."

Charlie's face blanched then. "Shit! Sorry, Max. I didn't mean anything by it." He reached out to me and I let him take my hand, knowing that he hadn't meant anything by that throwaway remark.

"I know. That's why, though. After I caught chlamydia from Jared the whole thing stuck with me. I just can't feel clean at times. I know it's irrational because I was treated and I'm fine but..."

"That was college, though. You were young, and well, dumb. We all were. I'm just lucky I didn't pick up anything either."

"It wasn't just that though. It happened just before my birthday, remember?" Charlie nodded. "Well, I tried to get in contact with my mom." His eyes widened. "I didn't tell you, but she had moved. Left no forwarding address. Her number was disconnected."

"Fuck!"

I couldn't contain my bitter laugh. "Yeah. So being rejected and catching an STD after my boyfriend cheated and turning twenty-one with no family was great."

"I'm sorry, Max."

"At least I had you."

"You'll always have me." He sounded so certain. No room for doubt but that didn't mean that I was sure of my place in his life. Especially if this all went wrong. Still, I reached for reassurance. "Really?" I could hear the fear and longing in my voice.

"I'm not going anywhere."

"That's not all though, Charlie." I pushed down my worry to get it all out. "No one has accepted me so I've never really had things the way I want them."

"I want us to be different. To keep talking when we need to say things. I want you to be comfortable enough to ask for what you need."

"It's not that simple. I..."

"Tell me," he pleads.

"I...I can't." I buried my face in my hands.

"Then," Charlie moved closer, running his hand up my thigh, "How about you show me how you need it to be?"

I lift my head to stare at him. "Really? Just like that?" I couldn't seem to process what he wanted, my brain on the fritz from the sensation of Charlie's wandering hand.

"Absolutely." His hand paused and he squeezed lightly, "Look, we need to do what works for us. Communication is great, but sometimes just showing me what you need for you to be happy is what will work better. D'you know what I mean?"

I nodded since his words made sense. Being open with Charlie was easy because we had a solid foundation to work from. The only reason that we hadn't talked about sex before was that I hadn't wanted to listen to him talk about fucking other guys while I'd been in love with him and wishing it were me instead.

Standing, I took his hand and pulled him towards my room, sensing that we were on the cusp of something but unwilling to slow it down. I needed this as much as I needed air. We needed to reconnect physically. True, it was quick to be jumping into bed but also felt completely natural to put my trust in Charlie, in what we were building, to take that step. Once we did this, there would be no going back.

The window was open to allow the scent of the cleaning products to dissipate and I dropped his hand to head over and close it, pulling the blinds down partway for privacy.

Kicking off his shoes, Charlie got on the bed and sat himself against the headboard.

I pulled off my t-shirt and dropped it to the floor, padding over in bare feet and sweats to him. My heart was beating a mile a minute as I tried to put on a brave face. I could trust Charlie. Even if he didn't want things the way I did, he'd meet me halfway. We could work through it together.

Climbing onto the bed, I straddled Charlie, leaning in for a kiss.

"Show you, huh?" I whispered against his lips.

"Yes," he breathed before pulling me flush against him.

Charlie surrendered to my kiss. My hands ran through his hair before pulling his head to angle it the way I wanted. His moan reverberated through my body and I couldn't help but rock against him.

His hands roamed my back, pulling me tighter against him. I could feel his arousal against my own.

Each of his reactions showed me just how right I was to trust in what we had. He was as into this as I was. It wouldn't always be as easy as this, but I just had to believe in us.

Every tiny moan was ratcheting my arousal higher and higher until I had to lean back and take a deep breath.

The dream of having him under me, as desperate for me as I was him, didn't compare to the reality, and I wanted to pinch myself to prove this was really happening.

I moved back to tug at his shirt, silently telling him to remove it. The shirt quickly joined mine on the floor and I was able to run my hands over the bare expanse of his chest, feeling smooth skin pulled taut over firm muscles. Weeks working with Henry had given him great definition and one day soon I'd spend all day mapping his body with my fingers and mouth.

I caressed and kissed over his chest, worshipping every inch, nipping at each nipple in turn, working my way down, and scooting back to pull him down on the bed.

He chuckled at my manhandling and followed my directions. The heat in his gaze seared me and I shucked off my sweats and opened the button of his jeans.

The bed rocked as Charlie hastily kicked his legs free of his jeans. "Fucking skinny jeans were a bad idea," he groused, making me laugh. Flinging the offending item to the floor, he stretched out with a quick grin.

"Better," I told him with a smirk as he lay waiting in his black boxer briefs, his erection tenting them, a damp spot visible in the material.

I paused for a minute just taking him in and feeling the heat between us ramp up as we studied each other. How did I express this next bit?

"I like to top," I told him simply if a bit abruptly.

"Cool, I like to bottom." He winked at me and I couldn't contain the burst of laughter.

Resting my hands on his thighs I said, "I'm being serious."

"So am I. I just don't do it very often. People tend to assume."

I gave him a knowing look. "Do they now?" sarcasm drenching my tone.

"Fair." He laughed and pulled me close to kiss me quickly. "I guess I'm guilty of making that assumption too, or I'd never thought seriously about how things would work between us. I would have asked though, just in case I was wrong."

"I believe you." I pulled him in for another kiss, addicted to his taste. "This is when, usually, guys would get annoyed because being practical 'ruins the mood,'" I said when I pulled away from the kiss. Charlie's lips were wet and slightly swollen. His pupils dilated until only a thin ring of blue remained.

"Hmm, want me to go clean up? Do you have stuff?" He read my thoughts far too easily.

"Yeah, there's a kit in the bathroom."

"Want me to stretch a little, too?"

I had a glove on hand for that and I held it up in question.

"That might actually be hot. I can pretend you're a doctor giving me a prostate exam." He grinned before moving into the bathroom.

"Where's the—? Oh, found it," he called.

While he was busy prepping, I removed my sweats and briefs and got the lube and a condom from the nightstand.

I lay back and waited casually stroking my cock back to full hardness. I'd thought that I'd cut the desire between us like I had so many times before, but Charlie had surprised me with how open he was to working with my quirks.

He appeared, fully naked and stunning, in the doorway and my skin burned with the heat of his approving stare. He was still fully erect, a bead of precum on the tip of his cock.

I reached for him as he approached and I moaned into his mouth at our kiss. He settled next to me on the bed and we used the moment to explore each other's bodies for the first time.

Charlie picked up the condom from under his hip, opened it, and rolled it on. I gave him a puzzled look. "So I don't get cum on the sheets."

He grinned and I shoved at his shoulder, then turned back to the nightstand to get another. It should have put a damper on the mood, but it didn't. I loved that Charlie wasn't showing any sign of disapproval at how I needed things. Every touch he gave showed how much he wanted this, wanted us.

He took the condom from me and carefully rolled it on. He then handed me the lube and the glove.

"I really want to feel you stretch me."

"You do?"

"Yeah, it's a bit kinky with the glove, I'm into it." He gave a cheeky grin, lightening the mood.

I slipped it on and lubed up a couple of fingers as Charlie moved flush against me, taking my lips in a hard kiss, his hands moving to grip my ass and grind our dicks together.

We both groaned at the contact and I moved my lips to his neck as I ran a gloved finger down his crack. I circled his hole, rubbing it lightly as Charlie gasped and writhed against me. His mouth moved over my shoulder and collarbone to my Adam's apple. He sucked on it with a moan as my finger breached him.

I moved it in and out, going deeper each time until I felt he was ready for another. He panted at the second and I went slowly, unwilling to hurt him in my rush to get inside him.

My cock ached and dripped inside the condom, but my pleasure came second to Charlie's.

When he relaxed around the two fingers, I gently moved them in and out, scissoring them carefully.

I worked him over for a few minutes until he got impatient with me. "More." He demanded, yanking on my head and giving me a bruising kiss.

Adding a third, I pushed deeper than before and Charlie cried out when I tapped his prostate.

"That's enough, I'm ready."

I made quick work of removing my fingers and taking off the glove, turning it inside out, and dropping it on the floor next to the trash can I was aiming for. I must have winced a little at my aim because Charlie craned his neck to look, then laughed.

"I'll get it after," he told me as he moved onto his back and raised his legs, planting his feet wide.

Raising to my knees, I paused to just look at him. Charlie was spread out on my bed before me, his face flushed with arousal and his pupils blown wide. The moment was heavy between us until Charlie's foot pressed into my ass in a silent plea to get moving. I added more lube to my cock and moved between his legs.

We both groaned as I entered him, going slowly to allow him time to adjust. The pressure around my length was amazing, it felt like an out-of-body experience to realize I was doing this with Charlie. He was under me trying to pull me in with his feet on my ass.

I came down over him as I was fully seated inside him. Kissing him lightly, I asked, "Okay?" He nodded and I began to move.

At first, I thrust in short and shallow movements. As his body yielded to mine, I pushed in deeper, but still slowly.

My lips met his and we panted against each other's mouths as I began to pick up the pace with his urging.

He started to move his hips, meeting me stroke for stroke. His hands dug into my back and I pumped harder.

Every movement was divine. Sweat covered our bodies as we undulated together, the room filled with the sounds of panted breaths and whispered cries of pleasure.

There wasn't an inch of space between us and Charlie groaned as his cock rubbed against my stomach.

"I'm close!" I pulled back a little, grabbing at his hips to change the angle, instantly making him cry out at the next thrust. "There!"

Concentrating on keeping that angle and trying not to cum before him, I drove in hard, again and again. Charlie grunted and groaned with each thrust, his fingers digging into any part of me he could reach.

"Oh my god!" he yelled as I nailed that spot over and over. I was sure that I'd be left with bruises but I couldn't find it in me to care. Nothing had ever felt as good as this. Charlie saturated all of my senses and I never wanted this to end.

Sweat dripped from us but I couldn't stop. I felt the tell-tale tingle of my approaching release but I tried to hold it back, putting Charlie's needs before my own.

All too soon he cried out and came. His inner muscles clamped down on me, my thrusts slowing as bliss filled me and I filled the condom with my own release.

I collapsed onto Charlie breathing hard, and he gave a sleepy laugh. The motion made me groan as he tightened on my sensitive dick.

Grabbing at the condom, I pulled out of him carefully. I made quick work of removing the latex and picking up the glove, disposing of them in a tissue. I cleaned up Charlie too, using a wet wipe to remove the traces of lube and cum.

When the clean-up was taken care of, I sat on the edge of the bed, suddenly unsure, until Charlie snaked an arm around my waist and pulled me next to him.

I turned over onto my side to look at him, stroking his hair out of his eyes. "Okay?"

"That was amazing," he said with a sleepy sigh, cuddling into me.

"Yeah."

He opened an eye and looked at me. "Yes."

"Okay. Nap, then dinner?" I wrapped my arms around him and he burrowed into my chest.

"Sounds perfect." He muttered the words against my chest and quickly fell asleep.

I pulled a blanket over us, our skin a little chilly now the sweat had dried, and settled my head on a pillow. I watched him sleep for a few moments, still in shock that this was real. Charlie was asleep in my bed after some of the best sex I'd ever had. I'd never have imagined that we'd fit together as well as we did. All my worries drifted away.

After kissing his forehead, I closed my eyes and followed Charlie into sleep.

Chapter Twenty Seven

Max

T he nap seemed to do us both a world of good. I woke to Charlie stroking a lightly calloused hand down my back in a teasing manner. A slightly goofy smile shone on his too handsome face.

I studied him in the fading light, the gleam in his eyes affectionate. I ran a finger down his nose, noting the almost invisible bump from where he'd broken it in the car accident. Then I booped his nose. "C'mon, shower then dinner."

My scrambling to get out of bed was slightly impeded by getting tangled in the blanket. I hit the floor with an "Ooof," and Charlie bellowed with laughter before dashing off to get in the shower first.

When I joined him under the warm spray, he checked me over for injuries before pulling me into a kiss.

I'd never imagined that it would be so easy, effortless really, to be with him. Everything great about our friendship had transferred to our relationship. Sexually we seemed compatible too, though I worried about how easy that had gone and didn't trust it to last.

We jacked each other off under the water of the shower, no worries about mess there, before rinsing off and getting dressed. None of my clothes would fit Charlie, he was about four inches taller than me and his muscle gains had meant he was far wider too, so he went commando in his jeans.

I made us some dinner and we chatted about the café or the gym but not about how weird I'd been on our dates. I knew that I owed Charlie more of an explanation than I'd given him, but part of me just hoped that it wouldn't be an issue.

We sat in silence for a while as we finished up our meals until Charlie broke it.

"It'll be fine, you know. We'll find what works for us." He smiled before turning serious. "You just have to speak up for what you want. The same goes for me, if I don't like something, I'll tell you." He paused. "It's all about communication and compromise, or so Evan says."

We both laughed.

"You're right, though. We just have to keep talking." I reached for his hand. "Thanks for not laughing earlier."

"Why would I laugh? You want to be safe and you don't like cum everywhere. You've got a point."

"No, I meant about me topping. I don't get to do it very often but I enjoy it more, for...uh...reasons."

"I was being honest. I love bottoming. I just didn't do it often for hook-ups because they look at me and see a top." He shrugged. "Seems like we're a perfect fit that way. As for the condoms thing, I'm happy to do that for as long as you need. It'll take a bit of getting used to for blow jobs if you even do them." He looked at me and I nodded. "But the point is that we'll talk it through and once we get used to what the other likes then we'll be golden." He gave me a grin that stretched wide across his face before slinging an arm around me and pulling me close. He pressed a kiss to my temple.

"As much as I want to spend all night with you, we both have work in the morning and I'll need clean clothes. I should head home."

"Want me to drive you?"

"Nah, I'll get a ride-share." He looked hesitant for a second and my heart clenched. "Why don't we see a movie on Tuesday? Maybe you could pack a bag and stay overnight with me?"

Relief washed over me, and I gave what I was sure was a tremulous smile. "I'd like that."

We'd worked together the next morning, keeping a careful distance until we shared our break in the office. Most of it had been spent with me pinned against the door as Charlie owned my mouth, my hands in his hair. I was sure our rumpled appearance later had set tongues wagging, but we'd decided to keep our relationship quiet, at least at work, until we got used to what we were.

It probably didn't help matters that Charlie had appeared that Monday an hour or so before his therapy appointment with Evan, to have lunch with me.

We'd eaten in a locked office and then Charlie had slipped under the desk, produced a flavored condom, and proceeded to suck my brains out via my dick. I'd been ready to return the favor, since Charlie had bought plenty of condoms, but a knock on the door had put an end to that plan.

Our third date, since I was including our meal at Charlie's apartment as a date, went well. We ate out at a great fusion place and watched the newest blockbuster action movie. An easy brainless watch so we could relax after a busy couple of days.

"Still okay to stay over?" Charlie asked as we left the theater to head to my car.

"Yeah, I have a bag in the trunk." We leaned against the car enjoying the night air after the humid theater.

"Great, so...we both have tomorrow off. Henry had me come in today instead since I knew you were off. How about we go to the amusement park? Go on a ton of rides and hit up the arcade?"

Seeing his excitement ratcheted up my own. "Yes! That sounds like an amazing plan."

Charlie leaned in close, pressing me against the car, and kissed me sweetly.

"I have to say that I never thought that having you as a boyfriend would be this good, or this easy, Max."

"D'you think it's because we were friends first?" I asked as I rubbed my hands up and down his back.

"Hmm, maybe," he said as he rested his head against mine and I soaked up his nearness. I loved the feeling of him against me. I'd never get used to it or take it for granted.

With a final kiss, Charlie pulled away. "C'mon, it's getting cold, let's go back to my place."

"And get cozy in bed?" I suggested.

"Sounds perfect."

Henry was on the sectional watching some sort of sport on the T.V. when we got back to Charlie's.

Not wanting to be rude, I sat near him and tried to make conversation with him. We had literally nothing in common apart from Charlie, but I needed to make an effort with the guy who could replace me as Charlie's best friend now that I'd had the promotion to boyfriend.

It was like pulling teeth trying to get him to open up to me and Charlie saw my growing frustration. "C'mon, let's go to bed. We have a lot planned for tomorrow."

With that Henry showed some interest and asked, "What you got planned?"

"Max and I are having a date at the amusement park."

"Sounds like a good time."

Just in case Charlie asked Henry along, I yawned loudly and Charlie insisted that we get moving.

"Are you too tired for anything or should I clean up?" Charlie asked me quietly as we entered his bathroom to brush our teeth.

"Hmm," I considered my options as I wound my arms around him and rested my head against his shoulder. "I didn't get a chance to blow you yesterday. How about some lazy blow jobs and sleep?"

His head slumped and I worried that I'd disappointed him until he chuckled. "Thank goodness, because I'm too tired for much of anything else. Today was long."

I squeezed him lightly, moved aside to brush my teeth, and headed into his room.

Charlie had made the space comfortable and cozy with a navy comforter over crisp pale blue sheets. The rug was set at what I assumed was his side of the bed since it was closest to the door. The brushed silver lamps I'd picked out looked great on each nightstand. There wasn't a whole lot of personality in the room yet, but he was slowly making the space his own.

I circled the bed and flopped down with a sigh, the bed frame groaning ominously.

It gave another groan as Charlie joined me on the bed. We both turned to another series of noises and laughed at the ridiculousness of the situation.

"I'm going to have to fix that before you sleep over again," Charlie said with a grin as if it was my weight that was causing it to make such a racket.

Moving closer so I could kiss him, I circled an arm around him. The feeling of his mouth against mine was intoxicating and we soon got lost in the kiss and wandering hands.

"We'll have to be very careful," I told him after I pulled away. Charlie's lips were damp and there was a slight flush on his cheeks.

I slid down the bed slowly, kissing every inch of available skin, and let out a relieved breath when the thing didn't collapse under me. Charlie moved to touch me, to try and reciprocate.

"No, hands-off," I told him. "This is just for you, don't worry about me." I explored the tight muscles of his stomach and chest with sucks and nips, pressing kisses and running my fingertips over his smooth skin. He had a small smattering of dark chest hair that I couldn't help but tug on, making him gasp and me grin. I never wanted this to stop but knew we needed to get some sleep. I loved having Charlie moaning underneath me. I reached the band of his deep red boxer briefs and stopped, causing Charlie to groan. "Condom?"

He reached up a hand to fumble in the nightstand and grabbed a box. Selecting one at random, he passed it to me.

After carefully removing his underwear, I gave him a firm stroke, pulling back his foreskin. Then opened the foil wrapper and rolled the latex over Charlie's hard length

I wished that things were different, that I didn't have so many hang-ups, because I wasn't sure that I'd be able to do this even with the clear results Charlie was sure to get in the next couple of weeks. What would he think when I tell him that I just don't like the taste of cum? That it was a real turn-off for me and I'd rather stick to condoms despite the faint taste of rubber?

Pushing those intrusive thoughts aside, I focused on my man stretched out and waiting, his focus entirely on me. My toes curled at the heat in his eyes and I vowed to make his wait worth the while.

Starting slowly, I licked from root to tip, circling the mushroom head, working the shaft up and down before moving back to the head. Charlie moved his hands to hold onto my head before second-guessing himself.

"You can touch me, just don't hold me down, okay?"

He nodded, looking flushed and wrecked.

I worked him harder, taking him deep into my mouth before opening my throat to allow him deeper. His hips stuttered with aborted thrusts.

"Fuck my throat, I can take it."

My words unleashed something in him and he began to thrust into my mouth, his hands cupping my face before one landed under my jaw so he could feel his cock in my throat.

It was difficult to remember to breathe through my nose and to relax, keeping my throat open to the onslaught but I loved the way that Charlie was using me, how he'd abandoned his constraints to seek out his pleasure. My cock was hard and leaking in my briefs, but I wasn't seeking release, this was all for him.

Habit had Charlie muttering, "Close!" as his orgasm neared. I could see him through my watering eyes; he looked almost feral as he chased his climax.

He groaned as his cock pulsed in my mouth, the condom keeping the salty liquid from me.

Slumping back, Charlie pulled me up his body to press a kiss to my mouth.

"Gimme a minute and it's your turn."

Slipping from his grasp I said, "Relax, that was just for you." I removed and disposed of the condom and went to wash my hands.

When I returned to the bedroom, Charlie looked asleep, his chest rising and falling slowly. His skin still glittering with sweat in the lamplight.

I crept into bed next to him, moving delicately to not jostle Charlie or the bed frame. I managed to pull the covers over us and wriggled close, completely content.

Minutes passed in silence, the usual noise of my brain quieted. Then Charlie turned and wrapped me in his arms and I slipped into sleep.

Chapter Twenty Eight

Charlie

By the end of the week and after an amazing date where we spent all day at the amusement park, I was more than ready to shout about my relationship with Max from the mountain tops. Being with him made me feel so steady. It was so unlike the feeling of being drunk and out of control. Max made me feel like I could accomplish anything as long as I had him by my side.

Hand in hand, we entered the busy bar that Andy and Will favored, each scanning the crowd for my family or either of the birthday people.

This was a big test for me. I'd been sober for nearly six months but had yet to really be tested. Being around a lot of alcohol, where no one would question what I had in my hand, was a lot to think about. Nerves had been building the closer we got to the party. If it wasn't for Andy, then I wouldn't have put myself through this.

Andy, birthday person number one, was easy to spot, surrounded by friends with Will at his side. He wore a crown with "Thirty" written on it, tilted at an angle so it came off careless and fun rather than spoiled royal. Happiness shone from every pore as he greeted guests and laughed at jokes.

I'd made a promise that I would come to the party for a little while. It was technically for both Andy and Abby, but

Mom had invited more people from Andy and Will's office than people he and his sister actually spent time with.

The place was packed and though the band had yet to start up, it was difficult to hear anyone over the cacophony of voices.

Wanting to make sure Mom knew I was there, I made a beeline for her, tugging Max close behind me.

The feel of his hand in mine was the only thing keeping me in the building. It wasn't that I wanted a drink, more that without alcohol to muffle everything, it was too much. Too loud, too many people, even the scents of different perfumes mixing was making me feel hemmed in and anxious.

Max pulled on my hand so I stopped and he popped up on tiptoes to speak in my ear, "Just let your Mom know that we'll head out to the balcony."

I sent her a quick text of our plans and let him pull me in that direction.

I couldn't remember being here before, it was all a bit vague, but I knew that Max had been since it was the place where Will had found him and taken him home.

My heart sank when I realized how selfish I was being, making Max return to a place with such bad memories just so he could support me.

I pulled on his hand a little so he would stop moving and he turned to look at me. He must have seen some of my guilt in my expression because he hooked his free hand around my neck and pulled me down for an achingly tender kiss.

Shouts and hoots went out around us but I pushed them all away to pull Max closer and deepen the kiss. I could kiss him forever.

A tap on my back broke me from the moment and I turned, tucking Max close into my side, to see who had interrupted us.

"Hey, Mom."

"Charlie. Max. It's good to see you both, though I'm surprised that you came." Mom's tone was clipped, though her words were polite. I knew that she disagreed about me moving out but I thought she'd gotten over it. It seemed like either she hadn't, or she had imagined up some way to blame Max for all the changes in my life, judging by the ridiculous glare he was getting from her. I wasn't having this.

"Mom, can we maybe talk tomorrow?" I could hear the exasperation in my tone. "Today is about Andy and Abby, and not about how you don't approve of my choices."

Her gaze softened. "Come by the house for brunch tomorrow, Charlie," she said, completely ignoring Max at my side.

I feel Max stiffen next to me. "Mom…" I warned. "You're being unnecessarily rude and hurtful."

"Darling, I haven't seen you in weeks!"

"I needed some space, Mom. I've called and checked in."

"You missed family dinner."

"So did Will and Andy because they didn't want to leave Lucifer so soon." I'd known the cat was an excuse not to have to go. I'd visited them at home with Max so I could meet the cat I'd be looking after in a few days. Will and Andy had trusted me with cat-sitting so that Will could take Andy on vacation. It was a big step for my brother, letting me stay in his home and trusting me with Andy's precious cat.

"Max can come too if that's the problem," she said grudgingly.

"Mom!" I rolled my eyes at her, "You need to apologize now and we can talk this through properly tomorrow." Turning to Max, I asked, "Do you want to do brunch? Honestly, because we don't have to."

Neither of us was working a morning shift and I looked to Max to see if he was on board with that idea. He gave a small nod, looking slightly reluctant. Mom's disapproval was hurting him and anger welled inside me.

"We'll see you tomorrow, but Mom, you need to get over this idea of Max being responsible for my past behavior. You're being hurtful by putting the blame for my decisions on him. He's done nothing but care for me and support me until I made that impossible. Think about that, please."

Max squeezed my hand and drew closer to me so that he was pressed into my side.

At the movement, my mother's eyes softened a fraction, but it wasn't enough for me to want to put Max through more of her crap tonight. We were too new for all these pressures. We should be enjoying the honeymoon period, the discovery and joy of finally being together instead of having my family disapproving.

"Mom!" came a call over the din of the bar. "I need your help."

Together we all turned to see Will gesturing at Mom. He threw a wink at me when she turned to repeat her brunch invitation. So, not all my family was against me being with Max.

The outside area was blissfully cool after the heat and crush of the inside and it was easy to find a free table.

"D'you want a soda?"

Max headed for the bar, leaving me for a brief second before my brother took his seat. "Sorry about Mom," Will said. He looked truly apologetic. "I've been trying to get her to see things from your side. From the way Andy and I see things."

"How do you and Andy see things?" I asked, curious. Will's attitude had changed so much towards me since I'd left rehab.

"Y'know what? It's a whole thing. A process I've worked through in therapy and I'll save you the details, but basically, I see how you've always been on the outside of us looking in. Even when our father didn't need you at the company, he still made you give up what you loved and come and work for him. You've never been the same since then. Of course, Alex and I didn't make things easy with our drama. You chose me and I rejected you."

I couldn't help but flinch at his words. He'd nailed it all. The constant striving to be noticed.

"It doesn't make it right, what I did with Ethan," I told him, my voice raw.

"No, but you inadvertently saved me from him." He paused, "Look, we've been over this. We can't change it, and I'm so impressed by how you've tackled rehab and rebuilding your life. It hasn't been easy, I'm sure, but you're doing it." He reached over and put a hand on my shoulder, giving it a quick squeeze before dropping it back onto the table.

Tears threatened to spill over and I pushed them back with serious effort. Will looked away, pretending not to notice how his words affected me.

After I cleared my throat I said, "Thank you. For giving me a second chance."

"The way I see it, everything since you woke up in the hospital has been you taking your second chance. You didn't need to do anything. Not rehab. Not the apologies. You could have cut your losses here and moved away. I thought about that, y'know?"

"You did?"

"Yeah. Before we got together, Andy and I hooked up a lot and I was still carrying around all my issues, so he ended it. After that, I thought about leaving, but he gave me a second chance. We all deserve them at times."

The conversation dropped as Max came to join us.

"Listen," Will said as he rose to stand. "I just wanted to say that I'm so glad that you two are finally together. Andy and I are so happy for you both."

The tension on Max's shoulders slipped away as a smile graced his face. "Thanks Will, that means a lot."

"I'll go get Andy and Abby so you can do gifts and then you can make your escape if you want. Can't be easy being here for either of you."

"That'd be great, thanks."

Max and I sat and had our drinks under a patio heater and enjoyed the relative quiet until Henry burst through the doors with a face like thunder.

Henry saw us and quickly made his way in our direction. "I'm heading out. I just wanted you guys to know. I can't stay here. See you later?"

We looked between ourselves and then nodded at him. "Okay. See you at the apartment." As quickly as he'd arrived, he was gone, exiting around the side of the building rather than going through the busy bar.

A few minutes later, Andy, Will, and Abby joined us at the table. I caught Abby's protestation, "I can't leave Josh for long, I promised him a dance."

"Where's Henry?" Andy asked as he scanned the growing crowd outside.

I looked at Max, wondering if I could sugar-coat it. "Um... he left."

Andy immediately looked disappointed, letting out a soft, "Oh."

Noticing the frown on Will's face, I sent a questioning glance his way.

"Pete's here. With a guy."

Well, fuck.

"Did no one know he was coming?" Max asks Andy.

"Pete said he'd try to be here for the party, but he didn't say for sure he would come. I emailed him the invitation just in case and I warned Henry it was possible, but I hardly expected him to show up with a guy in tow." Andy sounded hurt and I couldn't blame him. Pete not giving any warning couldn't have worked out worse.

Max looked at me, trying to communicate something silently. A bit slow on the uptake with worrying about Henry, it took me a minute to realize that Max wanted me to give the gifts over so we could go home and check on my friend.

I gave each of the twins their gift bags, although Abby protested at getting a gift at all. "It's just something small and you're family," I said to placate her.

Each opened the parcel containing one of the photographs I'd taken of them at Christmas. Andy with Will sharing a private moment surrounded by family. Abby and Josh sharing a kiss under the mistletoe. The frames that Max had chosen worked perfectly.

"Oh," came the soft exclamation from Abby when her eyes landed on the picture. "Thank you! This is lovely."

Andy and Abby showed each other their pictures, complimenting me on my skills which had a blush rising in my cheeks. Max sent a fond smile over the table and in that moment, I wanted it to just be me and him, but I had to be a good brother-in-law-to-be and spend some time with Andy before we could leave. Not that we'd have any time to ourselves unless we went to Max's apartment and I didn't want to leave Henry on his own.

Twenty minutes later, Max and I were slipping away from the party after making the rounds quickly. Pete had looked at us, me in particular, with interest. Brad and Dylan, Will's other gym friends, were friendly and kind. Brad offered a, "look out for Henry, would you? I'm worried about him." He then frowned at Pete's guest who had wrapped himself around Pete, looking like a barnacle as he clung to Pete, rather than a date.

Alex had ignored my attempts at civility and was a problem that I was going to have to deal with sooner rather than later. We didn't have to get along wonderfully, but we needed to be able to be in the same place together without issues for the sake of our family.

Mom had pressed a kiss to both mine and Max's cheeks with a reminder about brunch, which gave me hope that she would listen to us. Max had given her a sweet smile that she had returned, so there appeared to be a thawing there. Maybe something of what I'd said had gotten through to her.

There would be no giving Max up. I'd give up my whole family before I'd do that because he meant more to me than anyone ever could.

After another round of hugs and cheek kisses from Andy and Abby, a surprisingly long and tight hug from Will, we were out the door.

Chapter Twenty Nine

Max

The last thing I wanted to be doing post birthday party was dealing with friend drama, but Henry was hurting and Charlie had been asked to look after him.

We returned to their shared apartment less than an hour after Henry had left the party and found him sitting on the sectional with a beer in hand. He must have visited a liquor store after leaving the bar since I knew the apartment was dry.

He'd changed into sweats and looked like he'd showered off the bar smells, but the air hung heavy around him. His emotions had turned the atmosphere brittle.

I attempted to make myself comfortable not too far away from him and Charlie grabbed us sodas.

"Want to talk about it or put a movie on and pretend tonight didn't happen?" Charlie inquired.

"Movie." Henry all but grunted out.

I figured we'd start the movie and he'd get halfway before telling us what was going on in his mind. Most people just needed a few moments to figure things out before they spilled the beans.

Charlie picked up the remote and flicked through the offerings before selecting a dumb action film that wouldn't require a brain to follow along.

Sure enough, Henry caved quickly and we tuned out the action bursting from the screen to listen to him properly.

"Okay, so it's complicated…" He ran a hand over his face. "Just after I broke up with my last girlfriend, Gemma, something happened."

"Is that the girl that you went to our cabin with?" Charlie cut in and I gave him a look. It was Henry's turn to open up.

"That's her. She accused me of having feelings for Pete and said that Pete was in love with me. It was crazy weird between me and Pete for a few weeks after and then around Thanksgiving he came to my parent's house with me. It was the first time we'd been around each other alone in a while. So, we had a few beers and shot the shit." Henry trailed off and was quiet for a bit. "I don't know what happened. I guess, I just felt this draw to him. I'd been missing him hanging around and he was finally there.

"Then I leaned in and kissed him."

I don't know which one of us gasped, but Henry flushed. "He pushed me away and started going crazy. Saying I couldn't play with him like that. A whole bunch of stuff." Henry gave us an imitation of a casual shrug but it was plain to see the hurt was still there.

"Pete left and we didn't speak for a week. He sent a text asking for some space and I let him be. Then after a bit, he wanted to meet up. Look, long story short was he said he didn't want to be an experiment and needed me to figure out if I liked guys. I married pretty young, so Pete said I didn't get to explore my sexuality the same way he did. So he said to explore and figure it out and then come back to him."

Henry stopped for another drink of his soda. I'd switched out the beer once he'd finished the first bottle, figuring we didn't need a drunk and morose Henry on our hands.

"I tried to figure out dating. I checked out guys in the gym and the bar. But it's a lot. Then at Andy and Will's engagement party, I got a little drunk and kissed Pete again. He was furious and hurt and I felt like shit. After we argued, he left the party and made plans to travel. Just picked up and left. He left me a message saying we needed space and we'd talk when he got back, but I needed to figure myself out and he wasn't going to do that for me."

Henry hung his head, but we both still heard him mutter, "Then he turned up with that guy and didn't say a word to me."

My heart hurt for Henry. He'd been left to question his sexuality for months completely alone, with the others of the group pulling away from him after Pete had left so suddenly.

I got that the others blamed Henry, and they were right, it was technically his fault that Pete left. But none of them had thought to wonder what had happened that two friends were suddenly unable to be in the same room together?

Henry admitted that he was only part of the group because they met in his gym and Pete was close to Andy. He felt like he was their friend by default and that had only gotten worse when Pete had left suddenly to go traveling.

There was no one that could understand what he was going through for him to turn to, which is why his friendship with Charlie was so important to him. He'd finally had someone who wasn't a part of all the drama and bullshit that had surrounded him and Pete.

It was then that I felt a burst of anger towards Pete. As a bisexual guy, he knew that sexuality was a spectrum, and though there were labels, not all fit right for everyone.

Maybe Henry had developed sexual feelings towards Pete but having him "test" his attraction to guys on other people was so ridiculous, not to mention dangerous.

In my fury, the words burst out of me. "I'm so mad that I can't think just now! Let me get this straight, PETE wanted YOU to test out if you're attracted to him or just guys in general, by having you go out and try and pick up a man? Is that right?"

Henry looked worried and taken aback by my anger.

"And what would happen if someone started something with you and didn't stop when you wanted them to? It isn't safe to be so new to this and go out looking for a hookup! Guys would eat someone like you for breakfast. Like, there are guys that hunt for gay virgins!" I ran my hand over my face, worry for Henry and irritation at Pete at war in my head. "At least tell me you haven't signed up for an app?"

Henry visibly flinched and Charlie groaned. I let out a sigh.

"How's that working out for you?" Charlie voiced aloud the thought we seemed to share, the drawl of sarcasm heavy in his tone.

"I...uh...put it on mute after a couple of days. There were a lot of messages." I'd bet on quite a bit more than a lot. Jesus.

It was my turn to groan. "You put down that you were questioning your sexuality, didn't you? That you wanted something either no strings or low key, right?"

Finally cluing into where the problem came from, Henry covered his face with his hands. His shoulders started to shake. At first, I thought he was crying, but soon little puffs of laughter were audible. Tears streamed down his face and I couldn't help but grin at Charlie and shake my head.

"Dude, if you need help then all you need to do is ask, but really all you need is a couple of gay friends to test some theories on you."

That stopped Henry cold. "Test me? How d'you mean?"

I looked to Charlie for help, unable to articulate the ideas I was having and needing his support. We'd played this game before with curious college friends. He gave me a gentle smile, showing me he was on board with what I was thinking of doing. It was only a kiss, after all.

"I think what Max is suggesting is something simple. Like a kiss. Maybe see if you have a type. Nothing too wild. He's not suggesting you have sex with one of your friends. Right?" He glanced at me and I nodded empathetically. "You can tell a lot about a kiss."

Henry looked stunned. "You can?"

Charlie and I both nodded and I gazed at him to check if what I was about to do was going to upset him. Inside, I was a mix of bravado and fear. I knew that I could be about to make a really big mistake, but I couldn't back out now.

Charlie winked and I let out a relieved breath. This didn't mean anything, I was just helping out a friend.

Pushing Henry back onto the sofa, I clambered into his lap facing him.

"What?" He managed to get out as I leaned in.

"Relax," I interrupted, "We're just testing out some theories unless you're really uncomfortable with it. If you're worried about Charlie, then don't. Charlie's okay with it, aren't you babe?" I turned around a little so I could look him straight in the eye without leaving Henry's lap.

"As long as I get a turn too, I don't mind at all. This is kinda hot, actually."

"See?" I turned back to face Henry, leaning in a little closer, "If you don't want this, I'll stop right now, but if you're at all curious, then this is something safe. We won't hurt you or push you to do anything you don't want to."

He thought it over quickly and there was no faking the interest and heat in his eyes. Henry was into the idea of kissing me and my boyfriend.

I got a thrill every time that I thought of Charlie holding that title. His place in my life was far more permanent than something as fleeting as a boyfriend, but it was too soon to think of things like that.

My knees were starting to ache from sitting in this position so I prompted Henry a little, "So?"

He answered by leaning forward to meet my lips. Unprepared, it was just a tiny brush of lips and not a real kiss, so I reached out and placed a hand at the back of his neck so I could control it better.

Our lips met a second time. Henry's lips were full, warm and so soft against mine. We kissed close-mouthed for a few seconds before his tongue probed against my lips and

I opened to it, allowing it to explore my mouth. I took control again, my tongue twining with his, taking the kiss even deeper. Instinctively, I rocked against Henry and his growing arousal and he released a moan against my mouth.

The noise shocked me and I pulled back quickly like I'd been electrocuted and I moved off Henry's lap, glancing at Charlie for reassurance that I hadn't ruined everything between us.

Charlie looked at me with lust in his gaze and adjusted himself. "That was hot and clearly Henry was into it."

We both looked at a shell-shocked Henry as he also adjusted himself. "Damn! That was something else."

I couldn't hold in the laugh that escaped me. Henry and Charlie smiled at me and then looked at each other. I saw the interest there, though more on Henry's side. Charlie just seemed curious, which was a relief. I was willing to bet it was more of a game to him, but there was a trickle of unease at how willing Henry was to kiss Charlie. Henry led this time, shuffling closer to Charlie and bracketing his face with his hands, pulling Charlie closer until their lips met.

They were striking together. These large men locked in an intimate embrace and their kiss quickly escalated into something passionate where Henry and I were more exploratory and tender. Henry cupped Charlie's throat as he dominated the kiss and Charlie had given himself up to it. Small sounds of pleasure escaped from them both.

It was Charlie that broke the kiss. He pulled back and then dropped a quick, chaste kiss to Henry's lips so that it didn't look like a rejection. His eyes flitted to mine, and I saw worry there.

Henry slumped back in his seat and I cursed myself for starting this experiment. All I wanted to do was take Charlie to his room and get inside him, show him that he belonged to me. Unfortunately, we had to help our friend through his identity crisis.

"You okay?" Charlie asked him.

Henry let out a deep breath, "Yeah. I guess there's no question. I'm into guys."

"Yeah, no doubt there," I teased, trying to get out of my head and lighten what we had done. "I felt how much you were into it."

Henry blushed crimson and I resisted the urge to tease him further.

"It was easier with Charlie, but I think that it's because I know him better and he let me have control." Henry rubbed the back of his neck, the conversation making him uncomfortable.

It was my turn to blush. "Uh, yeah...I like being in charge."

Charlie laughed and the tension that had been building broke.

"So we're all okay?" Henry checked. "Because as much as I love you guys, I don't want to be a third, or break you guys up. It's Pete that I want if I haven't missed my chance or fucked things up beyond all repair."

I didn't want to answer for Charlie but shrugged at Henry, "All's good here." Lie. "It was just a safe way to test things out. I know you've kissed Pete but that only says that you're attracted to him, not guys in general. You reacting to us, well, that says it might be guys as well as women."

"What Max said. I know you aren't interested in us like that, but it's still good for the ego that we can get you hard." Charlie let out a laugh at the expression on Henry's face.

"Well," Henry said, rising from the sofa, "I'm off for a cold shower. You guys have fun."

Chapter Thirty

Charlie

I didn't know where the rest of our night was going to go. I certainly hadn't expected to be making out with my roommate while my boyfriend watched. Especially after watching him make out with Henry, too. Jesus that had been hot. I'd wondered at the lack of jealousy, but if anything, it was a turn-on to see them together like that and know how Max was affecting Henry. This wasn't going to be a common thing, I didn't want a third in our relationship and I was sure Henry felt the same way. It wasn't either of us he wanted, regardless of his body's reaction.

Max turned to me. "Bed. Now."

Yes, sir.

I was so turned on that I couldn't think straight and before I knew what was happening, Max had me pinned to my bed.

"Here's what's going to happen. You're going to take off all your clothes and lie back on this bed. I'm going to tie you down and work you over until that kiss with Henry is a distant memory and my name is the only one you remember." Max's voice was low, barely restrained need turning the words into a growl.

A moan escaped me and Max moved back, knowing he had my full focus.

"Are you on board with that, Charlie?" Max stared at me, looking for any hesitation.

Nodding frantically, I began to strip out of my clothes quickly but was stopped with a hand on my chest. "Words, Charlie."

"Yes. I want that."

"Good. Do you want to give me a safeword?"

"Traffic lights." I paused and he looked at me for clarification, "Red for stop. Yellow to slow down and check-in. Green for go."

"Perfect. Get those clothes off, then."

In my haste to strip off my jeans, I nearly tripped over my feet. My cock was achingly hard, and if I didn't calm down now this was going to be over before it started.

Settling against the pillows in the center of the bed, I placed my hands on either side of my head and waited for Max to find what he was looking for in my dresser.

He returned to my side with some silk ties. I'd kept some of the business wear, my suits and ties, from all the meetings I'd held while running the clubs. A deep part of me wondered if I'd kept them in case I returned to the clubs, but I knew that wasn't going to happen. The lingering sadness at that realization had evaporated.

Max quickly tied my hands firmly to the wooden frame of the bed. Henry had helped me fix the frame a couple of days ago so it no longer squeaked and groaned at every movement. I tested the restraints. There was some room for movement, but not a lot.

Then Max grabbed a pillow and placed it under my hips, angling them for easier access to my hole.

Coming down on top of me, he took my mouth in a bruising kiss, opening my mouth with his tongue to probe deep inside. We stayed that way for a long time, Max still clothed moving against me as he explored my mouth with his tongue, occasionally nipping at my lips and making me moan.

Left breathless, I pulled my head away to break the kiss and moaned at the nips and licks to my neck, along my collarbone, and down to my left nipple.

Max tortured and teased it for a long time while his fingers teased the other. All the while, I gasped and moaned.

He switched nipples, giving the right the same treatment until I was begging for him to give my cock attention.

Instead of heading down my body as I wanted, Max came back up for another deep kiss. The taste of Henry was long gone and only my Max remained.

Max pulled away this time and I groaned in frustration. I wanted him in me, on me, owning me completely.

He lavished kisses down my neck and chest again, before traveling further south. Kisses, licks, and nips were traced along my torso and lower abdomen as I tried to buck and move to get him where I needed him. His tongue laved the sensitive skin between my thighs and groin, avoiding my straining shaft altogether.

There was a devilish smirk on his face when I begged. "Max, please!"

Time became meaningless as he did as he said he would, working me over while leaving my dick hard and untouched. Being tied to the bed added extra depth to the sensations, to the whole experience. It made me focus on every movement that he made.

I was panting and leaking for him, ready to beg, when he rolled a condom down my length and took me into his hot, wet mouth. I hated that we had to use condoms for blow jobs but was determined not to let my poor choices in the past affect Max, so I had picked up flavored ones to make it more appealing and I could still feel the perfect suction on the head, the way his tongue moved down the shaft.

As Max sucked me, he used a glove and lubed fingers to open and stretch me, still taking his time and leaving me desperate. He looked me in the eyes as he sucked me deep, two fingers inside me and I could see the need there.

My hips thrust gently, working me deeper into his mouth and then back onto his fingers. Max added a third, twisting them and pressing against my prostate, making me cry out.

All I could think about was him and the way that he lit up my body with overwhelming sensations and I felt the familiar tingle of an orgasm.

"I'm close!"

He pulled his mouth off my cock and stilled his fingers, his other hand rubbing soothingly up and down my thigh as I calmed. I wanted to curse. I just wanted to cum but Max didn't look ready to give up his game. He hadn't even undressed yet.

Instead of returning to my cock, he moved up my body again, keeping his fingers inside, but they were still.

He kissed me, the strawberry taste of the flavored latex on his tongue before he broke away to use his free hand to remove his shirt, fumbling with it with only one hand.

"Should've taken my clothes off first," he muttered under his breath.

I groaned as I felt his bare skin against mine. Firm, smooth, and hot in the cool room.

Taking breaks in between to remove more clothing, I nearly sobbed when he eased his fingers from my body. I needed something filling me and he didn't look ready to give me his dick. After he was completely naked, he slicked up his fingers again, checking that I was stretched enough for him.

Max lavished more attention on every part of my body except my cock again until I wanted to sob with how much I needed the orgasm that felt just around the corner.

He removed his fingers gently, quickly disposed of the glove, and rolled on a condom. Checking, "Still green?" Looking for my nod before pushing in slowly.

Even with how much he'd worked to get me ready, his girth still required him to go slow and allow me the chance to breathe and relax against the stretch.

Fully seated, he paused until he felt my inner muscles give way.

Max stretched out on top of me. He kissed me softly, the simple touch of lips expressing so much of his feelings for me, before starting to thrust gently, slowly, making love to my body with soft exhalations in my ear.

"So good. You feel so good around my cock."

Moving deeper, harder, he kissed under my ear. "I could be inside you all day. God, you're amazing."

We worked together, rocking and kissing, his hands roaming my skin, into my hair. He grasped the strands, pulling them to angle my head to meet his mouth. The kiss became desperate, his hips driving into me at an increasingly faster pace.

He moved back, resting on his knees, pulling my hips up onto his cock harder. Pulling and pushing on my hips, his fingers biting into the skin there, leaving marks as he worked me onto his cock. The angle was perfect, hitting my prostate with every increasingly savage thrust. His balls slapped against my ass, the grunts, and groans animalistic as we worked towards our climax.

I wanted to hold him, to be able to touch him at all. I wanted to jack myself, my orgasm stuck on the precipice.

"I'm close!" I warned and he drove his cock into me faster and harder still, adding the bite of pain that sent me spiraling closer but it wasn't quite enough. "I...need..." Moaning and panting, I couldn't voice my thoughts. All I could focus on was the feel of him inside me, so thick and hard.

"Me too," he panted and gave me what I needed. He grasped my cock, stroking it in time to his movements.

Within seconds, my orgasm exploded from me, cum filling the condom I still wore. I had a distant thought about easier clean-up before everything faded. My vision spotted and sounds vanished as I was bathed in sensation.

Max's movements stuttered as my muscles clamped down on him and after a few more hard pumps of his hips, he came too, slumping back and pulling out of me gently.

All I could do was lie there and relish in the post-orgasm haze as Max pulled himself together, then pressed kisses to the slightly red flesh under the ties as he worked me free.

After removing both condoms, he slipped into the en suite bathroom and grabbed a small towel. Tenderly, he wiped me clean and now that I was able to touch him again, I pulled him into my arms and stroked my hands down his back. I grabbed the towel off him, chucking it in the direction of the hamper, and tightened my hold on him

He sighed contentedly, settling his head into my neck, and quickly fell asleep.

Chuckling, I pulled the cover over us and lay thinking about the events of the night. The scenes were on repeat as I worried over what each would mean for the future of my friendships and my relationship with Max.

Would he be so cool with the Henry kiss in the morning? While rationally I knew that he had been the one to instigate it, I wondered if maybe it had been a test. Perhaps I was meant to protest at him making out with Henry instead of taking my turn.

Max must have sensed my growing distress as he held me closer and pressed sleepy kisses to my neck. I heard my name but not all of what he said, but I heard the affection there.

All I could do was try to relax and trust in what we had.

Chapter Thirty One

Charlie

Cracking my eyelids the next morning, I was met with a general feeling of unease. Max had drifted from where he was usually curled up against my side. His back was to me and he was scrolling something on his phone.

"Morning," I said.

"Morning, what time are we meeting your mom?"

I checked my phone for messages and sure enough, there was one from Mom with the time and place for brunch.

"We've got just over an hour," I moved to reach for him but he slipped from the bed.

"I'll go grab a shower then."

As he circled the bed, I clasped his wrist. "Everything okay?" There seemed to be a wall building between us that I didn't understand.

"Everything's fine but we don't want to be late. Your mom already has issues with us." He pulled away and quickly entered the bathroom, the snick of the lock loud in the silence of the room.

Max didn't take long to shower and he tried to lighten the mood with teasing as he pushed me towards the bathroom, but it was off somehow. Gone were the kisses and touches I was becoming accustomed to.

We entered the busy restaurant with plenty of time to spare, but not enough time to talk. I was just getting up the courage to speak to Max about the weirdness between us when Mom was shown to our table.

Max rose first and kissed her on the cheek in welcome. A pleased smile graced her face.

"Hello Mom, you look nice," I said as I also rose to greet her with a hug.

The server approached and took our orders and we sat in silence for a moment.

Mom finally broke it. "I owe you both an apology for my behavior last night. I'm very happy that you are together as a couple and didn't want to give you the impression that I wasn't. However," I suppressed an eye roll. "I was surprised and didn't feel that Andy's party was the place to tell the family such big news."

While I knew Andy was okay with it since he and Will already knew, I wasn't about to point that out to Mom, since that news would go down like a lead balloon. "Point taken Mom. I'll apologize to Andy for making a scene at his party." It was easier just to placate her. "So you're happy Max and I are together?"

"Of course I am! I may have worried about the timing, but I've had some discussions with Evan. He thinks that Max is a very stabilizing influence on you, and I agree with that. I just was so worried about you before, but you look so happy. I don't think I've ever seen you so content."

"Being with Max is better than anything I've had before," I said to her while looking directly at him. His eyes widened. "He's helping me realize my dreams. Did I mention that he encouraged me to sell my photos in a store that sells work by local artists?"

"Really? Oh, darling, that's amazing news! Thank you, Max, for being the push that he needed."

Max blushed and stammered a few denials and fell silent.

Mom dominated the conversation between us for the rest of brunch, which was only broken when Max had to leave to get ready for work.

"Will you be okay getting home?" Max asked me. "I have to rush. Kristen needs me in earlier."

"Everything okay?"

"Yeah, it will be." His tone was off again, slightly curt in a way I didn't get. Was it just that he didn't want to discuss his business in front of Mom?

He leaned in and pecked my cheek, the barest brush of lips. He'd been sitting next to me the whole time but had kept a careful distance. I'd touched his thigh under the table and he'd flinched, so I'd withdrawn it.

"I'll call you later," I called to his retreating back which he acknowledged with a wave.

"Is everything okay with you two?" Mom asked delicately.

"Yeah, he just has a lot going on at work." I shrugged, trying to brush off the hurt I felt at Max's dismissal.

"So, do you have a key for Will's place? I'm looking after the cat."

Mom gave me a look that said she didn't appreciate the change of subject, but I let it go. "No, darling, you can get one at the concierge desk. They know that you will be staying though, so you should have no issue getting in tomorrow."

After spending some time with my mom, I returned to my apartment in time for Henry to head off for work. He flushed a fascinating shade of red when he spotted me.

"Henry, it's fine. There's nothing to be embarrassed about. It was a one-time experiment."

"So we're okay?"

"Of course."

"And Max?"

He must have seen my hesitation because his face fell. "Dammit, that's the last thing I wanted to happen!"

"We were fine when we went to sleep. I think that there's something else going on." I tried to placate myself and my friend at the same time with my words. There had to be something more to Max's weird behavior. He hadn't texted or replied to any of my messages.

"Tomorrow I'm heading to Will's for a few days. He's asked me to look after Lucifer while they are away.

"That's great that he asked you. Must mean things are better between you two."

"Yeah, Andy has helped. With him there between us, he translates, if that's the right word. He makes us understand each other better. Acts as a go-between a lot, or did at first, but yeah, we're getting there. Never thought that would happen."

"Well, that's great. I gotta go, see you later."

I sat and tried to watch some TV when Henry left, but couldn't settle on anything. I worked on the final touches of the photo book, emailed them off, and then printed a bunch of pictures to sell in the store I'd visited with Max. The owner had been in touch a couple of times to confirm the details, and I planned to visit the next day before work at the gym to drop them off.

Throwing myself into work didn't stop me from wondering what was happening with Max. There was still nothing from him and I'd stopped messaging, hoping that he just needed some space to figure things out.

I went to bed late that night having heard nothing from him, worry eating at my gut.

Chapter Thirty Two

Max

Anxiety was a nasty beast. It can eat away at your sense of self and make a person act in ways they wouldn't usually. At least that was what I tried to justify my actions with.

There was no excuse for ignoring Charlie. If I wanted our relationship to work then I needed to let him in. My main worry was how much was too much?

The way that he and Henry had made out with each other in front of me had stuck in my brain the whole night as Charlie lay sleeping next to me. For my own sanity, I had moved away. My dreams, when I had slept, had been full of images of Charlie leaving me for Henry, who was easier to deal with. Henry was new to being with a guy so didn't have all my hang-ups, so he was the better, easier choice in my anxiety-ridden brain.

It wasn't fair on Charlie, since he'd given me no reason to think that it hadn't just been an experiment. For all I knew, his body's reaction was more to do with me watching, having watched me kiss Henry first.

I knew I was being ridiculous but then I'd woken early to texts from work.

Kristen: The register is short again. I need to check the cameras but will have to wait until you and Heather are in.

Max: Damn, I thought that this was over with

Kristen: Me too but it isn't. You able to come in early?

Max: Yeah. NP

Worrying about my business had distracted me the whole time during the meal and I knew that I'd hurt Charlie with my distance and probably had given Alice a reason to tell him to break up with me. Not that he would. Not before talking to me, anyway.

I arrived at Books & Biscuits a couple of hours earlier than planned and Kristen and I spent a few hours locked in the office going over security tapes from the previous day to check where the shorts had occurred. We then spent time doing inventory until we had to stop.

Kristen was exhausted by five, having opened, so I sent her home and promised to look at as much footage as I could while Heather took over the book inventory.

The LGBTQIA section that Heather had suggested was really coming along, the sales were great and I was gradually giving her more responsibility, so I knew she could handle the inventory while I checked over other things.

We closed on time, but I stayed behind to review more footage, not leaving until really late, far too late to be messaging Charlie.

I flopped into bed utterly drained, though guilt prickled at the back of my brain.

Monday passed much the same way, with Kristen, Heather, and I looking through our records to see the extent of the problem. We were missing a fair bit of cash over a number of weeks. Not only that but books and other kinds of merchandise that we sold. Even with having a suspect, it would take weeks to sort through it all to hand over the evidence to the police and file a claim with our insurance. The whole thing was a nightmare.

I did message Charlie to apologize for the day before. We messaged back and forth a bit but I worried about how my words were coming across. They didn't sound the same and I worried about the damage I'd caused by ignoring him.

"Hey, stranger!" A familiar voice called out when I entered my apartment that evening. A fog of fatigue had settled over me and I just wanted to swallow down some food and go to bed. I needed a decent night's sleep and worried I'd only get that once I'd patched things up with Charlie and I could sleep next to him again.

"Hey, who are you again?" I asked

"Funny," my roommate Xavier said dryly. "I'm sorry I haven't been around much, but things with Carla are great."

"Hey, no worries."

"How's things with you and Charlie?" I must have made some sort of expression. "What happened?"

Xavier and I might not have been really close, but we'd lived together for a couple of years and had a decent friendship. He was pretty open and since he was bisexual, I could talk to him about dating without worry. I quickly explained the last few days and he sat silently for a bit.

"You already know what you need to do, Max."

"I know! But I'm just...worried."

"Probably about nothing and you know that."

"Yeah, you're right but..."

"But, nothing. You need to speak to him and clear the air. First, though, you look wrecked. Get some sleep and speak to him tomorrow.

"I'll call him first thing."

"Good. Listen, I'll try and be around more. Now that you are with Charlie, maybe Carla will come over more."

I laughed. "I can't believe that she ever thought that there was something with us."

He chuckled too. "I know! Love isn't rational, though."

Didn't I know it.

The first thing I did that morning was call Charlie. We were both on shift at Books & Biscuits later so I knew I had to sort things out.

I wondered how long it would take him to answer, or if he'd avoid my call, but he picked up right away like he'd been waiting for my call.

"Max, what's going on?" he asked immediately.

"I'm sorry. I guess I just freaked after the Henry thing."

"It was your idea!" Charlie sounded upset.

"I know! But after I kept thinking about how much more he seemed to be into it with you and that he'd be better for you than me."

"Better? How?"

"Well...he might not have the same hang-ups as me about sex." My voice was small. I hated admitting how vulnerable the whole thing left me feeling.

"Max..." There was silence on the line while Charlie decided what to say. "Henry isn't you. I'm not attracted to him whatsoever. The reaction I had to him was because you were there watching. Watching you and him was hot as fuck, but I didn't think you were going to drop me for him."

"No?"

"No! As for the sex stuff, I honestly don't care if we use condoms for the rest of our lives. We do what works for us. I love what we have."

My heart tripped over the word love. My feelings for Charlie were massive. I was sure that I loved him, but it was too soon to express that. We were too new for that depth of feeling.

"I love it, too. You make me so happy Charlie."

"So this is done? No more avoiding me or my calls?"

"Yeah, I'm sorry. I honestly just got caught up at work and then it was too late."

"Okay, so what's happening at work?"

"It doesn't matter. I'll sort it out."

"Max..."

"It's fine."

"Okay, well I have to go to therapy, but I'll see you later?"

"Yeah, I'm on shift with you, see you later."

We ended the call and I felt marginally better than before but was I concerned I'd stepped in it with Charlie at the end. He'd sounded frustrated.

Chapter Thirty Three

Charlie

Frustration boiled in me at Max and his evasiveness. I hadn't heard from him for more than a couple of texts in days, and then when I tried to help by asking what his problem was, he'd brushed me off.

If we were going to move forward in our relationship, then he had to treat me as an equal partner. I had things to offer in a partnership. I'd worked with a bunch of different people in the clubs, and I knew how to handle staff issues.

Instead, I'd been dismissed.

"Charlie, you can come in now," Evan called into the waiting room of his office.

"Hey, Evan," I said as I took my usual seat. I wasn't about to tell him the Max stuff, so I asked his opinion about selling my last club. All the Max stuff was too fresh in my head and heart, and I didn't want to spew words at Evan because I wasn't sure what I thought or felt about the whole thing. I needed to work through it a little on my own first. Then I'd speak to Evan if Max and I couldn't figure it ourselves.

"You've already made the decision," he said simply.

"Yeah. I'm not going back there. I've started selling my photos. And through Andy's sister, Abby, I've had interest from people wanting headshots."

"Headshots?"

"She works in the theater. She's a costume designer, but some of the actors saw some of my photos that she's shown them, and want me to do their headshots for promotion."

"Is that something that you are interested in?"

"I am, yeah. I'm thinking about doing some night classes at the university to brush up on what I'd already learned and do shoots on the side."

"What about Farmer's Fitness and Books & Biscuits?"

"I'd obviously cut back. I barely work at either, they can manage without me."

"Do you feel okay about that?"

"Yes. I feel like they gave me something the last few weeks. Stability. A reason to leave my mom's house. I'll still work over the summer, but in the fall, I want to start classes."

"That sounds great, Charlie."

I tensed as I approached Books & Biscuits for work. There was just a sense of foreboding. I didn't think that Max and I had cleared the air well enough and it was going to blow up in our faces.

Max was in the office when I went in, pouring over CCTV footage of the store, with pages of notes strewn around him and a frazzled look on his face.

"You okay?" I asked, worried for him.

"Hmm, yeah. It's fine."

Kristen entered the office. "Max, I've got the last of the inventory from Heather." She passed him a tablet.

"Fuck!" He muttered running his hands through his hair. He fiddled with the CCTV controls again and pulled up an image.

"What's going on?" I asked them both, taking in their tense forms.

"We've just found proof that one of the staff is stealing," Max said, disappointed and angry.

"Want me there as backup when you deal with it?"

I could almost see his hackles raise. "I've got it. I don't need you to back me up. I can manage to run my business!" he snapped.

Kristen looked between us and started to interject.

"Right. Okay. Noted." I said simply before leaving the office.

There was a second when I thought about walking out but I was going to be the better person.

"You know he didn't mean to snap," Kristen said soothingly when she joined me behind the coffee counter. She went to place a hand on my back but withdrew it when I moved away. I didn't need coddling.

"I know, but it still hurts." I got to work on the orders that had begun backing up. Max and Kristen needed to train the others to work the machine better. I often got stuck doing it when I was on shift and the repetitive motions got boring. I needed my brain occupied.

Max stayed in the office for a couple of hours. I'd begun to wonder if he was just trying to avoid me.

"I'm sorry, Charlie," he said quietly as I entered the office during my break.

"I don't know what's going on in your head, but you can't speak to me like that and not expect a reaction."

"I know. I'm sorry."

"Figure your shit out, Max."

"I'm trying to apologize!"

"Then do it properly. Do it three hours ago when you said it." My voice had raised to a shout and Max's face was flushed with what could be anger or shame.

"I haven't got time to baby your feelings, Charlie. Go home, it's quiet out there. We'll talk tomorrow when we both have calmed down."

"But…"

"No, Charlie. We're not doing this now. I need you to go home before you make this worse."

"Me?"

"Go home!"

My heart sank to my feet. He was telling me to go. How badly had I fucked this up?

"Max…" I could hear the tears that were welling in my voice.

Max had turned away. He wouldn't look at me. "No, Charlie. Just go home. We need some space."

Chapter Thirty Four

Charlie

This was stupid. Ridiculous and completely idiotic.

Thumping the bottle of vodka on the counter, I took a seat in one of the chairs at the tiny kitchen table and glared into space.

So we had fought. Our first one as a couple and unlikely to be our last. It wasn't as if we were going to break up over what was essentially a stupid fight.

We had wanted to keep work and our relationship separate, but blowing up at each other in front of Kristen was hardly keeping it quiet.

I looked at the bottle again. The now-familiar itch was teasing me.

Did I really want to throw away months of sobriety over something so small? To give up Max over an issue that could be easily handled? So he'd asked me to go home and had spoken to me like I was a child. I was hardly acting like an adult by having a temper tantrum and buying booze. Max had been right to push me away. We'd both needed to calm down.

How did I expect to stay sober if something so small was going to trigger a bender? Because it would be a bender. If I took so much as a sip of that vodka, I wouldn't be stopping until I passed out or the bottle was empty. More than likely, I'd be unconscious after all these months without a drop.

Months and months of hard work would be undone if I gave in right now.

In my head I ran through the exercises I'd been taught in rehab before picking up the bottle and putting it back into the bag.

Instead of berating myself over buying the bottle, I applauded myself for not opening it. For seeing that I was falling into patterns of behavior from before and for having the strength to say no to temptation.

A fight was a normal stressor and I'd fallen back into my usual coping mechanisms. That was fine, but I hadn't taken a drink and that was great.

Andy and Will had gone up to the lake house and I was pet sitting Lucifer, so there was no one here to listen to how much of a big deal this was. Evan would likely answer the phone, but the guy was my therapist and not my sponsor. It wasn't in his job description to take evening calls from his clients. He'd offered time and time again to be my sponsor but I'd declined every time. I was one hundred percent sure that I didn't need one because I knew I had people I could call.

I'd made friends at Books & Biscuits. I had my family, for the most part. There was Henry and his sister, Holly, if I needed someone to talk to. Except none of them were Max.

Max was literally the only person that I should be calling. I needed to apologize for not backing off and giving him the space he clearly had wanted. Then I had to show him that I wasn't just going to fall down at the slightest provocation. I was better than that.

Pulling up Max's contact on my phone, I started a video call. I needed to see his face and search it for any sign that this was too much for him. That I was too much for him.

If I thought for a second that I was harming him in any way, I'd take a step back. His happiness was more important to me than my own.

The call rang for a few seconds before Max picked up and his wary face came into view. I couldn't tell where he was, and the background was too dark to discern anything. It maybe looked like he was in his car but I couldn't see well enough to be sure.

"I'm sorry, Max."

He looked at me in stunned silence for a second. "Why? I shouted at you. I wouldn't discuss something with you and I treated you badly. I've felt like shit all day!" Max looked like he'd cried at some point. His hair was disheveled like he'd been tugging on the white-blond strands.

He needs a haircut, I thought fondly.

"Me too," I replied. My heart hurt with how much I wished we were face to face and not using screens.

"But I really think that having the time apart to calm down was a good idea," he added.

"Maybe it is, but Max, you can't say that you baby me. We need to be equals. If you are struggling with something, you need to know I'm here to help carry the load. You need to talk to me or this won't work out." I spoke plainly. It was something that had carried over from the stuff with Henry. Max didn't open up to me about his feelings a lot. I'd never really noticed it before. He didn't rely on me emotionally.

"I know, but you have to remember I've been on my own for a long time, Charlie. You know what it was like growing up with a mom that medicated herself with booze." Max's face was conflicted like he didn't want to bring up the idea that I had things in common with his mom.

"I know, that night when we fought, you said you didn't want me to turn into her. Bitter, lonely, and drunk." Max looked startled that I remembered that conversation from half a year ago.

I shrugged. "It stayed with me this whole time. You have to realize that I'm not her, Max. I won't give up on you. If you need help, I want to be the one that you turn to." My voice rose with desperation to be understood. "I want to be there for all the good and the bad stuff that will come at us, but you have to let me. You aren't alone anymore, Max. You are my family. Did you know I said that in the hospital? When I asked for you, they said family only and I told them that you were. As far as I was concerned then, you were my ONLY family, except for maybe Matty."

Max laughed through tears. "Charlie, you are my family! I just don't know how to be in one, so you'll have to teach me. I'll probably make more mistakes along the way."

I gave him a smile full of affection. "We all make mistakes. In fact, I made one earlier." He tried to cut me off. "Not at Books. Something else." Fuck! This was hard to get out. "So, I'm sorry. I, uh, also need to be honest. I, um... bought a bottle of vodka."

"What the fuck? Charlie, no!"

"I didn't open it," I protested, trying to back down from going on the defensive. My own actions had put me in this situation, and Max had every right to react the way he did. He'd told me what would happen if I drank again.

Max had turned pale with fear and shame filled me at being the cause of it.

"Look," I said, turning the camera to the still-sealed bottle in its bag. "Unopened and staying that way. I'll give it to one of Will's neighbors or something. I promise that I'm not going to fuck this up. I felt like an idiot the whole walk back here and an even bigger one in the liquor store. Not sure what I was thinking."

"You're at Will's?"

"Yeah, I'm cat-sitting, remember?"

He face-palmed, running his hand slowly down his face. "This week has been a mess, I swear."

"What's going on?"

"I'm sitting outside your apartment block. Have been for half an hour trying to get the courage to come up and apologize."

Laughter burst from me. Relief made me feel giddy. Max and I were quite the pair.

"Text me the address. I'll come over." Max demanded.

"You don't have to," I hedged, I wanted him here more than anything. Lucifer was cute and all, but not as cute as my Max. Didn't snuggle nearly as well, either.

"But I want to. We aren't ending our first argument with us being apart. I want to go to sleep with you holding me close, knowing that we're okay." There was the softness that had been missing in his gaze earlier.

"I want that, too." I was sure that he could hear the honesty in my voice even if he couldn't see it clearly in my eyes. I needed him with me but hadn't wanted to ask him. I didn't want to be a burden. Max had enough going on.

"Okay then, but you need to make us some food because my stomach was in knots earlier and I haven't been able to even think about eating."

"I can do that." I smiled at him. "I'll raid Andy's kitchen."

"Andy's, not Will's?"

"Have you ever had Will's cooking?"

"Uh...no? Yeah, no."

I laughed again, overjoyed at how quickly we'd gotten over this bump. "Be glad of that. He's lethal in the kitchen." I changed the subject. "Can you stay over?" The words were a rare show of vulnerability from me and almost stuck in my throat.

"Already planned on it. See you soon." Max ended the call with a shy smile and a weight lifted from my chest. If he could look at me like that, then we would be fine.

Raiding the cabinets quickly for a meal idea for us yielded an easy-to-make rice dinner since there weren't many gluten-free options for Max. Andy kept things pretty well stocked otherwise and I was impressed at the equipment he'd brought to the apartment. Most of it had to be from when he lived alone. I knew he'd learned to cook with his mom working so much when he and Abby were kids.

I'd learned out of boredom. There had been a boyfriend just after I left college that was in culinary school, and he'd taught me some basic things. After we'd broken up, I'd still messed around in the kitchen some. I found it relaxing.

Recently I hadn't had much of an opportunity to cook since Mom had ruled over her kitchen, and when I was with Max we ate a lot of takeout.

The food was ready when the front desk called to say Max had arrived. After giving permission, I looked for Lucifer and shut him in Will's room before leaving the door ajar for Max to come right in.

He found me in the kitchen, plating up our food. Coming up behind me and wrapping his arms around me, his head resting on my back just below my shoulders. I sank into the feeling for a second, just enjoying the feeling of us being close.

Squeezing and then patting his hands as a signal to move back, I worked on grabbing the silverware and getting glasses for water. "Can you grab the plates and I'll get the rest?"

"Sure, do you want to eat in here or the dining room?"

"Wherever you like. I need to let Lucifer out of Will's room."

"I can do that."

"It's the only door that's closed."

We talked while we ate, and the scene was domestic and comfortable. We'd done this kind of thing a hundred times before, but it was different now. The changes were clear in the warmth of Max's gaze and his foot against mine under the table like we had to be touching even in such a small way.

Lucifer, still in a snit with me, had decided to sit in the chair next to Max so he could be petted and loved on.

When Andy had sent pictures of Lucifer in the family group chat, I couldn't believe that Will had gotten the cat for Andy, but the beast was cute. When it wasn't sulking, anyway.

Once we'd eaten and cleaned up the kitchen, we settled on the sofa, another thing from Andy's old place, to stream something. Max loved true-life stories and documentaries so it was easy enough to find something to watch.

Snuggled up with Max might have been my favorite place to be. The earlier argument was forgiven if not entirely forgotten; we just needed to communicate better without getting upset.

Although things between us were back to normal by the time we decided to go to bed, by unspoken agreement there wasn't anything other than lazy kisses between us before we drifted to sleep with me spooning Max.

The emotional closeness was all that was necessary and far more important to me than just getting off.

It rocked me to my core that I now had something so much more valuable to me than sex. I'd give up sex, give up anything, for nights just holding him close.

Chapter Thirty Five

Max

Charlie and I hadn't been asleep long when I heard the sound of the door opening and Lucifer yowling.

"Shh, Lucifer, here puss." An unknown voice spoke.

I went to shake Charlie only to see that he was raised up trying to listen.

"Who is it?" I whispered.

"No idea," Charlie said in a low voice, more a rumble than actual words.

Whoever it was wandered into the kitchen and ran the faucet, opening cabinets before finding what they were looking for.

"Could it be Andy or Will back?" I asked quietly.

"No, they aren't back for another couple of days."

"Unless they came back early?"

"We'd recognize their voices." Charlie pointed out. Then he moved to the nightstand and picked up his phone. "Fuck, it's dead. I'm going to go look. Stay here." He rose from the bed, throwing on a t-shirt to cover his bare chest. Both of us had slept just in our underwear.

"What? No! I'm coming with you." I quickly got out of bed picking up my discarded shirt as Charlie waited for me at the door.

We crept along the hall towards the living space and quietly towards the kitchen where there was the sound of someone singing to themselves.

Red hair glinted in the low lights under the cabinets as Pete turned, startled, and dropped the glass he was holding.

"Holy fuck!" he screamed.

The glass shattering had Lucifer darting under the sofa and a whole litany of curses coming from Pete.

"What the hell? Why are you here?" Charlie demanded, frowning at Pete as the other man stood surrounded by glass.

Pete swayed slightly and I noticed that his blue-gray eyes were glassy. "Didn't Andy call?"

"Phone's dead," Charlie muttered as he squatted and started picking up the glass.

I stooped to help, but Charlie stopped me. "Go check on Lucifer, don't let him come through until this is cleaned up."

Nodding, I searched until I found the poor animal looking balefully at me from where he had huddled.

"It's okay baby, come here." I got on my hands and knees to try and tempt him out with pats. The furry beast was a sucker for some loving and soon enough I'd tempted him into my arms.

Lucifer was calm enough by the time Charlie and Pete exited the kitchen that he stayed in my arms, not picking up on the tension between the two as Charlie stalked by.

"I'll be back in a second," he said tersely. I didn't take offense, knowing I wasn't the cause of Charlie's mood.

Pete slumped into a recliner close to the sofa and I could see a small smirk on his pretty face. His features were delicate in an angular face, with sharp cheekbones. I wondered how he had fared in the military looking like he did, almost delicate. Pete had served with Henry for years, but I didn't know what role he'd played in their squad.

He yawned and stretched, his sweater raising and showing a pale, firm abdomen. He was watching me as much as I was watching him. It was distinctly uncomfortable since I didn't know what to say. We'd never actually met before, and here Pete was crashing Andy's place while Andy was out of town.

A stale smell of alcohol surrounded Pete and his clothes were creased like he'd fallen asleep in them. At the apartment door was a beaten-up backpack that probably contained Pete's other clothes. He was clearly here to stay.

We sat in silence for a few minutes, and if Lucifer hadn't been comfortable, I would have retreated to the bedroom to hide.

Charlie returned, his expression carefully blank. "Andy says that he's sorry he didn't tell you that he couldn't reach me. My phone had died. He also says to take his and Will's room, the sheets are fresh." He looked at me. "Could I speak to you for a minute?"

I moved Lucifer higher into my arms and stood slowly. I paused at the recliner and tried to give the cat to Pete, but he howled and jumped down running away.

"Obviously not a fan," Pete drawled. He looked between me and Charlie. "Not the only one, either."

Charlie and I exchanged a look but didn't contradict him. Taking my hand, he pulled me into the bedroom we'd been sleeping in, shooting Pete a dirty look over his shoulder that he likely missed. Pete was fully reclined in the chair, his head back.

"I called Henry too since I don't want either of us to stay here with Pete. He reeks of booze and I just don't like the guy."

"Me neither. Lucifer loves everyone and is scared of Pete. What do we do about him?"

"Andy and Will are cutting short their trip. They'll be home this afternoon. I'll text them and say how Lucifer is; maybe they will leave earlier."

"Good plan. I feel bad about tonight, but I don't want to stay here with Pete." I twisted my hands together, feeling anxious about the welfare of the poor cat. He'd been at a shelter for months and this was his home. It wasn't fair for him to be scared.

"No, me neither." Charlie gave me a commiserating look. "We can ask Henry to stay and keep an eye on the cat if you want?"

"Unless we send Pete to Henry's?"

"Do you really want Pete in my room? Or Henry for that matter?" He raised an eyebrow at me.

"Fair point."

Charlie's phone buzzed with a call.

"It's Henry," he said, answering the call. "Hey, are you here? I'll go buzz you up. Listen, would you mind staying here for Lucifer? He's terrified of Pete."

I could hear Henry's rumbling laugh. "Cats just hate Pete. I can stay."

"Great," Charlie pulled his phone from his ear and asked, "Would you mind changing the sheets for Henry, I'll come help in a sec."

"Sure, no problem. Where?" Charlie understood my question easily.

"Hall closet. Back soon." Charlie lifted the phone again as he headed toward the door.

I was just pulling the sheets off the bed when I heard Pete's angry voice. "What's he doing here?" Moving into the hall, I saw Charlie standing between the two former friends talking quietly to them both.

"Andy said he was worried about you and Henry was able to come stay with you and keep an eye on Lucifer, since you're clearly not a cat person. Max and I are going to head out."

"No, I'll go," Pete insisted and he went to pick up his bag.

"Not trying to be funny, but where are you going to go? Andy said you didn't have anywhere else until you get an apartment," Charlie fired back.

Henry froze at that. "I thought you were with that guy, what's his name?"

"Derek. But that's over since I caught him fucking someone else." Pete bit out.

A tiny tendril of sympathy wove through me and then I remembered how he'd treated Henry and I dismissed it. Then I felt guilty because no one deserved to be cheated on. God, I was a mess.

The trio moved to the kitchen and I went back into the spare room we'd been sharing to finish changing the bedding. Lucifer was lying in a puddle of the sheets looking very smug. So I joined him on the bed, allowing him to rub against my face and purr in my ear. I was going to have to get myself a cat. Maybe one day, if things with Charlie went well, we could do that together.

Chapter Thirty Six

Charlie

It was the early hours of the morning before Max and I returned to my apartment. We could have gone to his place, but Xavier was home with Carla and I wanted some alone time with my man.

He'd been half asleep, snuggled with Lucifer when I'd gone to help him with the sheets and he'd sleepily suggested we get a cat one day, too.

The idea of having that, a home with a pet, that security, burned in me. I wanted that so badly and just needed Max to have the confidence in our relationship that I did. There wasn't a thing about him that I didn't love, though we were a while away from, "I love you's."

Max needed to feel more secure first, so once we got into my room I went about showing him how I felt.

It started with soft kisses and touches as I stripped him of his clothes and laid him out on the bed. His hands reached for my clothes but I pinned his hands above his head.

"This is just for you, just enjoy. Keep your hands there."

Max reached up for the spindles of the bed frame and wrapped his fingers around them tightly.

"We're going to play a game," I told him, teasing my tongue over a pale pink nipple, causing it to harden. "You are going to tell me each thought you had that made you think this wouldn't work." Max shivered under me as I sucked the hardened bud and then laved my tongue over it. "Then, I'm going to show you that they don't matter, that I'm in this a hundred percent. Okay?"

I kissed over to the other nipple and began the same treatment before pulling away. "I need words, Max."

His hands flexed around the wooden frame before he said, "Yes," in a breathy voice. His cock was hard against my fabric-covered leg. I was still in the sweats I'd thrown on earlier.

"Good." I stretched up to grab supplies off of the nightstand then took off my t-shirt.

Heat filled Max's eyes as his gaze traced my chest. The approval was a balm to soothe the hurt from that afternoon.

I came down over him, skin meeting his chest, causing him to gasp. I took his mouth in a deep kiss, needing a hit of the taste of him.

We broke apart and I moved down his body, worshiping every inch apart from his straining wet tipped cock.

"Words, Max." I reminded him.

"I, uh…" He started haltingly. "I worry that I'll never get over my hate of cum. That because I hate the taste, you'll get sick of blow jobs with condoms on." He shuddered and I ran my fingers over his straining length.

"Go on," I prompted as I opened the foil and rolled the condom over his dick.

"I'm scared that you'll think I'm selfish if you can blow me without a condom and I won't do the same to you when we're tested."

The thought rattled around in my head as I took him into my throat, causing him to jerk up from the mattress and let go of the frame. Was it a big deal to me? Not really, it was something I could live with if it bothered him so badly.

I rewarded his honesty and openness with several hard sucks, taking him to the root each time and running my lips over the frenulum as he eased out again, making him buck and groan out my name.

Pulling off his cock, I ran my hands over his thighs so I could look into those gorgeous blue eyes. "I really don't think that will bother me, but I promise to say if it does. I like things as they are and your blowjobs are amazing."

"I can try to swallow," Max blurted.

I wrapped a hand around him and stroked again as I moved up to kiss him, to give him comfort without words that I loved what we did together.

Max pulled away from the kiss, fear filling his expression, tears on the brink of falling. "I'm worried that you're going to be disappointed with our sex life. That I'm too vanilla for you, but I just can't bear the taste and the feel of cum inside me. I might manage to rim you, but I don't know how I feel about it being done to me. I'm terrified you'll give up on me because I have so many hang-ups."

"Oh, baby." I wrapped my arms around him and held him to me tightly as I processed his words. My body covered his and I spoke into his neck between kisses. "I don't need you to swallow me down or to fill you up to enjoy what we do. You give me so much pleasure with just kisses. If you never wanted sex again, I'd manage." I tried to joke. "I'd just get reacquainted with my hand."

I felt his little chuckle. "Really?"

"Sure, babe, we have to do what works for us." I sat up a little so we were eye to eye. "If that's condoms, wipes, and gloves until we can't get it up anymore, then so be it. The flavored ones aren't bad."

He laughed again and squeezed me close. "You're the best boyfriend I've ever had."

"Not all that hard," I teased.

He laughed again. "I'm not all that hard now either." He indicated towards his softened cock.

I removed and discarded the condom on his limp member. "Shame, I had such plans for you." I kissed him deeply, my hands roaming his body and his cock began to thicken once more against my hip.

Reaching for the lube and another couple of foil packets, I shed my sweats and stroked him to full hardness before sheathing him again. I covered myself, also preferring not to get spunk everywhere, and picked up the lube.

I kissed him as I worked myself open, panting and grunting into his mouth as I stretched enough to accommodate his girth.

Max's cock wasn't long but had plenty of girth so I needed three fingers before I could even think of taking him inside me.

He'd given up holding onto the bed and his hands roamed and teased as our kisses became more frantic.

He pulled away from my mouth, lips moving over my neck as he tried to see what my hand was doing. "Damn that's hot, I can't wait to be inside you."

Deciding I couldn't wait much longer I removed my fingers, smearing the lube there onto his shaft then wiping my fingers with a wet wipe. I pushed him onto his back and climbed on top of him, positioning his cock at my hole and slowly inching him inside.

We groaned in unison as my ass met his thighs and I began to ride him slowly. I impaled myself on him over and over, working up a sweat, thighs burning as I moved. I couldn't get enough of the feeling, the way that Max looked at me as if in awe that we were doing this.

He reached his hands around to my ass, running a finger over my rim, feeling his cock move in and out of me. "Fuck that's hot. You're so tight around me. I wish I could see my dick fuck into you." He sounded wrecked.

"There's a mirror over there," I said looking behind me. "Raise yourself up and you can see it."

Max raised his head, bunching all the pillows under his shoulders to see. Spotting the mirror on the closet door at the perfect angle to catch the action on the bed he groaned. He planted his feet and thrust up as he watched, panting. "Jesus, that's hot."

Our bodies moved together as he watched us in the mirror and I concentrated on him. We gasped and moaned, the room filled with the sounds as sweat dripped from us. All I could feel was Max, this deep connection and feeling of rightness.

I lost all sense of time as I reveled in the feeling of Max's cock, hard and stretching me just perfectly. His hand moved over my length, adding that twist at the top that made me gasp.

I felt that tell-tale tingle rapidly approaching. "I'm coming," my words strangled as my orgasm stole all my senses.

"Charlie," Max groaned in my ear as he pulled me against him and pumped his hips deep into me, once, twice, before stilling.

I let him take my weight for a couple of seconds before moving slightly to the side.

Max kissed my lips, the tip of my nose, and then my forehead. My eyes closed at the adoration in the action.

Max carefully pulled out of me, grabbed some tissues, and disposed of the condoms carefully before nuzzling into my arms.

"Shower?"

"Hmm...in a minute."

We basked in the afterglow before washing each other gently in the shower, trading kisses the whole time. The act felt important. Full of care and something I'd never had before. Something I'd never give up.

As I pulled him into my arms later, I realized I was in love with Max, and what he called his hang-ups were just quirks that didn't bother me at all. He wouldn't be my Max without them.

Chapter Thirty Seven

Max

Charlie looked worried as he walked up to Books & Biscuits. I caught sight of him walking in quickly, a folder under his arm, as I set out the sandwich board with today's specials outside the café.

Taking a minute to look at him before he noticed me, I cataloged the changes in him over the last few months. He'd filled out with eating better and his training sessions in the gym. I could see the benefits of his therapy with Evan in the way he walked tall, no longer weighted down with shame over his past.

While we hadn't shared those three little words, I would soon. I couldn't hide my feelings anymore. I'd thought I'd been in love with him before rehab, all those years with him as my best friend, but that love paled in comparison to what I felt now. My love for him had grown and changed as he had. It was deeper now, entrenched in the knowledge that we could get through anything together and keep our friendship intact. Now that I knew what it was like to be inside him, to have him accept all my quirks, I couldn't imagine being with anyone else. I also knew to my bones that my feelings were returned. There was no fear of rejection. He needed me just as much as I needed him.

Charlie caught sight of me then, a grin lighting up his handsome face. I could stare at him for hours, and I probably had over the last few weeks, since that night at

Andy and Will's place. As he drew closer, I could see the affection in his eyes and it settled that little bit of doubt that always lingered. A product of constantly being pushed aside by my mom.

He pulled me into a tight hug and leaned back enough to press a kiss to my lips in full view of everyone in the café and those walking the streets.

There came a whoop from inside that I was pretty sure was made by Kristen and the customers laughed.

Charlie grinned before sobering. "There's something I have to show you. I don't want you to worry, I have a plan. Well, if you agree anyway."

With no idea what was going on, or if I was going to like his plan, I suggested that we head into the office and chat so that nothing was overheard.

There must have been something in our expressions as we crossed the café because nothing was said by anyone inside and their eyes followed us carefully.

In the tiny office, there was only room for a couple of file cabinets, a battered old desk, and a few chairs. Automatically I sank into the large faux leather computer chair and Charlie took an armchair on the opposite side. "What's going on?"

"First of all. My test results came back and they are clear, but that doesn't mean I want to change anything about how we have sex. Let's just play it by ear, okay?"

I nodded. "I got mine back too and same. It's a relief that you don't want to change anything because I'm not ready."

"Probably for the best, it might be a stressful few months soon."

"What d'you mean?" I asked, starting to get worried.

"That's my other piece of news. Your building, the café, and everything are being sold."

It was probably just as well that I was sitting because I felt weak in the knees with that bombshell, my mouth gaping as I took it in. My mind whirred with questions and I didn't know where to start.

"Max!" Charlie's words didn't register, though I was certain he'd been speaking the whole time as my brain tried to process.

"Max, listen. I have it all handled." He waited until I met my eyes before carrying on. "I've been looking to buy some property for a while. I need to move out of Henry's. I love the guy but it's awkward with us all together and we all knew it was short-term." I went to interject because I knew that Henry was his only other friend and I didn't want to make things weird.

Charlie stopped me, putting up a hand. "I've been putting off buying since there hasn't been anything that caught my interest." Checking I was still with him and getting a nod in return he continued, "I think I should buy the building."

"What? There's no way you can afford that. I know you made a decent profit from the clubs but..."

Charlie cut me off. "I did, and I've also sold the last club." He gave me a look to stop me from speaking. "I've been holding onto it as some sort of symbol that I can make successful things as if a year down the line I'll manage to go back to it. There's no chance of that. I'm always going to be in recovery.

"With the sale of that club and the money from the other clubs, I can manage to buy the whole building. That means the café, bookshop, and two apartments above."

He started to look hesitant as if I wouldn't like the next part of his grand scheme. "Then I thought I could make one part a photography studio and the other part an apartment to live in."

"That sounds amazing Charlie! I love the idea of the studio, but what about Books & Biscuits?"

"Well, you'd just pay rent until we pay off a loan to do some renovations that are needed to make the apartment a home for us."

We.

Us.

Did that mean?

"Charlie, are you asking me to move in with you?"

"You noticed that, huh?" He gave me an almost shy grin. "Yes. I want us to live together. I'd be happy to wake up to you anywhere, but doing this, buying the building for us, keeps your business safe and allows me to start mine knowing you are nearby if I need you. What do you think?"

"Have you run the numbers? What does Alex think?"

Rolling his eyes he said, "Of course, I've run them. I worked in finance before, remember? I've seen your accounts and you're doing pretty good. There's room for improvement of course, but maybe we could freshen up the place or play around with the layout when we own it."

"You keep saying we." I point out, "But you'd be paying for this. It'd be your building."

"Ours. Your name goes on it, too. The money you pay for rent will pay the loan and will be considered as your investment. I want this to be a partnership."

"But I don't bring anything to the table here," I protested, worry filling me.

"Max, you've built up a business from scratch and kept it running successfully for nearly four years now. You've got the experience that I need about building a business from scratch. In the clubs, I had managers that had done it all before. They were established, all I had to do was improve them."

I didn't want him to downplay his success, he'd done great things with his clubs and it had suited him at the time. I wanted to say something but he carried on, giving me reason after reason why he felt that this would work.

"You've had to deal with staff in a way that I've never had to do. I'm a long way off from needing some help in the studio but you know how to market yourself. I wish you wouldn't downplay what you have to offer." He reached for my hand. "I have all this money and I need somewhere long-term to live. I can't live with Henry forever. What better place is there than an apartment with the man I love and my best friend? Especially if it helps you."

"You love me, huh?" I grinned at the easy way that he'd admitted his feelings while I got up and went over to his chair and clambered into his lap. I pressed a kiss to his lips and thanked the universe for giving me such a good man to love. I ran my fingers through his hair and he leaned into the touch.

"You know I do. I know you love me, too. It's in everything you've done for me. I just didn't see it before." he said quietly as we basked in this precious moment.

He squeezed my hand before pulling it back to rifle through the binder. "Unfortunately, we are in a time crunch. We have to decide today." He put the folder down again, giving me a hug and another kiss.

"So you're serious about this?" I asked as I returned to my chair and sat back, thinking about the possibilities. A clear mental picture forming. "And Alex thinks it's a good idea?"

"Alex thinks it's a solid investment but thinks we need a prenup."

We both make a face of disgust at the idea of marriage.

"I don't want to get married," I said firmly. "That might change, but I don't right now. I love you, Charlie, so much, and I'm starting to picture what you want to build. I have to admit, it's gorgeous. Us living above the bookstore. Your studio above the café." Pausing, I thought my words through. "I don't think that we need to be married for that though. Is there some sort of contract that we can sign for if things go wrong?"

Charlie laughed and drew out a thinner folder from the binder he had left on the desk between us. "We're on the same page. I knew we would be. This is what Alex suggests. This," he passed me the document, "is for if we don't marry and have a prenup. Basically, it's a document stating that you'd be my tenant and have a share in the ownership of the building. Books & Biscuits would operate as yours and the rest as mine but we really need to go to a lawyer to go through all the finer details. I just need your go-ahead so we can put in an offer. Since you're the only tenant just now, we get the first refusal. You just have to acknowledge that I'm acting for you."

This was our defining moment. I could feel it. If I said no to this, to something he clearly wanted, then it would show a lack of faith in him. He'd clearly done his research and he was so excited by the prospect of us moving forward with it. His eyes were lit with infectious joy and I knew I'd agree to anything to never see that dim because of me.

"Make the call. Let's do this."

Chapter Thirty Eight

Charlie

The summer had seemed to almost vanish in a blink. Max and I had been ludicrously busy with all the renovations that were needed to the building.

After consulting with some of our friends, we'd agreed that my photography studio needed an elevator like the one at Farmer's Fitness so that it was inclusive of disabled people.

Since Max and I had discussed fostering down the line, we decided an elevator up to our apartment above the bookstore was also a good idea.

The plans had been approved quickly, much like the sale, so we arranged for work to start as soon as it could.

Unfortunately, we'd had to close the café for a couple of days with the dust from the bookstore's extension creating havoc and mess everywhere.

The staff had appreciated a few days off, some still dealing with the revelation that Finn, someone hired at the same time as me, had been stealing from them as well as Max's business. The police had been involved given the amount of cash and stock missing, but Finn had vanished, likely tipped off by one of the other staff that he'd been found out.

"Max? You back here?" I called as I moved to the newly finished staff area and separate office at the back of the building. I'd come through the bookstore, the shelves being put together by the staff in preparation for the books part of Books & Biscuits reopening the next day.

"Yeah," came his distracted-sounding voice. All the upheaval was wearing on him. Some of our apartment was finished enough to live in while we did the rest of the work over time, but we had thought about waiting until we got back from our vacation before we moved in together. I'd had a change of heart about that. Max needed looking after and would take on too much if someone didn't stop him.

I entered the office, catching sight of Max bent over, looking through invoices strewn all over his desk. His hair was tousled but not in that sexy, just got fucked kind of way, but as if he'd been pulling on the strands.

"What's wrong?" I asked coming up behind him.

He startled and dropped the papers he'd been rifling through.

"Holy fuck!" He pressed a hand over his heart. "We need to put a bell on you!"

I laughed but sobered at the strain around his eyes and in the twist of his mouth.

"Come sit down and tell me what's up."

He obliged me, not by sinking into his new desk chair, but by clambering into my lap and nuzzling into my neck.

"There's so much to do and there's so much mess!" he wailed into my skin.

I could feel the tension in his body leech away as he cried against me as if just talking about his problems was helping.

"There's so much to do and it's so expensive!" he continued.

My man had reached his breaking point with the whole thing.

"Do we need to be here just now?" I asked softly, smoothing his hair and rubbing his back.

He shook his head. "No, Kris is here and she told me to go home, but there's so much work that still needs to be done."

"Does it absolutely need to be finished today? The staff won't have anything to do but restock books tomorrow and make some coffees." I stroked his hair. "That reminds me, I moved the machine. Denver helped. That thing is a beast of a thing to lift."

"Thanks, Charlie."

I pressed a kiss to his head, the white-blond strands soft against my lips.

"Come on, I want to show you something."

He didn't hesitate but his movements were sluggish. He'd been working all kinds of hours trying to organize everything. I led him out of the office, out the shiny new staff entrance at the back of the building, trying to avoid any of the staff that were milling about, and along to the entrance to our apartment.

"What are we doing here?" Max was adorably confused.

"It's finished, for the most part. The top floor can wait, but we can't. I had them finish the kitchen and bathrooms so that we can move in."

"But I thought we were waiting until after we got back from Mexico?"

"That's a few weeks away. I want to live with you now."

Max smiled. "I want to live with you, too."

"Good, because I had Henry help me take some of our things from my apartment. My old apartment."

"Is Henry going to be okay with you leaving early?" Max asked, his voice filled with concern for our friend.

"I've paid up until after my brother's wedding, not that he needed me for rent, and I've also still got some stuff there. We don't have much in the way of furniture yet, and I dunno about you, but I was sick of the back and forth between places."

"I am too, but I was trying to put the business first..." He sounded conflicted.

"Well, we have to put ourselves first sometimes and now is one of those times. So, this is how it's going to go. We're going upstairs, in the elevator since it's on, and having a quick look around. Then we are having a nap," I told him firmly.

"A nap?" He raised a brow at me.

"You are exhausted. So yes, a nap. Then maybe a blow-job. We can check on everyone after."

He leaned into me, dead on his feet. "That sounds great, actually."

I unlocked the door to the lower lobby of our building. Stairs went up on the left to another vestibule. It led to a hallway that connected our apartment and my studio. In front of us was the elevator that I'd been so glad Henry had suggested getting put in earlier. I'd been so grateful not to have to carry boxes and boxes of my belongings up the stairs. Max had a box of his own of things he'd left at Henry's so at least he had some clothes to wear after our nap.

The elevator had been expensive, but since it connected to my studio too, it was worth the investment long term.

We ascended fairly quickly and I led Max to another door, our main door, and unlocked it, Max having found some energy in his excitement to see the place livable.

We'd had the place taken down to the studs and reorganized the layout, giving us a spacious open plan kitchen and dining area. A TV room was in the center and our master bedroom was also on this floor. The whole third floor was for kids, or if the plan didn't work out, we'd find some other use for the space.

Max and I looked around quickly. We still had a lot of things to buy, but we could order takeout and eat it in bed. I'd order after we slept.

The bedroom was finished aside from needing dressers and the rest of Max's things, and a few things I had at Mom's or Henry's.

Mom had snuck in and made up the bed for us, knowing that I wanted to spend the night in our new home. She'd been pretty great with helping with the renovation plans, giving us decorating advice. We'd reached a nice and steady point in our relationship, but I worried about her coping with Matty so far away at college.

"C'mon, let's shower before we nap," I suggested to Max and I directed him to our en suite bathroom.

Max gasped as he entered the room. "It's more than I dreamt of!" he exclaimed as he took in the large room.

"Here," I led him to a door, "a little privacy in case one of us is in the shower," I said, indicating the toilet.

Max bit his bottom lip worriedly and I pressed a finger against it to free it. "What's wrong?"

"It just…" he began, "can we really afford all this? Two rainfall showerheads, the open shower, the bench? It's a lot, Charlie."

"I know, but I think we deserve it, don't you? You work so hard and I want to give you this. I'd give you the world if you wanted it."

He melted against me, wrapping his arms around my middle. "I know and I love you so much for it. I'm just tired and not thinking straight. If I had more energy I'd be inspecting every inch of the place. I can't believe this is our home!"

"There's still work to be done on it, but I couldn't wait any longer to live with you," I told him as I helped Max remove his clothes, piling them in the corner to be dealt with later. His phone was chucked onto the bed where it disappeared among the pile of pillows that adorned it. Mom may have gone overboard with the bedding.

Max leaned into me, pulling my head down so my lips could meet his. The kiss started sweet, an outpouring of emotion, but I stopped it before it could deepen.

"Just a shower until you have a nap. You're dead on your feet," I told him firmly.

After washing Max gently, I wrapped myself in a towel before gently and carefully drying him and helping him into some loose pajama pants.

I drew back the blankets and ushered him in, crawling in behind him. I fumbled for my phone, setting an alarm since there was no way we'd wake up until the next morning otherwise, then I drew Max into me, curled myself around him, and let him sleep.

The alarm vibrated next to my hand, not rousing Max, who was still sleeping soundly. I didn't want him to sleep too much in case he wouldn't be able to sleep later that evening, so I started stroking my fingers up and down his arm and whispering his name in his ear.

He began to wriggle at the ticklish sensation and his lips stretched into a smile, though his eyes remained closed.

"Time to wake up, sweetheart. I promised you food, remember?" I cooed into his ear.

His grin widened. "And a blow-job," he muttered, his voice hoarse from sleep.

"Hmm, can't forget that now," I said as I made my way down his body, pressing my lips to the skin of his lower abdomen as I pulled the pants he was wearing down.

Max wasn't fully hard, but I licked and teased him to full hardness while fondling his balls. I loved being able to do this without a barrier now. It wasn't so much a lack of trust in me that had Max insistent on them, I knew that, but handing him my clear results had certainly helped him relax a little. There were things he still didn't like and I was okay with that. I'd meant what I'd said, we had to do what worked for us.

Once he was fully erect, I went to town, licking and sucking him hard. This was going to be quick, something to take the edge off since we'd been too tired for sex the last couple of days.

I took him into the back of my throat and swallowed around him, pulling back so only the tip was in my mouth and swirled my tongue around it, then speared my tongue into the slit, reveling in the taste of precum.

Max moaned and gasped, letting out, "Oh, please," when he hit the back of my throat again. His hips jerked and he writhed as he tried not to push himself too deep. I gagged a couple of times, unprepared, and he tried to pull away but I laid a hand on his hip to keep him in place, enjoying the weight and feel of him in my mouth a little longer.

Pulling off him, I moved down and sucked on his balls. He groaned before I deep-throated him again, resisting the urge to play with him longer.

"Close!" he cried out as I increased the intensity of my sucking and he trembled as he shot his load onto my tongue. I swallowed it down and licked him clean as he whimpered.

Crawling up the bed again, I wrapped him in my arms, mindful not to kiss him just yet. He hated the taste of cum and now that we were going without condoms, I could suck him off without a barrier, but that left an aftertaste he couldn't deal with. I didn't care that he would suck me until I was close and pull off, or would use a condom if we had one in hand. Everything about our sex life was perfect because it was ours.

Since we'd admitted the depth of our feelings, saying those three words, everything had gotten better, deeper between us. That connection that had always been there was built on a solid foundation of friendship and had morphed into something incredible, indescribable. I could feel Max's love for me in every look and gesture. He was getting better about leaning on me and realizing when he needed help, but ingrained habits were hard to break. I just had to trust that he loved me and needed me.

Having my person rely on me made it easier to focus on the important things in my life. My book on my time in rehab was being published in a few weeks. I had bookings for photography sessions and the pictures that I'd printed were selling well. Once the studio was open properly, I'd cut out working at Farmer's Fitness. Henry had Pete to help out if needed since they were working on their friendship. The jury was still out on whether Pete deserved a second chance at calling Henry his best friend.

My thoughts wandered as I held Max and soaked in his afterglow. Seeing his pleasure was more than enough for me.

Max let out a contented sigh and stretched, turning towards me. "Your turn?"

"No, sweetheart, I need to feed you. Let's order some food."

"You sure? I can..."

"I'm sure. I just wanted to do that for you."

"You're too good to me."

He looked at me, that special expression only reserved for and given to me. One full of love.

"Not possible," I said simply and pressed a kiss to his nose.

Chapter Thirty Nine

Max

A week after the bookstore reopened, we were able to reopen the café, unveiling the extended space and the more expanded menu. I'd had to recruit a couple of cooks and kitchen staff, but with Charlie's projections, I knew that it would be worth it long term.

There was a grand re-opening with our friends, Charlie's family, and all the staff there to have a look around the new and improved Books & Biscuits. I'd almost worried myself sick with nerves over their responses but everyone had loved the extra room and all the little touches we had added to the place.

It had been tempting to change the name, to start this new era fresh, but I knew that our customers would still use the old name and rebranding was expensive. Plus, I wanted to continue to honor my friend, Eddie. We'd even squeezed in some tartan prints and some artwork of Scotland since he'd been so proud of his homeland.

Managing to get the renovations done in time for our trip away had taken the mental load off. I didn't just want to reopen and ditch the staff since I knew that we could be busier than normal with the locals wanting to take a peek at something new, or newer, at least.

I'd been right about that, but towards the end of a couple of weeks, the frantic pace had slowed some and we had a few more staff members, so I felt more confident about leaving them for a few days.

Charlie had given Kristen and Rachele the use of his family's beach house for a long weekend so that they could have a well-deserved break.

Selfishly, I wanted Kristen rested and fresh for when we went away since she would be in charge. I'd given her the promotion to manager that she so rightly deserved, making Heather assistant manager and in charge of the bookstore. I knew my business was in good hands with them and that we were building a great team.

They returned practically glowing with health and happiness. Kristen wrapped me in a hug. "You're the best," she said. "Thank you, we really needed that break."

I couldn't take all the credit. "Charlie's idea, I just made sure that you were covered."

Kristen went to hug Charlie next, surprising him and making him blush.

A few days before we were due to leave, I was in my new office sorting invoices when my phone rang with a strange number. Unsure who it could be and anxious it might be important, I answered the call.

"Hello?"

"Hey, Max," came a slightly familiar voice, "It's Andy, Will's fiancé."

"Oh hey..." It was strange to be getting a call from him.

"Look, I know this is out of the blue, but Will is taking me on a surprise vacation in a few days and I was wondering if you could look after Lucifer for me? He really likes you and Charlie."

My heart warmed with pride at being asked but fell when I realized I'd have to say no. "Oh, I'm sorry, Andy, but Charlie is taking me away for a couple of days, too. We need the break after all the renovations." I hated to lie to him but I'd been sworn to secrecy over the wedding. We all knew that Will's "last minute" vacation was probably going to be when they tied the knot.

Since I was the worst liar ever, Charlie and I had been avoiding the family in case I put my foot in it and told Andy what was in store. It had been fairly easy since we'd been caught up with everything going on with the business. I'd only had to hold it together during the re-opening since half of Andy and Will's office had turned up.

"Shoot!" Andy's voice brought me back to the conversation. "Never mind. I'm sure I'll find someone for him. I just don't want to put him in a cattery, y'know."

I nodded though he couldn't see me. "Yeah. He's a sweet cat." I wanted one of my own but things needed to settle down before I broached that subject with Charlie. "Sorry, Andy."

"It's okay. You and Charlie need a break, too. You've had so much going on this summer. It's only a few weeks before the book launch isn't it?"

"Hmm?" My mind was still thinking over Andy's cat problem. Then I had a sudden thought. "What about your neighbor?"

"Mr. Thomas?" Andy sounded confused.

"Yeah, doesn't he sometimes check on him during the day? He might look after him for you. He's in the building, so he wouldn't have to go far," I suggested.

"That's a great idea! Thanks, Max. Genius. I'll go ask!"

Andy said a quick goodbye and hung up, leaving me to pack for our trip, to his and Will's wedding.

Chapter Forty

Charlie

I'd promised to take Max to the beach, so I had to hope that the beach in Mexico was a good substitute for a trip to my family's beach house.

The resort that Will had chosen for his and Andy's wedding was stunning. A long stretch of exclusive beach and a massive building with all that we needed in one place. Separate honeymoon cabins dotted the areas surrounding the main building

We arrived ahead of the grooms by a couple of hours so we could set everything up for the surprise and re-proposal. Our bags were whisked away to our rooms and we were caught up in hurricane Alice, as my mom tried to organize us all for the arrival of the happy couple.

"Charlie?" My eldest brother, Alex, asked as he approached us. "Could we talk later?"

"Uh, sure," I hedged. Alex had been acting weird since I'd gone to him for advice about investing in the building that housed Books & Biscuits. There had been several "missed" calls, and I'd watched them ring. He didn't know that. A number of texts had followed, but I'd been so busy with the renovations that I hadn't done anything about them. Seeing him now, I felt kinda bad about that.

"What's that about?" Max whispered in my ear as he finished hanging the banner Will had shipped ahead.

The staff had offered to set everything up, but Mom had insisted that we play a part in it all and had taken over organizing the next few days. She had no doubt whatsoever that Andy would say yes to Will. They'd been putting off planning their wedding with how busy work had been and this was the ideal solution.

"No idea." I shrugged. I was curious but with the stress and upheaval of everything, I hadn't wanted to endure another lecture from my eldest brother.

"Charlie." There was a small admonishment in Max's tone. "You can't avoid him forever. What if he wants to make up?"

I thought about it. A year ago I'd have scoffed at the idea of making nice with my brother, but now, nearly a year after almost dying? Well, not having that hanging over me would be great.

Alex had been a puzzle I'd tried to figure out over a lot of therapy. We hadn't had an issue with each other, except that he'd taken Will's side and had never forgiven me when Will had. Was this him finally relenting?

An hour later we had our warning that the grooms were en route in their shuttle, so everyone dashed to their rooms to freshen up.

It hadn't surprised me that Will and Andy's friends had traveled to Mexico for this. They really cared about each other. What did shock me was how closely Henry and Pete stood together. Out of the corner of my eye, I thought I'd seen them kiss once, a blink and you'd miss it pass of lips. I made a mental note to pin Henry down and ask what was going on.

"Shower?" I suggested as Max and I entered our suite. I'd managed to snag one of the last suites, on the same floor as the grooms. I wanted us to have a memorable break.

"Great idea!" He pulled me towards the large bathroom and flicked on the water in the massive shower. There was room in it for several people and like ours at home, it had two showerheads.

My stomach fluttered when I thought about our home. The idea that I had something permanent with Max. Going to sleep with him every night was better than anything in the world. Any time I had a flicker of anxiety and wanted to reach for a drink, I thought of Max clinging to me in the middle of the night. His breath on my neck, the feel of his skin against mine. Then I found the strength to push bad thoughts aside.

We undressed quickly as steam filled the bathroom, leaving our discarded clothes on the floor.

I let out a groan as I stepped under the water, the tight muscles of my shoulders relaxing.

Max's eyes heated as he took me in and I stretched out a hand for him. He clasped it firmly and I pulled him towards me.

Our lips met, gently at first but quickly heating, my tongue probing his mouth, my hands in his hair, the damp strands sticking to my fingers.

Max pushed up on his toes, his cock brushing mine and making us both groan. His hand stroked me from root to tip and I bent a little to make us fit together better. Shower sex wasn't always easy with our height difference.

Max took our cocks in his hand, the water making us slide together better, but not smoothly enough. Picking up some shower gel, I drizzled some over his hand, slicking the way better and thrust up into his grasp.

I rested my forehead against his and watched as he worked us quickly, each aware that we had somewhere to be soon.

As my orgasm rose, I kissed Max fiercely, breaking apart only to moan his name as I came apart over his dick and hand. Max followed after.

We traded kisses and whispered endearments as we washed and got ready to join the others down in the lobby.

No one was shocked when Andy said yes a second time, though his asking Will was the official story, we all knew that Will had proposed the same day, ruining Andy's surprise. Will got to one-up him by surprising him with a fully planned wedding.

Max and I took time out from family stuff in the days that followed because he was worried about me being in such high-pressure situations. Though I avoided being alone with my mom or Alex, it was still a lot to deal with and I appreciated Max looking out for me.

It was his vacation too, so I made sure there were trips for us to take away from the others.

To give us all time to relax and sort out last-minute things, the wedding was scheduled for three days after the grooms arrived, which allowed time for bachelor parties and some much-needed pampering.

The day before their wedding, Andy and Will spent the day in the resort's spa while Max and I took the resort's bus to the nearest town and explored.

We ate lunch and dinner away from the others and soaked up the culture as we sat enjoying each other's company. We shopped in the local market, finding trinkets to take home to our friends and little things that we could keep in our apartment to remind us of this trip. We took endless photos of everything and I watched Max light up with delight at every turn.

I promised myself that Max and I would travel both to places unseen and places we'd been before, and explore them as a couple. That I would prioritize being with Max over making money, the way that my father never had. I wouldn't take for granted what we had, especially since there'd been a point when this had been a far-off dream.

The ceremony was beautiful and as I hugged my new brother-in-law, I said "Congratulations, and welcome to the family."

Andy glowed with happiness. "Thank you! This is better than I could have ever hoped for."

"You're just glad you didn't have to plan a wedding!" I joked as Max came up beside me, wrapping his arm around my waist.

"I really am. I'm so grateful Will planned all this." I could see the hearts in his eyes over his new husband.

"Well, I'm happy for you both. You guys are great together."

"Me too," Max said, leaning his head against my arm.

"Thanks. No wedding in the future for you two?" Andy asked.

We'd already answered this a lot recently. We shook our heads, "No," we said firmly and in unison, making us laugh.

Andy was called away by another guest and Alex took the chance to come over.

"Charlie? Can we talk now?" he asked softly.

I looked at Max, who gave Alex a side-eye and moved away to speak to Henry and Pete. Neither of us was hugely keen on Pete but he and Henry were trying to be friends again. Henry had even been on a few dates with a guy from the gym but I needed to catch up with my friend judging by the way he and Pete were looking at each other.

"Charlie?"

"Yeah, sure." I indicated to the edge of the room, away from the servers setting up for the dance and clearing away the remnants of our perfect meal.

"Look, I know you've been avoiding me and I get it but I wanted to clear the air," he said, looking contrite.

"Clear the air?" I repeated.

"Yeah, I'm well aware that it's past time for that."

I gave a humorless chuckle. "Just a little."

He gave me a look that suggested that he was pushing down his temper. "Did you know I was in therapy, too?"

My laugh was shocked into cutting off. "Therapy? That's just Matty to go now, huh?" I was being glib but I wasn't surprised.

"Around the time you ended up in the hospital I was already on a leave of absence from the company after Helena admitted she was pregnant by her new man." He paused, collecting himself. "I had a breakdown."

I went to interrupt, to say something comforting, my hand reaching for his shoulder.

"Mom kept it quiet since you were heading for rehab. Will knew some of it but he had enough going on and we were still working things out." His head hung low like he still held onto the shame of what had happened with Helena. As far as I could see, that was all done and dusted. Will didn't hold a grudge.

I gave in then and wrapped my arms around my brother. He sagged into the hold. "I'm sorry, Charlie. We could have lost you and I wanted to stay angry for something that didn't even have anything to do with me."

"Then why?" I asked quietly, even as I kept a firm grip on him.

Alex felt frail still. When I thought back to last year, he'd looked as bad off as I had. Thin, haggard and stressed, but he hadn't rallied the same.

"I needed someone to blame things on when I was sick of putting it all on myself."

"Alex." I squeezed him before stepping back and letting go. "How about this? We start fresh today. Everything that is done, is done. Helena and Ethan, they have nothing to do with now."

"But I still have Joe, and he's half Helena." Alex cut in.

"Yeah, I know, but we can pretend that we didn't all hurt each other. Will has, and we hurt him the most."

We turned to seek out our brother, who was watching us with an approving smile.

"Okay, that I can do." He grinned at me. "So I heard something about a book launch. Let me know when and I'll get a sitter for Joe."

"Really?"

"Yeah, a fresh start means celebrating my baby brother releasing a book. You've always been great at capturing someone's essence when you take their picture." Alex looked proud and fond.

My eyes filled and I had to clear my throat to get the words out. "You can bring Joe, it's a dry event and during the day. We're doing it at Books & Biscuits."

Alex smiled. "That's different."

I wasn't sure how to take that. "I'm taking my recovery seriously. You know this since you helped me sell my last club. I've cut all ties with that past and I just want to live a sober life with the guy that I love."

There must have been something in my tone, or perhaps that the volume of my voice rose because Alex rushed to soothe me. "I didn't mean anything by it. Shit! I'm sorry."

"It's okay..."

He interrupted, "What I meant to say is you always seem to know the right way to start an event. Celebrating a book launch in a bookstore is perfect. A dry one, when it's a book about rehab, is thoughtful and kind. I'm so proud of you, Charlie."

Alex embraced me quickly, but not before I saw a glimpse of tears. "Let me know and I'll be there, okay?" He squeezed my shoulder and moved away.

"Everything okay?" asked Max as he slipped his hand into mine.

"Perfect," I said, leaning down to kiss him. I explained my conversation with my brother and Max smiled sweetly.

"I'm happy things are better between you two now. Family stuff should be less stressful now."

Our conversation was paused as one of the staff announced it was time for the first dance.

It took a while to locate Andy and Will, who looked decidedly rumpled, and their friends catcalling as they made their way to the dance floor.

I pulled Max in front of me, resting my head on top of his as we watched the newlyweds move around the floor sharing kisses and exchanging words of love.

Halfway through the dance, other couples began to join them and Max took my hand, moving to join them.

It felt natural to dance with him in my arms, not as if this was our first dance as a couple, but like we'd done this a hundred times before.

We swayed to the song for a little while before it ended and switched to another slower number.

Max rested his head against my chest relaxing into my hold. "Thank you for all of this, Charlie. I never imagined that us being together would be this perfect, this good. You make me feel like I could do anything."

"You can, and I'll be by your side through it all. Always. You are all I need."

I could feel his smile against the skin of my throat.

"I love you, Charlie. So much, I don't even have the words for how much."

I wrapped him tighter against me, the feeling of home and love almost overwhelming in its intensity.

"Max, you have my whole heart, for all it's worth."

Epilogue

Two Years Later - Charlie

"**S**o you're telling me," I said as the woman tried to interrupt me. I held up a hand since I wasn't finished, "You're suggesting, that in order to be successful foster parents, that we get married?"

Our case manager pursed her lips. "Unfortunately, it is often the case that married couples get through the process faster. They are seen as a more stable environment." She held up a hand to halt Max's tirade. "It isn't how I see things, but," she softened, "I like you two and want to see you with a bunch of kids. You certainly have the space."

I looked at Max. We'd known that this was a possibility and I knew how much he wanted some kids around the place.

"We'll get married," he told her, with a smile at me.

"Today," I said firmly.

Miriam looked stunned. Our caseworker was a no-nonsense woman, aged somewhere between thirty and ninety. If someone said to me that she was immortal, I'd have believed them. She was constantly in movement somehow, always evaluating her surroundings, and she'd given us a glowing report when she had checked out our apartment. The city had stalled on us and it seemed that our lack of wedding rings was the last hurdle to fostering.

When she finally came to her senses she repeated, "Today?" in a faint voice.

Max and I shared a look. We'd discussed this many times over the last couple of years and knew we'd do anything to make our dreams a reality.

"Absolutely, I'll call and make an appointment at city hall now," I said.

"I'll do it," Max said, getting up, putting our cat, Belphie, down and squeezing my shoulder. He picked up his phone and left the room heading into the kitchen. Belphie followed after him, always eager to be wherever Max was. We'd gotten him from the same shelter that Andy got Lucifer, but Belphie had been a tiny ratty-looking black kitten, shot through with gray. Since he'd been so small when he'd arrived at the shelter he didn't have a name. Max wanted to go with the demon cat name theme, hence Belphegor, or Belphie, as he was lovingly called. He only got his full name used on him when he was a brat.

The apartment remodel had been finished for about a year. We'd paused on the upstairs bedrooms to give ourselves a break from all the construction. We did some traveling, visited my sister at college, and headed to Europe for a couple of weeks.

It'd been more of a working vacation for me, I'd taken my camera to get shots for another book, a kind of photo journal about living and loving with addiction. The book had sold well and my business was running steady enough to have a couple of staff.

"Are you sure about this?" Miriam's voice cut into my thoughts.

"We're certain. It isn't a surprise and something we've discussed in the past. We'll go to city hall today and get married if we can. Are you able to put it down on your evaluation?"

"I will. It bodes well for you both that you are willing to do this to gain approval. I can't see it being long before you have a placement." Her voice was saddened.

"Unfortunately, there are quite a few children in the LGBTQIA+ demographic that struggle to get a home for any length of time."

"Which is why we want to do this, for those kids in particular."

Her smile was approving. "I shouldn't say this, but I'm almost certain you will be rubber-stamped. The city is crying out for decent foster parents and you've set up everything so wonderfully."

Max came back into view. "Four o'clock and I have a list of the documents we need."

"Great, so what do we do now?"

"Well, we better invite some people, or there'll be murders!" He looked over at Miriam, "I'm joking of course, but we do need witnesses."

"Right, I'll drop a message in the family group chat. Thankfully Matty is still home for another few days."

Max gave me a look and directed his attention to Miriam. "Would you like to come?"

"Oh, no, I couldn't impose. I also have a full day of appointments, so I'll get out of your hair. Congratulations to both of you. I hope to see you soon."

I led Miriam to the elevator and said our goodbyes as Max went to our bedroom, looking for our best suits.

"Any particular color or just black? What ties?"

"Hmm?"

"Charlie! I need help picking."

"I think we should match as much as we can. I'm going to text the group and some of our friends."

Charlie: Max and I are getting married today at city hall. 4 pm. We would love it if you could join us.

I sent the message to the family chat that Alex, his girlfriend Sarah, Will, Andy, Mom, and Matty were part of. Then sent it to Henry, his sister Holly, and Heather from the café.

"Do you want me to message Kristen or do you want to call her? I told Heather, but I'm not sure who else out of the staff you'd want to be there."

Max popped his head out of the closet. "I'll offer to close Books & Biscuits early and they can all come if they want. The ones that need the hours can stay and close if there is a supervisor available."

"Reid's been going on about needing hours, so he'll probably stay."

Reid was someone that we'd found by chance and he fit in perfectly. He rented the one-bedroom above my photography studio for a reduced rate and took classes at the local university around his shifts at Books & Biscuits.

"I'll head down and talk to everyone. Kristen is down there now." He came over and gave me a sweet kiss and a grin. "Can't believe we're getting married."

I grabbed his hand to stop him from leaving. "Do you wish we'd done this before? Do you need a proper wedding? Because I'll give you anything you want. It doesn't have to be today."

He cupped my face and said quietly, "No, it's perfect this way. We don't need this, so it isn't a big deal. We already know we're forever. You make me happy every day and I love you."

"I love you, too."

Max disappeared downstairs as I noticed my phone was buzzing and buzzing on the bed next to me. There were at least a dozen notifications.

Andy: We'll be there!
Sarah: Us too
Mom: Call me
Matty: Mom is freaking, call her. I'll be there
Henry: Finally. See you at 4
Holly: Trying to get a shift change. Will try to be there.
Heather: I'll be there. Congrats!

My heart warmed at the responses and I took a second to bask in the happy feeling before calling my mom.

"Hey, Mom."

Max

I felt like I was going to vibrate out of my skin, I was so excited to get married. It was stupid to be so worked up about it, but I couldn't help it. I'd been perfectly happy with not getting married, it wasn't how I'd seen my future, but now that it was happening, I couldn't imagine a future where Charlie and I hadn't tied the knot.

Quickly closing the doors to both the bookstore and the café, turning the signs to closed, I gathered the staff and told them our news.

"Congratulations, Max!" Kristen said amid other congratulations, as she pulled me into a fierce hug. "I'll go call Rachele and see if she can get out of work. I'll need to change my clothes!"

"Go home. You have three hours to make yourself more beautiful and meet us there."

Kristen kissed my cheek and went to get her things.

I talked to each staff member in turn. Some hadn't been with us long, like Reid, which was one of the downsides of hiring students, so a few were happy to stay on until close.

"Reid, will you be okay locking everything up?"

He looked worried for a second. "Um, yes? I've done it before so it should be fine."

"Call if you have any problems, okay? You can come meet us after work if you want."

"Can I call you later and let you know?" I was worried his anxiety wouldn't let him come celebrate with us, but I wasn't going to make a big deal of it. He'd come a long way since I'd met him six months ago.

"Sure." I patted his shoulder before unlocking the doors again and returning to the apartment.

Charlie was on a call when I got back and it sounded like it was getting heated.

"No, that's not what we want. That's what you want. " A pause. "We are doing this today. Will you be there?" Another silence. "It's happening regardless." More silence. "Okay."

I heard his sigh as I approached him. "Your mom?"

"Yeah. She wants this big wedding. She doesn't understand why we don't want that."

I ran my hands through his dark hair and pressed a kiss to his forehead. "Who else is coming?"

"Everyone I messaged. I'm sure we've missed people, but at this point, I don't care."

I wanted some photos of the day and Charlie's assistant would be the perfect choice. "Did you call Asher?"

"No, he's got class until two. We were going to go over some editing this evening so I'll send a message once he's done. I'll call Izzy now, though."

"I'll make us some lunch and then we can get ready."

He stopped me. "Are you sure you want to do it this way?"

"I am. I've never been more certain in my whole life. Let's just get married today and sort out a weekend at the beach house as our honeymoon. I don't want something fancy. I just want you. Forever."

"You already had me forever, but this piece of paper will make it official I guess."

"I, uh, wondered..." Nerves halted my words.

"What is it? You can have anything you want." Charlie said simply, looking at me with such love and trust in his eyes.

"Could I change my last name to yours? Become a Petraki. I'm not overly fond of Davis."

Charlie's mouth hung open for a second and I resisted the urge to laugh.

"What? Of course, you can! I'd become a Davis for you if you wanted."

"No, I'm happy to leave that name and associations with my mom behind."

He kissed me, long and deep until we had to break apart for air. "I can't wait to marry you and make you Mr. Max Petraki." His smile could have lit up any room and I felt his joy in my soul.

"Looking forward to joining your family."

He pulled me close for a hug until his stomach rumbling reminded me about lunch.

"Make your calls. I'll feed us."

Charlie

Max and I left our building with over an hour to spare so that we could go and get rings. Though it was last minute, we'd made sure we looked dapper in our suits and had Asher take some pictures of us getting ready together before we left.

It was lucky that Asher had seen my text and had ducked out of class early or we'd never have gotten the chance to have that part of our special day documented.

I'd upgraded Max's car to a hybrid SUV that was highly recommended as a family car, and we took that to city hall before remembering to look for a jewelry store to pick out wedding bands. We'd done this all backwards, booking a ceremony first, but if we were going to be married then I was going to wear a ring. I wanted Max to wear one, too.

We were in luck, the jewelry store had two simple but beautiful platinum bands in our sizes. Max asked if we could return after the ceremony to engrave them with the wedding date, but the gentleman had the tools and ability to do it then and there.

It was amazing to watch a craftsman engrave our initials and the date into the bands and I left a hefty tip for the service.

City hall was busy and our group took up most of the waiting room. It was slightly overwhelming how quickly everyone had dropped everything to come and celebrate with us.

Mom and Matty both looked gorgeous, though Mom had to stop sneering at the venue. Matty kept giving her side looks and inching away.

"Hey," Alex approached, with his girlfriend, Sarah and Joe. "Congratulations, I'm happy for you both." Alex leaned in for a hug, followed by Sarah and Joe.

"Thanks for coming, glad you could make it." We shared a smile and I moved to greet the next group. Two years had made quite the difference with my eldest brother. We'd never be close friends, but we were something like it now.

Andy rushed me, clasping my hands after a fierce embrace. "I'm so excited for you both! This is such a you way to do it, too."

I laughed. "Thanks, I think."

"You and Max are as committed to each other as me and Will are. You don't need the marriage certificate to prove it, but it's great that you are putting those kids you want to foster before your ideas about marriage. I know how important it is to Max, to give a stable home to teens that have similar backgrounds as him."

"Is that why?" Mom cut in, she'd slowly gravitated towards her favorite son-in-law.

"I haven't said much about it at our family dinners, but Andy knows we've been going through the process to get approved to foster," I told her with a shrug. "We thought that not being married might be a stumbling block and Miriam confirmed it today. There's never going to be anyone for me but Max, he's been there for everything, so a piece of paper is meaningless to us. The city and the state, not so much." I shrugged again and Mom sniffled before folding me into a hug.

"Oh darling, this makes so much sense now! We'll have dinner at the house after. We can order in. All your friends can come." She moved away to make some calls, probably to the house staff to get everything prepared and I looked after her retreating back with a smile.

Henry and Pete approached and we shared hugs before Henry whispered in my ear. "You owe me fifty dollars." A reminder of our bet over two years ago.

I laughed. "Got it right here!" I handed over the bill before hugging my best friend again. "I'm glad you're here."

"Holly says she's sorry that she couldn't get away, there was no other management cover with me here, but she'll come see you guys soon."

Before I could reply, we were called into the room. The guests all went ahead of us to take seats and then I took Max's hand and walked in behind. Asher and Izzy had been busy taking photos of people as they arrived and both captured us as we walked down the makeshift aisle to the clerk that would officiate our wedding.

The ceremony passed in minutes, punctuated by either me or Max repeating the clerk's words, and finished with our solemn I do's.

The moment weighed heavy on us. We may not have wanted to get married before, but now it was happening, it felt so very real and important.

All the eyes in the room watched as we were pronounced husbands, and the clerk notified the room of Max's name change to soft exclamations from my mom and cheers from our friends.

Flashes surrounded us as we shared our first kiss as husbands, our arms wrapped tightly around each other, smiles on our faces as our lips touched.

I'd never been more sure of my place in the world; at the side of my best friend and husband.

The End

Acknowledgments

My alphas, Starla and Rachel, helped me make this a better version of itself and I'm so grateful for their advice. Thank you both.

My beta readers, Janet, Jennifer, and Brooks, for giving it another read and for the feedback.

Thank you, Kristen, for being a sunshine character and my editor.

Rachele, thanks for being Kristen's wife!

Heather, Sarah, and Izzy thank you for letting me borrow your names and for all of the support.

A big thanks to Kelly who listens to all my random book ideas. She gets texts when I get out of the shower with plot bunnies and helps them make sense without complaint.

Thank you to my family who let me write in peace for the most part.

A final thanks go to you, the reader, for taking a chance on my books. I really appreciate you helping me live my dream.

If you enjoyed this book, please consider leaving a review. Reviews help books be seen and are so helpful to writers. Thank you.

About Author

Jax Stuart is a Scottish-born author, mum of two and owner of a menagerie (two cats, a tortoise and 3 fish tanks of fish!).

She started writing her first book at age eleven but gave writing up for years. A big birthday last year prompted her to finally go after that publishing dream.

When she isn't writing, Jax is an avid reader and likes to spend time with friends and family.

You can find her on;

https://www.facebook.com/groups/1301563603574707
https://app.mailerlite.com/sites/preview/4625065
https://jaxstuartauthor.wixsite.com/website
https://twitter.com/stuart_jax
https://www.bookbub.com/profile/jax-stuart

Come join her reader group - Stuart's Syndicate.

Also By

So Worth More, Second Chances Series #1
https://books2read.com/u/m0BO00

An M/M second chance romance

Andy ends his friends with benefits relationship with his co-worker, Will, when he realizes that while it has plenty of benefits, it's light on the friends. He's sick of Will's rules and poor treatment but agrees to be friends, minus the benefits because he's still hung up on the guy.

Will gets the wake-up call he so desperately needed when Andy ends things and discovers that maybe Andy's feelings aren't one-sided but he's got a lot of healing to do before he can be the man that Andy needs.

So Worth More has some allusions to domestic abuse, mentions of former partners cheating, and a whole heap of family drama. While Andy does deserve better, Will does get there in the end. Told in dual pov with HEA.

So Worth More: The Wedding, Second Chances Series #1.5
https://claims.prolificworks.com/free/6Yvo60gZ?

fbclid=IwAR3MW3gPTNS8-_RmP-
Rc5lM_h7FoQD78pMf6AbjpdVyzW0xdXOcDwNaPAG4

An extended epilogue and features Andy and Will's wedding!

Growing Love
https://claims.prolificworks.com/free/KxiWrlQM

What started out being a short prompt for flash-fiction ended up being more of a serial. A Vet, a gardener and a garden center. Features a rescued hedgehog and is written in British English

Coming soon, It's Truth for Love, A Whitehills prequel and The Mage's Covenant, a paranormal romance.

Printed in Great Britain
by Amazon